She was free

But she could not thank him. She could not even say goodbye.

"Clarissa."

At the sound of her name, she spun back toward him. Her heart leapt, then dropped like a stone as she saw that he was holding the parfleche, extending it toward her with both hands.

Fighting tears of anguish, she walked slowly back toward him. His face was in full sunlight now, the jaw set, the blue eyes narrowed against the glare. What colossal, stubborn pride he had! If only he would speak, or even look at her....

As she reached out to take the rawhide case, their fingers brushed. The light contact of skin to skin blazed like a flash of gunpowder through her body. Struck by the sudden, searing heat in his eyes, Clarissa let the case fall.

In the next instant he had caught her in his arms....

Dear Reader,

What a perfect time to celebrate history—the eve of a new century. This month we're featuring four terrific romances with awe-inspiring heroes and heroines from days gone by that you'll want to take with you into the *next* century!

Wolf Heart is the fascinating, timeless hero from *Shawnee Bride* by Elizabeth Lane. Fans of Native American stories will absolutely love this authentic, emotion-filled love story about a boy who was orphaned at eleven and adopted by the Shawnee. Now a fierce Shawnee warrior, both in his heart and mind, Wolf Heart falls in love with a beautiful white woman whom he rescues from river pirates. Will their love transcend the cultural barriers? Will she live as his Shawnee bride, or will she return to the white man's world? Don't miss this wonderful story!

In *By Queen's Grace* by Shari Anton, Saxon knight Corwin of Lenvil heroically wins the hand—and heart—of his longtime secret love, a royal maiden. Antoinette Huntington is the unforgettable heroine in *The Lady and the Outlaw* by DeLoras Scott. Here, the English Antoinette has a romantic run-in with an outlaw on a train headed for the Arizona Territory.

Simon of Blackstone will steal your heart in *The Champion* by Suzanne Barclay, the launch book in the KNIGHTS OF THE BLACK ROSE miniseries. Simon returns from war to confront the father he never knew…and finds himself and his lady love the prime suspects in his father's murder.

Enjoy! And come back again next month for four more choices of the best in historical romance.

Happy holidays,

Tracy Farrell
Senior Editor

SHAWNEE BRIDE
Elizabeth Lane

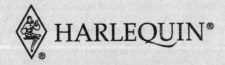

HARLEQUIN®

TORONTO • NEW YORK • LONDON
AMSTERDAM • PARIS • SYDNEY • HAMBURG
STOCKHOLM • ATHENS • TOKYO • MILAN • MADRID
PRAGUE • WARSAW • BUDAPEST • AUCKLAND

ISBN 0-373-29092-6

SHAWNEE BRIDE

Copyright © 1999 by Elizabeth Lane

Visit us at www.romance.net

Printed in U.S.A.

Please address questions and book requests to:
Harlequin Reader Service
U.S.: 3010 Walden Ave., P.O. Box 1325, Buffalo, NY 14269
Canadian: P.O. Box 609, Fort Erie, Ont. L2A 5X3

Author Note by Elizabeth Lane

Before writing *Shawnee Bride,* I did extensive research on Shawnee history and customs. Even with the best of intentions, however, it is difficult to know everything about a culture that is not one's own. If anything I have written here is found to be erroneous or offensive, I offer my apologies to the reader and to a people for whom I have nothing but the deepest respect.

I owe a special debt of gratitude to James Alexander Thom, whose fine biographical novel *Panther in the Sky* inspired the setting and background for Clarissa and Wolf Heart's story.

Elizabeth Lane

Prologue

The Valley of the Ohio, 1747

Seth Johnson bolted through the underbrush, terror fueling the strength of his eleven-year-old legs. Brambles clawed at his threadbare clothes. Roots and vines clutched at his ankles. His heart hammered in anguished fire bursts as he ran.

Behind him, the silence of the forest was even more terrible than his father's screams had been. Pa would be dead by now, God willing, and even if he wasn't, there was nothing that could be done for him.

The marauding black bear had come out of nowhere, jumping Benjamin Johnson as he crouched to reset one of his beaver traps. Seth had flung sticks and rocks and screamed himself hoarse in a frantic effort to distract the monster, but none of his boyish racket had been of any use. In the end, he had been left with no choice except to run for his life.

Was the bear coming after him now? If he paused to listen, would he hear it crashing through the undergrowth as its great black nose smelled out his trail? Seth could not risk stopping to find out. A charging bear, bent on killing, could run down the fastest man alive.

His bare feet, already large and rawhide tough, splashed into a shallow creek. He plunged upstream, praying the water would carry away his scent. His lungs burned. His breath burst out in labored gasps as he toiled uphill against the icy current.

Seth stifled a cry as his left foot slipped on a mossy stone, wrenching the ankle. Pain lanced his leg—a sharper pain, even, than the hot, flat sting Pa's belt had caused last night when Seth had dropped a jug of whiskey into the river. For what it was worth, at least Pa would never beat him again.

Grimacing, Seth stumbled out of the water, crumpled against the overhung bank and curled there like a clenched fist. He could not see or hear the bear. All the same, he felt the hair prickle on the back of his neck, a sure sign that danger was close by, and he knew there was nothing he could do.

Helpless, he shrank deeper into the shadow of the high bank. "Pa!" he wanted to shout. "I'm here, Pa! Come and help me!" But he knew it would be no use.

He was alone in a thousand square miles of wilderness. Worse than alone. This was Shawnee territory, his father had told him. The Shawnee were savages who would just as soon cut out a white man's innards and roast him alive as look at him. Better the bear than the Shawnee. At least a bear would kill him swiftly.

The way it had killed Pa.

The silence around him had taken on a dark weight of its own. The birds were quiet. Even the insects had stopped buzzing. A drop of sweat trickled along Seth's collarbone, cool against his hot flesh, as he waited.

He heard a sudden dry rustling sound. Then something

leaped off the bank, landing almost on top of him. Seth glimpsed a flash of bare brown legs and beaded moccasins. Then a rough, smelly blanket enfolded him, cutting off breath and sight. Powerful arms lifted him high. Wild with fear, he kicked, squirmed and punched the stifling darkness, mouthing every curse he had ever heard Pa utter. "Turn me loose, you filthy savage!" he screamed. "Let me go, or, so help me, I'll have your hide!"

It was then that Seth heard, through the blanket, a sound that sent a shiver all the way to the marrow of his bones.

The sound was laughter.

Chapter One

Fort Pitt, April 1761

"**E**nough of this foolishness, Clarissa Rogers!" The older woman's voice pierced the cool spring twilight. "It's getting dark! We should all be getting back to the fort!"

"I'll be there shortly! You go on, Aunt Margaret!" Clarissa tugged deftly at the long string, making the kite soar and dip against the roiling clouds. A storm was moving in over the spring-swollen river, the breeze was perfect for kite flying and she was having the most wonderful time of her life.

"You'd better do as she says." The lieutenant, one of three young officers who raced alongside her, scowled worriedly. "Look at the sky. It's going to rain any minute."

"*You* can go back anytime you want to." Clarissa tossed her head, loosening her red-gold curls to stream in the wind. She could not remember having felt so free—not, at least, in the seven years since her father had died, leaving her in the care of her dour older brother and their stern housekeeper, Mrs. Pimm. Junius Rogers had turned their once-cheerful Baltimore home into a gloomy, suffocating prison, banishing music, laughter and freedom. For Clarissa, this visit to her aunt and uncle on the Pennsylvania frontier was like a breath of fresh air.

Behind her, the stout ramparts of the fort rose against the sky. Stiffened by the breeze, the Union Jack, which had so recently replaced the French tricolor, snapped smartly from its pole on the blockhouse. On either side of the low spit of land, the river waters flowed brown with spring silt where the Monongahela and the Allegheny joined to form the Ohio. Flatboats, pirogues and canoes dotted the shoreline. Wooden shacks and lean-tos had sprouted around the fort's outer walls like mushrooms around a tree stump. This growing sprawl of taverns, trading posts and settler cabins had already taken on a name of its own—Pittsburgh.

Clarissa laughed as she ran, one hand bunching up her embroidered petticoat to save it from grass stains. She had no illusions about the reason Junius had sent her here. She was seventeen, of marriageable age, and he wanted her out of the way, safely wed to some promising young officer. It was a practical plan, for she was neither impoverished nor plain, and there were plenty of eager suitors here. But there was one thing Junius hadn't counted on. His headstrong young sister was having far too much fun to settle on any one of them.

"Clarissa, do come in now!" Her aunt's impatient voice broke the gathering darkness. "They'll be closing the gates soon, and Molly will be putting supper on the table! You can fly that ridiculous kite again tomorrow if you insist!"

Clarissa halted, causing two of her escorts to collide

in mid-run. Lanterns had begun to flicker above the ramparts of the fort and in the settlement below. Lightning flashed in the east and, as thunder stirred across the horizon, she felt a single raindrop wet her eyelid.

High above, the kite tugged compellingly at its string, wheeling like a brave white bird against the darkening sky. Clarissa gazed up at it for a moment, then sighed. ''All right,'' she called over her shoulder. ''I'll be there as soon as I reel in the twine!''

''*Now,* Clarissa!'' Her aunt's tone clearly indicated that she'd lost all patience. ''One of the young men can bring in your toy!''

''Oh…very well!'' Not wanting to try the good woman further, Clarissa turned and was about to hand the twine ball to one of her companions when a stiff gust of wind struck the kite. Jerking at its string, the kite took an abrupt dive. With a suddenness that caused Clarissa to cry in dismay, it plummeted straight down, crashing out of sight somewhere between the cabins and the water.

''I'll go after it!'' Second Lieutenant Thomas Ainsworth, the youngest of her suitors, was off at a run, following the path of the string where it trailed across the grass. It was Tom Ainsworth who had made the kite, whittling the sticks of white birch for the frame and mounting the lightweight canvas with a skill that bespoke years of boyhood practice. Clarissa was truly fond of him. If only she'd been blessed with a brother like Tom instead of the stingy, unsmiling Junius! How much more pleasant her life might have been!

''Do be careful, Tom!'' she called, shouting above the wind. ''I'll wait for you inside the gate, I promise! I won't let the guards lock up until you're back inside the fort!''

The young lieutenant gave no sign that he'd heard her.

He raced toward the waterfront, heedless of the lightning that snaked across the sky, heedless of the sinister growl of thunder. Clarissa gazed after him until he vanished into the misting rain. Then, picking up her skirts once more, she spun on her slippered toes and hurried to catch up with her departing aunt. The two remaining officers trailed after her like devoted puppies.

Clarissa was true to her promise. After sending the others on their way, she stationed herself in the shelter of the gate, under the watch of the soldiers who patrolled the parapets. This would not be a long wait, she assured herself. At any moment Tom would come bounding up the slope, grinning as he held the precious kite aloft.

She would kiss him, Clarissa resolved—a playful, sisterly peck that no one could possibly misunderstand. Then, perhaps, she would invite him to supper. That was the least she could do to show her gratitude.

Minutes crawled by, and he did not return. Clarissa grew restless and more than a little hungry. Through the dark mist of rain, her sharp green eyes could just make out the white string, which Tom, in his haste, had left lying on the grass. The string had not so much as moved.

What was taking him so long? Had he met a friend? A girl, perhaps? Had he stopped for a drink in one of those unsavory little dens that had sprung up along the waterfront? Didn't he know she was waiting for him?

Clarissa's young, untempered patience frayed and snapped. Ignoring the shout of the guard who saw her leave, she strode out of the gate and stalked across the green. What harm, after all, could it do to find Tom Ainsworth and give him a piece of her mind? She was already wet. As for danger, there could hardly be any menace lurking within a stone's throw of the fort.

The white string was easy to follow. It gleamed against

the wet grass in the eerie half-light of the gathering storm.
Clutching her skirts, Clarissa sprinted along its path.
There was no guarantee the string would lead her to that
inconstant rascal Tom Ainsworth, but at least, with luck,
she would find the kite.

By day, the shacks along the riverfront had a seedy
quality about them. Now, in the rainy twilight, every
black shadow seemed a living, crawling thing. Slivers of
lamplight glimmered through log walls. From somewhere
in the darkness a man coughed and swore violently. A
woman laughed.

By now the string had grown wet and muddy. Clarissa's eyes strained through the murk as she picked her
way down an alley. She was soaking wet and shivering
with cold. Her slippers were ruined, and her aunt would
likely be furious with her. Oh, what she would say to
Lieutenant Thomas Ainsworth when she caught up
with—

Her thoughts ended in a startled gasp as her foot
bumped something soft and solid. It was a man, lying
quite still, facedown in the mud.

It was Tom Ainsworth.

''Oh!'' She dropped to a crouch, her anger swept away
by concern as she saw the bloody red welt on his temple.
She seized his shoulders, desperate to rouse him. ''Don't
be dead, Tom,'' she prayed aloud, shaking him hard.
''Oh, please, don't be dead!''

He moaned, and Clarissa's heart welled with relief and
gratitude. ''Come on!'' She struggled to lift him. ''We've
got to get you back to the fort!''

His head turned then, and she caught the stark flash of
alarm in his eyes. ''Run, Clarissa!'' he whispered
hoarsely. ''Leave me and get yourself out of here!''

''Don't be a donkey!'' She gripped his shoulders, desperate to force him up. "I'm not going anywhere without you, Tom Ainsworth, and that's that, so you may as well just—*oh!*"

Rough hands seized Clarissa from behind, wrenching her up and backward. Her scream ended in a muffled gasp as a greasy palm clamped over her mouth, wrenching her jaw. She found flesh and bit down hard.

"Hell-bitch!" The slap exploded in her head, igniting hot glimmering rings of pain. She sagged against her unseen captor, dazed but still conscious. As her vision cleared she saw Tom on his knees, struggling to stand. A second man, clad in grimy buckskins, had materialized from the shadows. His moccasin-clad foot caught the side of Tom's head in a brutal kick. Tom crumpled in the mud and lay still.

"Let me go to him!" Clarissa writhed and twisted against the arms that clasped her like a vise. The stench of her captor's unwashed skin and clothes made her flesh crawl.

"Well now, Zeke, looks like we've got ourselves a feisty one. Pretty one, too." The man in buckskins fingered the knife at his belt as he looked Clarissa up and down.

"Damn good thing we got somethin' outa this," the man named Zeke growled. "Her boyfriend there didn't have enough in his pocket to make rollin' him worth our trouble. Leastwise, we can have ourselves a little fun. Wanna toss dice for who gets 'er first?"

Clarissa could feel his breath, rank and steamy against her bare shoulder. Gulping back her fear, she glared at the wiry man in buckskins. "Don't either of you touch me!" she snapped imperiously. "If the lieutenant and I don't return straightaway to the fort, my uncle, Colonel

Hancock, will have his whole regiment out looking for us. You'll both be hanged on the spot!''

''Now ain't you the uppity one!'' Zeke's grip tightened on her arms, hurting her. ''You won't be so high-an'-mighty once you've had us atween your legs, will she, Maynard? Hell, she'll be beggin' for it, like they all do!''

The man in buckskins hesitated, scowling.

''Maynard?''

''Shut up. I'm thinkin'.'' He scratched at his scraggly jaw. ''If what the girl says is true, we'd be runnin' a risk to take turns with her here in town. But if we was to carry her downriver with us...''

''Hell, Maynard, that's the best idea yet!'' Zeke responded with a whoop. ''Ain't nobody goin' to trail us into Injun territory. We can keep the little spitfire tied to the boat an' hump 'er whenever we want. Atween times, she can cook an' wash for us!''

Clarissa fought back waves of sick panic, forcing herself to stay calm. Her only chance of escape lay in keeping her head, she reminded herself. She would wait for the two men to lower their guard. Then, at the first opportunity—

''We're wastin' time,'' Maynard growled. ''Let's get to the boat.''

''What about the boyfriend?'' Zeke glanced down at Tom Ainsworth's limp body where it lay in the rain-spattered mud.

Clarissa's heart plummeted. She had been praying the young lieutenant was still alive and that someone would find him before it was too late. ''Leave him here!'' she urged. ''Look at him! What possible harm can he do you now?''

''Plenty if he ain't dead yet,'' Maynard snapped. ''And even if he is, folks who find the body might piece together what happened. Only place this young bastard's goin' now is the bottom of the river."

"Please." Clarissa strained frantically against Zeke's grasp. "Don't kill him. I'll do anything you say."

Maynard laughed roughly as he bent to pick up Tom's inert feet. "You'll do it anyhow, girl. As I see it, you ain't got much choice."

The storm's full fury was moving in, heavy rain whipping the river to a froth. Clarissa stumbled through the mud, pressed forward by Zeke's painful grip on her arms. Through the downpour she could make out the river's edge and the blocky outlines of the boats. Lanterns flickered through the darkness. Her heart leaped as she realized there were people on one sheltered deck—people who would surely not fail to heed a young girl's cry for help.

Maynard had looped his arms around Tom's feet and was dragging the young lieutenant facedown through the mud. Tom had not uttered a sound. Clarissa feared he was dead, but fearing was a far cry from knowing, and that uncertainty held her prisoner. If there was one chance in a hundred that Tom was alive, she could not break loose and abandon him.

"Step lively, now girl." Zeke chuckled as he prodded her down the long slope toward the water. "The sooner we get you downriver, the sooner the fun can start!"

Clarissa trudged through the storm, willing herself to bide her time. Her gown was soaked, her shoes and petticoat caked with mud. Her hair hung in her face and streamed down her back in long, wet ribbons.

"I'll wager you're a virgin," Zeke said, leering. "I can tell that much from the looks of you. Maynard an' me, we always share the goods by half, but only one of us can break that cherry, an' I aim for it to be me. I'm better equipped for it if I say so myself. Maynard, now, he's just a little feller, if you get my meanin'!''

Clarissa steeled herself against his vulgar prattle. She had no illusions about what this unsavory pair planned to do with her. Just last month her newly married cousin, Jenny, had confided in breathless whispers all the details of physical love between a man and a woman. The description had fascinated Clarissa then. But what Zeke and Maynard had in mind was far removed from love, and the very thought of it made her sick to her stomach.

The lanterns were closer now. She could make out the silhouettes of three men in their light. They were staggering around on the deck, laughing raucously as they lurched against each other. They were drunk, she realized with a sinking heart. Drunk, and probably of the same evil stripe as her captors. But right now they were her only hope.

Another twenty paces, she calculated, and the strangers on the boat would be certain to hear her. Clarissa moved like a sleepwalker through the dark curtains of rain, every nerve quivering. Her life, and the life of Tom Ainsworth, hung in the balance, at the mercy of luck and timing.

She could hear the rush and tumble of the rain-swollen river. The lanterns were very close now, the strangers on board caught up in their own drunken revelry. Clarissa's muscles tensed. It was now or never.

She spun hard away from her captor and plunged toward the lamplight. ''Help us!'' she screamed. ''For the love of heaven—''

She saw one of the men turn. Then, without warning, a huge bolt of lightning split the sky and, in its booming echo, something cracked against the side of her head. She felt an explosion of pain. The lights spun, quivered then vanished in a dizzying spiral of blackness.

* * *

She awoke to the motion of the river.

For the first few breaths, the throbbing pain in Clarissa's head seemed to fill the whole world. As her senses cleared, she became aware that she was lying on her side, her face pressed against a rough log surface.

Icy water surged between the logs, splashing her face and shocking her fully awake. Only then did she realize that it was near dawn. The rain was coming down in watery sheets, and the whole world seemed to be dipping and racing around her. When she tried to sit up, she discovered that her wrists were lashed to a support pole of a rude hut, built on to the log deck of a flatboat.

By the first pale light, she could make out a bulky figure at the rear of the boat. It was Zeke. Her scheme to rescue herself and Tom had come to nothing.

Tom! Where was he?

The thin rawhide cut her wrists, mingling streaks of blood with the rain as she writhed and twisted, her frantic gaze probing the shadows. When she could discover no sign of him, Clarissa knew, with a sickening certainty, that he was gone. She would never again see his eager grin. She would never again share his boyish laughter or watch his skilled fingers fashion a kite.

But there would be no time to mourn her friend. The boat was pitching crazily, spinning in the wild current. Zeke's curses rose above the howl of the wind as he wrestled with the tiller. As Clarissa watched, numb with terror, Maynard staggered around the corner of the shack. He was fighting for balance on the lurching deck. "Take 'er in to the bank, damn you!" he yelled. "We got to tie up till this devil storm blows over!"

"You take 'er in if you're so bitchin' smart!" Zeke

bellowed. "Blasted tiller ain't worth no more'n a stinkin' broom straw against this current! We're gonna founder!"

Clarissa tumbled sideways, the motion wrenching her bound wrists, as the boat careened around a bend in the river. She could hear Zeke bawling helplessly above the roar of the storm.

"Give me that!" Maynard shoved him aside and grabbed the tiller himself. He was calmer and possessed more skill than Zeke, but he lacked the weight to man-handle the pitching craft. "Don't just stand there!" he shrilled at Zeke. "Help me!"

As Clarissa watched the two men struggle, she suddenly became aware that the water-soaked rawhide thongs were softening around her wrists. Gritting her teeth against the pain, she twisted and sawed at the thin ties until, at last, they stretched enough to let her hands slip through. With every joint throbbing, she clasped the pole and clawed her way to a sitting position. Only then could she see the full scope of her peril.

Vast and black, the rain-swollen Ohio hissed between its banks. The flatboat shot along in the current, bobbing and spinning, out of control. Clarissa stared in helpless horror as a huge uprooted tree stump spun in an eddy and swept back toward them. She screamed as it swung to one side, then tumbled into the eddy again, missing the flatboat by a hand's breadth.

Zeke and Maynard, if they had heard her at all, were too busy to pay her any heed. They grappled with the tiller, yelling curses at the storm and at each other. This, Clarissa thought, would be a perfect time to slip over-board and make her escape—except for one bit of irony. In all the years of her sheltered Baltimore girlhood, she had never immersed herself in anything larger than a cop-per bathtub. She could not swim a stroke.

The racing current funneled around a sharp bend, tilting the flatboat almost on its side. Clarissa screamed again as the hut tore loose from its fastenings. She glimpsed Zeke's face as he hurtled past her to vanish into the darkness. Almost at the same instant, one corner of the boat struck something hard beneath the surface. The blow splintered the raft like a child's toy.

Logs, boards and supplies flew in all directions, propelled by the same force that catapulted Clarissa into the air. For a heart-stopping instant, she flew through rain-filled emptiness. Then her body slammed into the river.

Dazed, she sank beneath the churning flood. The current's icy embrace turned and tumbled her, sweeping her along like a helpless doll. Water filled her nose and roared in her ears. Something brushed her face—something cold and alive. Her body jerked with revulsion.

No! She couldn't die now! Not here! Not like this!

As terror replaced shock she began to struggle. Her bursting lungs drove her instinctively to kick her way upward. A sheet of lightning, distant now, flashed against the dawn sky as her head broke the surface. She gulped a mouthful of precious air and, with it, a choking quantity of muddy water. Bubbles burst from her lips as the current dragged her under again.

Debris from the wrecked boat swirled around her. Clarissa jerked with pain as a big log crashed against her ribs. Miraculously she felt it pushing beneath her, lifting her upward. Clasping the log with her arms, she kicked until she broke the surface once more. The floating log stayed beneath her this time, keeping her there.

Choking and coughing, Clarissa filled her lungs with air. She was alive, but her peril was far from over. The unbridled current was still sweeping her downstream. Tree limbs, boat wreckage and things she could not even bear to imagine bobbed and swirled along with her. In rare moments of calm water, she caught glimpses of the wooded shore. There were no settlements here—no houses, farms or forts. This was wilderness, a land peopled by bears, snakes, pumas and naked copper savages who would kill her for the pleasure of hanging her scalp on their lodge poles. Drowning was a pleasant prospect compared to what might happen to her on land.

By the time the morning sun crept above the trees, Clarissa's strength was gone. She lay across the log, too numb to hold on to the rough bark. Her red-gold hair streamed like a net in the muddy water, catching twigs, leaves and drowned insects.

Her mind drifted in and out of dreams. She fancied herself back in Baltimore, waking up to the mouthwatering aromas of scones, bacon and porridge. She imagined curling into the warm feather bed to steal one last delicious moment of sleep, then rising, brushing out her hair, slipping into her warm flannel wrapper and pattering downstairs to breakfast. This morning, even the sight of Junius's sour face filled her with tenderness. She smiled at him—

A sudden impact jolted Clarissa's body, shocking her awake. Her log had struck a sandbar that jutted out from shore within a sheltered curve of the river. The current was already washing the sand from around the log's end. Seconds from now the log would float free again, carrying her with it. There was no time to lose.

Gathering her strength, she dragged her bruised, chilled body off the log and rolled onto the sandbar. For a moment she lay there, gasping. Then, rousing herself, she crawled toward the bank. The sand gave way beneath her weight, leaving hollows of water where her palms and knees had pressed. A small snake—she had no idea what kind it was—slithered across the back of her hand and vanished into the river. Clarissa was too exhausted even to flinch.

Only when the ground felt solid did she allow herself to collapse facedown onto the grassy bank. The earth was cold against her aching body. Icy water dripped from the storm-lashed trees. A magpie scolded harshly from a branch, its call a sharp counterpoint to the chattering sound of Clarissa's own teeth.

For a long time she lay where she had dropped, too numb to move. Little by little, the sun crept above the trees. Fingers of light probed between the budding branches of birch and chestnut, warming her through her wet clothes. From an elderberry thicket, the song of a thrush bubbled on the morning air.

Raising her head, Clarissa blinked herself fully awake. Threads of vapor were curling upward from the rain-soaked ground. Her skirts were steaming themselves dry in the bright sunlight. The storm had passed, as all storms did, and a new day had begun.

The rushing murmur of the Ohio filled Clarissa's ears as she sat up and lifted a hand to her matted hair. Finding it hopelessly tangled, she swept the russet mass out of her face and sat clutching her knees, gazing across the sandbar at the muddy current, thinking how it had nearly claimed her. She remembered the storm and the two evil men who had vanished in the darkness. She remembered Tom Ainsworth, whose face she would never see again.

Clarissa slumped over her knees, shuddering in despair. How could a single careless moment so utterly destroy two lives?

At last she forced herself to sit up, pressing her palms to her burning eyes to stop the tears. This was no time for hand-wringing, she upbraided herself. She had no in-

tention of dying in this wilderness. She had two strong
legs and was quite capable of walking back to Fort Pitt.
If only she knew the way…

Suddenly she stared at the river.

What a silly goose she had been, sitting here feeling
sorry for herself! She was not lost at all. The flatboat had
come downstream. To find her way back to the fort, all
she needed to do was follow the riverbank upstream
again.

Setting her jaw, Clarissa staggered to her feet. She
moved awkwardly, her joints stiff, her bare feet swollen
and tender from hours in the water. Ignoring the pain,
she forced herself to take one step, then another.

Her mud-stiffened skirts clung to her legs. Her wet
petticoat dragged on the ground, hobbling her every
stride. She had scarcely gained ground when a sudden
misstep sent her sprawling again. The force of the landing
knocked the breath out of her. She lay gasping in the
mud, biting back tears of frustration.

I will not give up, Clarissa swore. If she had to crawl
all the way to Fort Pitt on her belly, she would do it. She
would survive to laugh again, to dance and flirt again, to
love, marry and bear a house full of happy children. She
would survive to grow old and wise, to cradle her grandchildren in her lap one day and tell them the story of her
great adventure in the wilderness.

Marshaling the last of her strength, she willed herself
to rise. Her right hand groped outward to brace her
body—only to freeze in midmotion as her fingertips
sensed an odd smoothness beneath their touch.

She glanced down and saw that her hand had discovered a shallow impression in the bare brown earth. Her
throat jerked as she realized what it was.

She was staring down at the long, broad print of a
leather moccasin.

Chapter Two

Wolf Heart watched from a stand of birch as the slender white girl scrambled to her feet. The panic in her wide green eyes could only mean one thing—she had discovered his tracks and sensed he was nearby.

His throat tightened as she hesitated, wheeling one way, then another. Her hair was a tangled cloud of flame in the morning sunlight. Her gown—the fabric too light and fine to be homespun—clung to her willowy woman's body in mud-stained tatters. She looked as fragile as the wing of a butterfly.

Wolf Heart had seen her clinging to the log as it washed ashore. He had melted into the trees as she crawled onto the sandbar, keeping out of sight as she collapsed, trembling and exhausted, onto the bank. A whirlwind of emotions had torn at him. This ethereal young stranger was part of a world he had long since buried, a world he had grown to despise. She and her kind did not belong here.

The girl spun away and broke into a limping run, headed toward the riverbank. Wolf Heart's blue eyes narrowed for an instant. As she vanished behind a clump of red willows, he stepped out of his hiding place and glided noiselessly after her.

Shadows flickered over his rangy hard-muscled body as he moved through the undergrowth. In this, the moon of mouse-eared leaves, the willows and birches trailed long catkins in the light morning wind, but the foliage was thin. The girl's hair blazed like a signal fire through the trees, making it easy to trail her even at a distance. Wolf Heart eased his powerful stride, giving her plenty of room. He had no wish to confront her face-to-face. Not, at least, until he had made up his mind what to do with her.

As he paused for thought, his fingers brushed the small deerskin medicine pouch he wore on a thong around his neck. It contained objects of his own choosing, small tokens of memory, family and courage. Wolf Heart's medicine pouch had been fashioned by his Shawnee mother, Black Wings. She had cut and stitched the leather, adding bands of fringe and fine quillwork to make it a thing of beauty. Inside it, Wolf Heart had reverently placed a tooth from the first bear he had taken, along with the bright indigo feather of a bluebird and, most important of all, his personal *pa-waw-ka,* a translucent shell he had seized from the bed of the ice-bound river during the ordeal that had marked his passage into manhood.

The medicine pouch was his badge of belonging, his proof to himself and others that he had abandoned all memory of Seth Johnson and become, in his deepest being, a true Shawnee. He had undergone the test and rituals. He had hunted bear, elk and puma, fought bravely against the marauding Iroquois and earned a place of honor among his brothers of the *kispoko* warrior sept. He had danced around the war pole. He had sung the death chant over Black Wings when she died of the coughing sickness. All this time, he had never questioned who or what he was—until now.

The coppery flash of her hair told him the girl was still running, darting in ragged bursts of speed along the bank of the Ohio-se-pe. She was headed upstream, toward the fort, most likely, or one of the grubby little settlements that pushed the white man's boundaries ever closer to the world of the Shawnee.

Wolf Heart had met a fair number of white men since the death of his father. There were the French who traded their guns and blankets for furs. There were the English redcoats who were becoming more and more common now that the British had seized the fort at the joining of the rivers. White men, yes. But any images of white women—including his own birth mother, who had died when he was six—existed only in the dimmest recesses of Wolf Heart's memory. He had never imagined, let alone seen, a fox-haired wisp of a girl like this one.

Any other Shawnee would have taken her prisoner by now, he reminded himself darkly. The tribe had sided with the French in this mad war against the English, making any English prisoner a trophy of war. So why then, when it would be so easy, had he not simply captured her? Was it her startling beauty that held him at bay? Was it the certainty that this girl would never survive captivity? Or was it something more subtle and disturbing—some long-buried tie of blood that even he could not deny? Whatever the reason, it troubled Wolf Heart deeply.

Far ahead now, he saw her stumble and go down in a patch of bog. His breath caught as she clawed her way upright then paused to glance back in his direction, her hair whipping the pale oval of her face. Her head went up sharply, and for an instant Wolf Heart thought she might have seen him. But then, just as abruptly, she wheeled and floundered on as before, dripping mud as she fought her way through the briars and willows that rimmed the flooded river.

The girl had spirit, he conceded. She was chilled, sore, exhausted and probably half-starved, as well, but she had shown no sign of flagging. Spunk and grit, combined with a healthy dose of fear, were driving her on, step by struggling step.

But for all her courage, Wolf Heart knew she could never make it back to her world alive. The journey was too long and too dangerous.

On impulse, he paused to examine her tracks in the mud. Crouching low, he traced the shape of one narrow imprint with his fingertip.

Where her foot had pressed, the damp brown earth was stained with blood.

Clarissa plunged along the bank of the river. Her ribs heaved painfully beneath the constricting stays of her corset. Her heart exploded with every beat, hammering the walls of her chest as she ran.

She had seen one fresh track. How many others had there been? How many pairs of savage eyes were watching her, even now, as she fled like a hunted animal.

A gust of wind whipped her long hair into her eyes, half-blinding her. She swept it back, only to feel the tangled ends catch on a low-hanging tree branch. A vision of the biblical Absalom, hanging lifeless by his hair, flashed through her mind as she jerked to free it. Any second now, she would feel the fatal thrust of an arrow in her back or, worse, the roughness of brown hands seizing her waist, dragging her off to an end so horrible she could not even imagine it.

She would die fighting, Clarissa vowed as she splashed through a patch of flooded willows. Whatever happened, she would not allow herself to be taken alive.

As she mounted the bank once more, pain shot through the ball of her left foot. She remembered, however dimly, stepping on something sharp earlier, but she had not dared to pause and investigate. Now the injury was getting worse. Her right sole, as well, had grown so tender that every step was agony. Sometime soon she would have to stop and wrap her feet, perhaps with strips of her petticoat. If only she knew where—

Clarissa's thoughts ended in a gasp as her toe stubbed against something soft. That same gasp exploded in a stifled scream as she looked down and saw the body of a man, clad in waterlogged buckskins, lying facedown in the long grass.

Her stomach convulsed as she recognized Maynard.

Her first impulse was to run, but when he did not move she swallowed her fear and stood staring down at him. *He's dead,* she thought. *He can't hurt anyone now.*

Flies swarmed around a blood-encrusted gash on the man's temple, but there were no other marks of injury on him. Most likely he had struck his head when the flatboat capsized, drowned while unconscious, and finally washed up here on the bank.

Clarissa battled waves of nausea as she crouched over the inert form, steeling herself to touch him. Maynard had been armed with a hunting knife. If that knife was still on him, and if she could get it, she would no longer be helpless prey. She would have a weapon to defend herself.

Maynard's dirty, wet buckskins reeked in the morning

sun. The stench swam in Clarissa's nostrils as she bent close, seized his arm and dragged him over onto his back. Yes, the knife was still there, large and evil looking, laced into the scabbard that hung from his belt. All she had to do was reach out and—

She froze as Maynard rolled his head to one side and groaned.

Panic seized her, and for an instant all she could think of was running away. But she needed the knife. She would have to get it now, before Maynard came fully awake.

She made a desperate lunge for the weapon, her fingers clutching at the leather-wrapped grip. For the space of a heartbeat, she had it. Then his sinewy hand closed around her wrist, twisting so hard that she cried out and dropped the knife.

"Well, hang me for a horse thief!" He grinned up at her, his small eyes glittering. "Heaven don't get no better than this!" He rolled to a sitting position, his free hand darting out to grab the knife from where it had fallen. A single joint-wrenching move spun her against him with the blade at her throat.

"You and me got some unfinished business, girl," he rasped against her ear. "And we're gonna finish it here and now!" His hand released her wrist and slid upward to fondle her breast. "Treat me nice, and you won't get hurt. Hell, you might even get to like it."

Clarissa struggled to keep her head. "We've got to get out of here," she whispered, her throat moving against the razor-sharp blade. "Indians—I saw moccasin tracks—"

"Nice try, girl." Maynard's arm tightened around her. "But I know this country, an' there ain't no Injun towns anywhere near these parts. An' even if you did see tracks, hell, plenty of white men wear moccasins, too. Now quit stallin', you little bitch, and git down on your back!''

The broad steel blade caught a glimmer of sun as he jerked her around and slammed her onto the wet grass. Clarissa lay rigid and trembling, praying for an instant's distraction when she might be able to catch him off guard. Maynard, she calculated, was capable of killing her, or carving her up so hideously that she would no doubt wish herself dead. If her timing was off, she would not get a second chance.

He was breathing hard now, muttering curses as he used his free hand to tug at the lacing of his breeches. The water had caused the leather ties to swell, and the knot was too stubborn to yield to Maynard's one-handed fumbling. Clarissa tensed as he grew more and more impatient. At last he spat out an oath and tossed the knife, point down, into the grass.

In a flash she was after it, twisting sideways, stretching to seize the weapon where it had struck. But she was not fast enough. With blinding speed, his hand had clamped hard around her wrist.

''Stupid little bitch!'' he cursed, twisting her arm so viciously that Clarissa felt her bones begin to separate, and she whimpered aloud in spite of her resolve. ''So help me, I'll fix you good!'' he rasped, snatching up the knife and raising it high for a slashing blow. ''I'll show you who's boss if it's the last thing I—''

Maynard spoke no more. She saw him stiffen and arch as if struck hard between the shoulder blades by some invisible force. Only as he pitched forward did she glimpse the arrow point protruding through the front of his buckskin shirt, right where his heart would be.

Clarissa's fear exploded into all-out panic as the lifeless body collapsed, still twitching on top of her. She

thrashed and kicked in a wild struggle to throw off the
horror, wanting only to be free of Maynard's smothering
weight.

Seconds passed, each one a small eternity, before she
realized that her ordeal of terror was only beginning.

The knife—it had been in Maynard's hand. She had to
get it before it was too late. Her fingers groped desperately along the wet ground where he would have dropped
the weapon. Her heart convulsed as she felt the tip of the
blade, cold and sharp against her fingertip. Gasping with
effort, she stretched to reach the handle. Her fingers
touched it, almost clasped it.

Then the weight of Maynard's limp corpse was
snatched off her as if it had suddenly sprouted wings.

The morning sun struck Clarissa fully in the eyes.
Dazed and blinking, she lay sprawled on the ground, her
muddy skirts ruched up to her thighs. She was aware that
Maynard's body had fallen to one side, but that was no
longer a concern. Her full attention was riveted on the
masculine figure who loomed above her, his features silhouetted by the blinding light.

Sun dazzled, her gaze dropped low, taking in long,
muscular, buckskin-clad legs. Little by little, her eyes fo-
cused upward, skimming the shadowed bulge beneath his
breechcloth, then darting abruptly to the feather-trimmed
tomahawk that hung at his waist and the elegantly crafted
bow balanced in his left hand.

Flinging herself onto her belly, she made another lunge
for Maynard's knife. This time her fingers closed around
the handle. She rolled swiftly, drawing in her knees and
coming up in a tight crouch, the weapon raised in defiance.

The stranger had not moved, but from her new position, Clarissa could see him more clearly. His powerful

chest and arms were bare except for the leather strap of his arrow quiver and a small decorated pouch that hung from a thong around his neck. His long wavy hair, decorated with twin eagle feathers at the scalp lock, was raven-black, tinged with an azure glow where the light fell on it. Flat silver ear studs, set into his lobes, glittered as they caught the rays of the sun. His eyes, shadowed by craggy brows, were—

Her thoughts scattered like alarmed birds as he took a step toward her.

Clarissa tensed, clutching the knife. She had vowed to die fighting rather than be taken alive. Now that vow would be put to the test. "Don't come any closer!" she hissed.

He took another cautious step, then one more. "Don't be afraid," he said gently. "I won't hurt you."

Clarissa was beyond hearing his words, let alone comprehending them. Her pulse exploded, pumping her system with the fury of a cornered animal as she sprang upward to meet this new enemy. The steel blade flashed in the sun as she struck wildly, blindly at the stranger's chest.

She heard him grunt as the razor edge skimmed his flesh. His huge hand captured her wrist, its momentum whipping her against him, where he caught and held her fast. Clarissa had dropped the knife, but she continued to fight like a wildcat, her hands clawing his chest, her feet kicking his solidly placed legs.

A glancing blow from her raised knee caught him off guard. Still gripping her waist, he stumbled backward and stepped into the entrance of a badger hole. His fall carried them both to the ground. They rolled in the grass, legs tangling, knees jabbing as he struggled to subdue her.

Their tussle had displaced his breechcloth. Clarissa felt

the masculine bulge brush her thigh. The contact triggered a disturbing tingle, flooding her body with rivulets of heat—but the sensation was swiftly dashed by terror. This man, this *Indian* would ravish her, she thought, just as Maynard had meant to do. Then he would use that deadly tomahawk to hack away her scalp, leaving her body here for the crows and buzzards.

He had managed to seize both her wrists and pinion them above her shoulders. Wild with fear, Clarissa twisted to one side and sank her teeth into the firm bronze flesh of his forearm.

"Stop it!" He jerked away, his voice raw with anger now. "Stop now!"

Clarissa went rigid with shock as the realization struck her. This half-naked savage was speaking to her in English.

"What…?" She struggled to form a question, but it was no use. The words died somewhere between her mind and her tongue as she found herself staring up into a pair of cold, angry eyes.

The irises of those black-centered eyes were a deep cobalt-blue.

Wolf Heart felt the girl's body go limp beneath him. Where his hands gripped her wrists, he could feel her pulse racing like the heart of a rabbit in a snare. She was still frightened, but at least she had stopped fighting him.

"I don't mean to hurt you," he said, groping for the words of a language he had spoken but rarely in the past fourteen years. "But if you bite me again, you will wish you hadn't!"

She stared up at him, her wide eyes the color of deep mossy pools. "You're a white man!" she whispered incredulously.

"No." Wolf Heart's reply was as cold as the chill her words evoked. "I am Shawnee."

Her gold-tipped lashes blinked as she strained upward. "But your speech, your eyes—"

"I was a white *boy* once, a very long time ago. I have never been a white man." Wolf Heart raised his body, aware, suddenly, that he was straddling her hips in a most unseemly manner. "If I let you sit up, do you promise you won't try to run?"

The girl hesitated, giving him a moment to study her thin heart-shaped face. She would be a beauty in the white man's world, he thought. But he had grown accustomed to the robust darkness of Shawnee women, and this pale creature seemed as out of place here as a snowflake in summer. Her skin was streaked with angry red scratches from the brambles. Her hair was matted with river weed, and one side of her face was crusted with a layer of drying mud.

"What a sorry sight you are," he said, the words springing from some forgotten well of memory. It was the kind of thing his white mother might have said to him as a child.

Her green eyes flashed with spirit. "And what kind of sight would you be if you'd been kidnapped, shipwrecked in a flood and nearly drowned?" she snapped. "Are you going to let me up?"

"I'm still waiting for your answer," he retorted gruffly. "Will you promise to stay put?"

"That depends."

"Depends?" Had he ever known that word? A heartbeat passed before it surfaced in his memory.

"My answer depends on what you mean to do with me," she explained as if she were talking to a backward child. When he did not answer at once, the fear stole back into her eyes. "All I want is to go back to Fort Pitt," she said in a small strained voice. "Just let me go. Is that such a difficult thing to do?"

Wolf Heart scowled as the dilemma he had wrestled all morning closed in on him. "Fort Pitt is many days' walk from here. These woods are filled with dangers, and you are not strong—"

"I'm stronger than I look!" she interrupted. "I came close to getting the best of you, if I say so myself!"

"You wouldn't come so close to getting the best of a puma or a bear—or another man like that one." He jerked his head toward the buckskin-clad body that lay in the grass, a stone's toss away. "But I'd wager you'd be more likely to starve, or drown, or maybe get bitten by a copperhead."

"You could take me back!" She strained upward against his hands, her eyes so hopeful that they tore at his heart. "My uncle, Colonel Hancock, would pay you a handsome reward."

"What would I do with money? I am Shawnee!" The words burst out of Wolf Heart, resolving his own question. Shawnee law demanded that all captives be turned over to the village council for judgment. To defy that law, to go against custom and set the girl free, would be an abnegation of his duty as a Shawnee warrior.

He willed his expression, and his heart, to harden. "You are my prisoner," he said. "I must take you back to my people."

"Don't be ridiculous! Your people are my people— white!"

"Sit up." Wolf Heart ignored the sting of her words as he jerked her roughly to a sitting position and bound her wrists behind her back with a strip of deer hide. She did not speak, but he could feel the anger in her slim,

taut body and see it in the set of her delicate jaw. When
he pulled her to her feet, she did not protest, but he knew
her mind was working. Given the chance, the girl would
make every effort to escape.

When he motioned for her to walk ahead of him, she
moved silently into place. She was footsore and hungry,
and he knew he was being cruel, but he did not trust
himself enough to treat her gently. Not yet, at least.

Abruptly she swung back to face him. Blazing defiance, her eyes flickered toward the dead man who lay
facedown in the grass, the arrow still protruding from his
back. "What about him?" she asked in a voice drawn
thin by fury.

"That one is past our help." Wolf Heart turned away
from the corpse, which was already beginning to attract
flies.

"I can see that," the girl snapped. "But since you're
a Shawnee, I thought you might be wanting to take his
scalp."

Wolf Heart glared at her, his temper stirring.

"Go ahead," she persisted. "He was an evil man, and
his death was no loss. Show me what a true savage
you've become!"

Her sarcasm cut as no blade could. Wolf Heart, who
had never killed a white man before, let alone taken a
white scalp, bit back the urge to seize her shoulders in
his hands and shake her until she whimpered for for-
giveness.

"Well?" she demanded, her eyes flinging a challenge.

Freezing all emotion, he caught her elbow, spun her
away from him and shoved her to a reluctant walk.

Clarissa stumbled along the forest trail, feeling more
dead than alive. Her blistered, bleeding feet were beyond

pain. Her stomach was a clenched knot of hunger and fear. Only anger kept her moving—that, and her resolve to make this self-proclaimed Shawnee pay dearly for having taken her prisoner.

"It's a lovely day for a walk, isn't it?" She tossed her hair, refusing to give him the satisfaction of hearing her complain.

Wolf Heart's only reply was brooding silence.

"I've always wanted to explore the wilderness," she persisted with mock pleasantry. "And what a splendid guide I have! A man who knows every bird, every tree—"

"That's enough!" His voice, behind her, was a low growl of irritation. "Keep that up, and every ear within a day's run will be able to hear you!"

"Oh, how nice!" She forced her miserable feet to a lilting skip and began to sing. "'In Scarlet Town where I was born/ There lived a fair maid dwellin'/ Made every lad cry well a-day/ Her name was Barbara—'"

"Stop it!" he snapped, his massive hand catching her arm and whipping her around to face him. "Do you want me to gag your mouth, tie your legs and drag you along the trail?"

Clarissa gulped back her fear, forcing herself to meet his blazing blue eyes. "Well, at least that might save some wear on my poor blistered feet!" she declared saucily. "Yes, indeed, why don't you try it?"

He shot her a thunderous scowl. Then the breath eased wearily out of him, and Clarissa knew she had won a victory, however small. "Sit," he ordered her gruffly.

"There?" She glanced toward a toadstool-encrusted log.

"Sit anywhere. I don't care. Just keep your mouth shut

while I tend to your feet. We still have a lot of walking to do.''

"How much walking?'' Clarissa sank on to the log, exhausted to the point of collapse but determined not to show it. "Where are you taking me?''

"To the place where I left my canoe.'' He crouched on one bent knee, his heavy black brows meeting in a scowl as he lifted and examined the bruised, blistered sole of her foot.

"And from there?''

"To my village, far down the river.''

"And what will become of me then?'' Clarissa's voice dropped to a choked whisper as the gravity of her situation sank home. This was no game, no idle contest of wit and will. This was a battle for her life.

He was bent low, his craggy features compressed into a frown as his fingers picked away the thorns and tiny rocks that had embedded themselves in her tender flesh.

"You didn't answer me,'' she said, feigning boldness. "What will happen when we reach your village?''

"You will be brought before the council,'' he said slowly, his eyes on his task. "And you will be tried.''

"Tried?'' Clarissa's body gave an involuntary jerk. "Tried for what?''

He glanced up at her, his eyes the icy blue of a frozen lake in winter. "To see if you are worthy,'' he answered.

"Worthy?'' Clarissa could feel her heart fluttering like a trapped bird inside her rib cage.

"Yes,'' he answered in a low voice. "Worthy to live.''

Chapter Three

Wolf Heart caught the subtle widening of her eyes. He saw the terror that glinted in their clear green depths. He felt the tension in her slim white foot where it balanced on his bent knee. The girl had courage. Perhaps too much courage for her own good.

At first, when she had defied him, even teased him, he had thought her merely foolish. Now he saw that she was well aware of her danger. Even so, she hid her fear, masking it with boldness.

"Tell me," she demanded, fixing him with a brazen gaze. "What is your name?"

"In your tongue, my name means Wolf Heart," he said, bending close to twist a stubborn thorn from her heel. She winced as it came free, the small wound oozing blood. How could she have walked so far on those sore, tender feet without a whimper of complaint?

"I mean your real name," she persisted annoyingly.

He froze, scowling up at her. "I just told you my real name."

"All right, then, your old name. Your Christian name."

"Seth Johnson." The long-forgotten syllables were

hard to form. They left him wanting to rinse out his own mouth for having spoken them.

"My name is Clarissa. Clarissa Rogers," she said lightly, as if she were meeting some swain at a party. "May I call you Seth?"

"No." Wolf Heart carefully brushed the last of the dirt and twigs from her left foot, wishing she would be quiet and leave him alone. But, he sensed she was formulating more questions, and he knew that she would allow him no peace until she had her answers.

"Since you're bound to ask, I was adopted by the Shawnee when I was eleven years old," he said. "They raised me as one of their own. I *am* Shawnee, and my true name is Wolf Heart."

A quiver passed through her fragile body as he lifted her right foot, cradling it, for the space of a heartbeat, between his big rough hands.

"And did the Shawnee try you as they will try me?" she asked, lowering her voice to a taut whisper.

"Yes." He worked a small, sharp stone from the ball of her foot and used his finger to stanch the bead of crimson blood it left behind.

"Tell me about it," she said. "I want to be ready."

"When you need to know, then I will tell you." He gazed down at her bruised, bleeding legs, trying not to think of the gauntlet and what it would do to her pale flesh. At that moment, he wished with all his heart she could be spared the ordeal. But that was not the Shawnee way.

"Are you hungry?" He spoke into the gulf of silence that had fallen between them.

"I could probably force myself to eat a bite or two." Her eyes glittered defiance. "Untie my wrists, and I'll help myself to whatever you're serving."

Wolf Heart hesitated, then shook his head, knowing he could not trust those swift hands of hers unfettered. "First I will finish with your feet," he said decisively. "Then I will feed you myself."

He drew his own steel hunting knife and saw her shrink back from him, her eyes as startled as a doe's. Without speaking, he seized a handful of her ragged petticoat and began slashing a strip as wide as his hand from around the hem.

Her spunk returned as she realized what he was doing. "You owe me for one fine English petticoat!" she bantered.

"I'll pay you in food." He finished cutting the strip and began wrapping it in tight layers around her foot. The cloth would wear out rapidly, but at least it should protect her bleeding soles long enough to reach the canoe.

The girl watched him in tense silence as he worked. *Clarissa.* His mind toyed with her name, turning it over like a glistening river stone. It was a flower name, a name that whispered of pink satin ribbons, dancing slippers and tea in thin little china cups. Clarissa.

"What happened to your family?" she asked, the question pushing into his thoughts. "Did the Shawnee kill them?"

He shot her a glare. "No. I was an orphan. Even that is more than you need to know."

"I'm an orphan, too," she said, studying him with those disconcerting eyes. "My brother Junius sent me to Fort Pitt to find a husband."

"And did you find one?" He had finished wrapping her left foot and started on her right. He was looking down as he spoke and, thus, was totally unprepared for the responding tinkle of laughter. It was a musical sound, as light as the trill of a bird. He glanced up at her, half-startled.

"Find a husband? Gracious, no!" she exclaimed, her pale cheeks dimpling. "Unless, of course, you'd be willing to fill the job. Junius isn't fussy. He just wants me out of the way."

Wolf Heart bent his attention to the wrapping of her foot. Shawnee girls could also be bold and saucy. That he knew all too well. Yet this fragile creature, bruised, starved and probably frightened half to death, was the most impudent female he had ever met in his life. Her spirit moved and astounded him.

But he could not soften toward her, Wolf Heart admonished himself. This intriguing prisoner was not his to judge. She belonged, even now, to the people of his tribe, and he could not let himself be swayed, either by her fragile beauty or by her white blood. Her fate was out of his hands.

"You need to eat." He reached into the small parfleche that hung at his waist, drew out a thin strip of smoked venison and thrust it toward her.

"Ugh! What's that?" She drew back, wrinkling her elegant nose in distaste. "It looks awful and smells even worse!"

"It's just deer meat," Wolf Heart said irritably.

He tore off a small chunk from the dark, dry slab. Her gaze widened sharply as his fingers moved the morsel toward her mouth. "It looks raw," she said, shrinking away from him.

"Smoked and salted. Try it."

She shook her head in a show of defiance. This, Wolf Heart swiftly realized, was to be a contest of wills. "How long has it been since you ate?" he demanded.

"What difference does it—" Her question ended in a

choking sound as he shoved the sliver of meat into her
open mouth, seized her jaw between his two hands and
held it shut. Inches from his own, her green eyes blazed
like a bobcat's.

"You are going to eat if I have to stuff this down your
throat!" he said in a low, menacing voice. "Now chew!"

Her gaze shot daggers as he held her, his fingers framing her temples, his thumbs bracing her jaw. She smelled
of river moss, and her cheeks were as soft as the petals
of the wild hawthorn blossom. A vein throbbed beneath
the translucent skin of her throat.

Wolf Heart found himself growing acutely aware of
her body and the way the mud-stiffened bodice of her
gown had molded to her small, perfect breasts. He remembered their savage struggle on the riverbank, her
slim legs tangling so wildly with his own. Even now, the
thought of it triggered a freshet of heat that trickled
downward to pool in his loins.

This was not good, he lectured himself. Being this
close to her was filling his head with thoughts that would
only weaken his resolve and make everything more difficult. Clarissa Rogers was nothing but a red-haired bundle of trouble. She was the kind of female who could get
under a man's skin and fester there like a blackberry
spine. He would be a fool not to keep a safe distance.

With a sharp exhalation, he forced himself to let her
go. She sagged backward, her gaze searing his senses.

"Very well, I won't force you to eat," he said evenly.
"But you're going to need all your strength in the days
ahead. Your life will depend on it, Clarissa. That much
I can promise you."

For an instant her pride wavered. Then a single tear
glimmered in her angry eyes. Without a word, she began
to chew the venison he had given her, gingerly at first,

then with ravenous hunger. Her swanlike throat jerked as she swallowed.

Bit by bit, he fed her nearly half of the smoked venison. She might have eaten it all, but Wolf Heart feared that so much meat on an empty stomach might make her sick.

Her eyes watched him guardedly as he replaced the leftover meat in the parfleche. She had not uttered a word the whole time she was eating. Only now, as he stepped back and motioned for her to stand, did she clear her throat and speak.

"Don't expect me to thank you for the food," she said. "If you really want my thanks, you'll untie me and let me go."

"You wouldn't last a day out here on your own." He stepped back onto the trail and waited for her to take her place in front of him. She moved obediently ahead, then swung angrily back to face him.

"Are my chances any better with the Shawnee?" she flared. "What if I don't pass my so-called trial? What if I'm not judged worthy to live? What then? Why don't you just kill me here and now?"

Wolf heart met her eyes, steeling himself against the fear in their green depths—the fear that was already eating away at his conscience. He remembered his own boyhood ordeal, the stark terror that had kept him on his feet and driven him through the gauntlet. Maybe it would be the same for Clarissa. Her delicate body housed a fighting spirit, that much he already knew. But would it be enough?

She glared up at him with the ferocity of a trapped animal, and for an instant Wolf Heart was tempted to reveal everything she would be facing. He swiftly

checked himself. Knowing would only heighten her fear.
It would only serve to worsen her ordeal.

He forced himself to give her a hard look. "Turn
around and walk, Clarissa," he said quietly. "We have
a long way to go."

The canoe lay at the river's edge, concealed by a
thicket of overhanging willows. Fashioned of birch bark,
the brown inner side facing outward, it was an elegant
little craft, as sleek and graceful as the point of a spear.

The sight of it filled Clarissa with a mingled rush of
relief and dismay. Wolf Heart had set a grueling pace on
the trail, draining every drop of her endurance. Bone
weary and sore, she welcomed the prospect of resting her
battered feet. But reaching the canoe also meant they
were nearing the Shawnee village where she would face
a fate so terrible that he had refused even to speak of it.

Tossing her hair out of her eyes, she slumped against
a tree. She could feel Wolf Heart's keen blue eyes watching her every motion, but he had not touched her since
their encounter over the meat. He had scarcely spoken,
in fact; not even earlier, when she'd insisted that he turn
his back while she squatted wretchedly in the grass to
relieve herself. He had shut himself away to become as
silent and mysterious as the forest itself.

His sun-gilded body glistened with sweat as he bent to
slide the canoe into the river. Except for his eyes, this
man, christened Seth Johnson, could have passed for a
full-blooded Shawnee. He had dark bronze skin overlay-
ing a lithe, muscular body. His flowing black hair and
liquid way of moving blended with the elements of wind
and water, sunlight and shadow. His face was satin
smooth with no trace of beard. How could that be? Cla-

rissa wondered. Perhaps later she would ask him—if she lived long enough.

The canoe lay rocking gently in a shallow bed of water. "Climb in," Wolf Heart ordered her gruffly. Then, seeing that she would not be able to balance in the wobbly craft with her hands tied, he straightened, moved close to her and began loosening the knot of the leather thongs that bound her wrists.

Clarissa stood very still, her heart hammering as she felt the brush of his fingertips and the stir of his breath in her hair. His skin smelled lightly of rain and wood smoke. She fought the strange compelling urge to strain forward and taste him with the tip of her tongue.

For the space of a breath, time seemed to freeze. Then the leather thong fell away, freeing her arms. He stepped back as Clarissa rubbed the circulation into her tingling wrists.

"No tricks," he warned her gruffly, "or I'll truss you up like a dead deer and sling you into the bottom of the canoe."

She nodded, more in acknowledgment than promise. If any chance arose to escape, Clarissa knew she would take it.

He crouched to hold the canoe's edge until she could sit down in the prow, facing forward with her muddy ragged skirts piled around her. "Hang on to that cross brace," he said, his glance indicating a smooth wooden bar in front of her. "There's some rough water out there."

She twisted back to look at him. "You don't have to do this," she pleaded. "Let me go and forget you ever saw me. I'll take my chances in the woods."

The only answer to her plea was the subtle tightening of Wolf Heart's jaw.

Clarissa felt the canoe scrape the bottom of the shallow inlet as he took his place behind her and pushed off with the paddle. Swiftly they glided out into the flooded river.

Clarissa gasped as the flood-swollen current struck the canoe, sweeping it into an eddy, swirling it around and around like a windblown leaf. She clung white knuckled to the brace, spray lashing her cheeks as the bow dipped and danced through the water. Haunted by the nightmare ride on the flatboat, she battled rising waves of panic.

Behind her, she could hear Wolf Heart laboring with the paddle. She could hear the deep, steady passage of air in and out of his powerful lungs. He was not afraid, she suddenly realized. He knew the river's nature and how to use it, how to move in harmony with the current, not against it.

Clarissa felt her fear easing. She leaned forward, the breeze lifting her hair as the water foamed along the narrow bow. Her hands kept their tight grip on the cross brace. Except for the persistent churning of her stomach she could almost believe she was going to survive this wild ride.

Moments later they shot out of the rapids and entered a calmer stretch of water. Clarissa slumped over the bow. "Are you all right?" she heard Wolf Heart ask.

"I'm just dandy," she snapped, feeling dizzy and nauseous. "For someone who's been half-drowned, force-marched barefoot through the woods, stuffed with half-raw meat and taken on a giant whirligig ride, I'm doing magnificently! Now, if you'll excuse me—"

She leaned over the side of the bobbing canoe and proceeded to lose everything he had so insistently fed her.

Behind her, dead silence had fallen. In the midst of that silence she heard Wolf Heart chuckle. The sound was so deep and warm and startling that, for all her miserable condition, it sent a shock of pleasure through her body—pleasure that was swiftly replaced by outrage. Shawnee or white, this backwoods ruffian had no right to laugh at her discomfort.

She turned around and shot him a malevolent glare, only to see him grinning broadly at her. "Clarissa Rogers, you're a caution," he said.

"A caution?" She shook her head at the homeyness of the word, coming as it did from a bare-chested savage with silver disks in his ears and two eagle feathers jutting from his scalp lock. "I have no idea what you mean by that!"

Sunlight rippled on his massive shoulders as he maneuvered the canoe expertly around a large boulder. "You've been through enough to undo most white women," he said. "But you still haven't lost your spunk."

"I can see you don't know much about white women!" Clarissa huffed, still feeling light-headed. "Did you expect me to swoon? Did you expect me to whimper and cry like a helpless little ninny? For your information, I'm way beyond that now. I've long since had all the crying scared out of me!"

Turning her back on him, she frowned down at the greenish brown river, wondering how deep it was. If she could touch bottom, she might be able to wade ashore and flee into the woods. She would be taking a dangerous chance, but even drowning could prove to be a kinder fate than the unknown terrors awaiting her in the Shawnee village.

"Where do you come from?" she asked, resolving to bide her time and wait for exactly the right spot in the river. "Your speech, some of the things you say—you

don't sound as if you started life in a log hut on the
Allegheny.''

When he did not answer, Clarissa realized she had
stepped on to forbidden ground. As a man who had buried his past, Wolf Heart was clearly uncomfortable with
her question.

''Very well, if you won't talk, I will,'' she said, setting
out to distract him with chatter. ''My father was a cloth
merchant. He owned one of the finest shops in Baltimore.
He and my mother were very happy, as I recall, but she
died when I was six, and the rest of my upbringing was
left to our housekeeper, Mrs. Pimm.''

She spoke into the breeze, letting her words float back
to the brooding presence behind her. ''My father passed
away seven years ago, and, of course, my brother Junius,
who was already grown, inherited the house and the business. We never did get on well, Junius and I. He's made
no secret of counting the days until I take my dowry and
leave him alone with his precious, moldy, old ledger
books.''

Clarissa glanced back over her shoulder to see if Wolf
Heart was listening. His stony face had assumed a mask
of studied indifference.

''My dowry includes a fine ten-acre parcel of land just
outside the city and fifty pounds in gold,'' she continued,
ignoring his silence. ''All of it, of course, will go to my
husband when I marry.''

Her voice trailed off as it struck her that, in all likelihood, she would not live to bestow her dowry, or herself, on any future husband. Her land and money would
go to the penny-pinching Junius, to gather dust with the
rest of his possessions. Her bones would lie in unmarked
earth, somewhere in this alien wilderness, unmourned
and unremembered.

Tears blurred Clarissa's sight. She blinked them furiously away, determined not to show emotion before her grim captor. Straightening her shoulders, she cleared her throat to speak again, but no words would come. Her hands whitened on the cross brace as the silence grew more and more oppressive.

"I was born in Boston." Wolf Heart's voice, low and husky behind her, sent a tremor through Clarissa's body. "My father was a schoolmaster, a good and gentle man until my mother died. Then he took to drink, and that changed everything."

He lapsed into silence once more, and Clarissa sensed the struggle that raged inside him. He was not a man who revealed himself easily, that she already knew. This slow opening of his past left her strangely touched, as if, in exchange for her empty prattle, he had presented her with a rare and valuable gift.

Quiet minutes passed, broken only by the ripple of the water and the calls of morning songbirds. At last he cleared his throat and spoke again, each word laced with the pain of memory.

"The whiskey turned my father into a violent, foulmouthed stranger. The more he drank, the more he cursed and beat me. I should have run away, but I was only a boy, and he was all the family I had.

"After we lost our home to the moneylenders, he began having grand dreams about making a fortune in the fur trade. He hired both of us out until he'd saved enough for traps. Then we headed west—farther west than any reasonable white man would have gone alone. We were trapping beaver near the mouth of the Little Miami when a bear came charging out of the willows. She grabbed my father before he could even turn around." Even now, Wolf Heart's words quivered with self-blame. "I couldn't

save him. All I could do was run for my life.'' He emp-
tied his lungs in a ragged exhalation. ''The boy named
Seth Johnson died that day. He was reborn as a Shawnee.''

Stillness lay like a wall between them, growing thicker,
heavier. ''The Shawnee found you and took you in?''
Clarissa prompted when she could bear it no longer.

''They offered me everything I thought I'd lost,'' he
said. ''Family. Honor. Kindness. A life filled with meaning and purpose.''

''And when they put you on trial—'' a bitter undertone
had crept into Clarissa's voice ''—did you prove yourself
worthy to live among them?''

''Yes.''

She strained to hear his half-whispered reply.

''As I have had to prove myself many times over. Even
now.''

The canoe shot forward as he drove the paddle hard
into the current. Clarissa stared bleakly ahead—trees,
willows and water blending into streaks of muted spring
color. She knew now why Wolf Heart had taken her prisoner, and why he would never let her go. To show compassion for a white captive would prove, to him and to
all his adopted tribe, that he was not a true Shawnee. He
would be an outcast, torn from a world he had come to
know and love.

She could expect no mercy from him.

They were passing through a level stretch of river.
Here the floodwaters had crept outward across the bot-
tomlands to form a lake, so calm and glassy that the
current was scarcely visible. Clarissa stared down at the
clouded water, wondering what lay beneath it. Surely,
with the river spread so wide, it could not be more than
a few feet deep in any spot. Better yet, the bank on the

near side was thick with brush and willows. If she could reach them, it might be possible to duck beneath the water, then surface and hide in the shelter of the trailing branches until Wolf Heart gave her up for drowned.

Clarissa's mind reeled with the daring of her idea. It was a reckless scheme, to be sure. But a fighting chance at escape was better than no chance at all.

She glanced back at Wolf Heart, hoping to catch him off guard. He was watching her intently.

"How far is your village?" she asked in a ploy to lure him back into conversation.

"Not far." His paddle rippled through the silky water. "We will be there before sundown."

"You were a long way from home when you found me," she ventured. "What were you doing?"

"Trailing a bear."

"A bear?" Clarissa's reflexes jerked. She imagined herself lying unconscious on the riverbank, the monstrous beast lumbering out of the trees to sniff at her inert body.

"It came to nothing," Wolf Heart said. "I lost the trail not long before I found you."

"At least you won't be coming home empty-handed." Clarissa made a show of finger-combing her matted curls, drawing his gaze upward as, beneath her skirts, her legs shifted for the leap to freedom. Her pounding heart seemed to fill her whole chest and throat as she tensed, then sprang upward and hurled herself out over the surface of the river.

For the barest instant she hung suspended between sun and water. Then the cold strangling wetness closed around her and she began to sink. Her kicking feet groped for the bottom that, by all reason, should have been within easy reach. It was not there.

Too late, Clarissa realized how wrong she had been.

The river was far deeper here than it had appeared from the surface, and now its strong undertow was pulling her down. Her bursting lungs released a trail of bubbles in the darkness. Her mouth gulped for air and took in water. Her legs and arms thrashed frantically as her oxygen-starved mind began to dim.

She was already beginning to drown.

Chapter Four

Wolf Heart cursed under his breath—a white man's curse—as his prisoner plunged over the side of the canoe and vanished headlong into the brown swirl of water. His annoyance was directed more at himself than at Clarissa Rogers. He should have known she would try something like this.

His first impulse was to dive in after her, but he swiftly checked himself. To jump into the river would mean losing the canoe and all his provisions. It would be easy enough to paddle to shore ahead of her. That way he would be there waiting to confront her when she staggered, dripping and exhausted, onto the bank.

He turned the canoe broadside to the current, expecting at any moment to see Clarissa's head bob into sight, her russet hair streaming behind her like a long wet foxtail as she stroked through the water. The undercurrent was strong in this part of the river, but the bank was no more than a stone's throw away. A good swimmer would be able to cover the distance in a few minutes' time. And surely, if Clarissa was not a good swimmer, she would not have jumped.

Seconds passed, measured in long deep breaths and

expectant heartbeats. More seconds crawled by, and still she did not appear. Wolf Heart's instincts shrilled in alarm as he realized something was wrong.

In a flash his lean body knifed into the river, leveling out an arm's length below the surface. Water filled his vision, so murky with silt that he could barely see his own hands, let alone any sign of Clarissa.

Sick with dread he stroked deeper, heading downstream, the way the current would have carried her. The boyhood ordeal by which he had earned his *pa-waw-ka* served him well now. Every morning, for four long winter moons, he had forced himself to dive naked into the frigid river. On the final day, with the whole village looking on, he had made three dives, the last one carrying him beneath the ice to the Ohio's dark bed, where his searching hand had clasped the translucent shell he carried now in his medicine pouch.

That long dive came back to him now as he groped for Clarissa's slender, elusive body. He remembered the fear, the darkness, the deadly cold. As he had once found his *pa-waw-ka,* he knew he had to find her.

Lungs bursting, he surfaced at last. His eyes scanned the milky surface of the river as he gulped air, then dove again. Could she be playing with him, hiding somewhere out of sight, laughing behind her hands as he searched frantically in the water? He would not put that past the little vixen—but no, a black inner certainty told him the danger was real.

The current was rougher here. Wolf Heart could feel its pull as the river swept him toward an outcrop of rocks. If he did not find her soon...

His pulse leaped as his fingers brushed a mass of flowing hair, long and fine and silky to the touch. He seized it, and in the next instant felt her head, her throat, her face. He reached lower and caught her waist. She did not respond.

With a wrenching tug, he pulled her body clear from where it had wedged between two underwater boulders. She drifted beside him, as lifeless and unresisting as a doll, as he kicked for the surface, made a final upward lunge and broke with her into the sunlight.

Clarissa lolled in his arms, blue from lack of air. A vein pulsed along the curve of her throat, but she was not breathing.

He plunged for the shallows, lifting her in his arms as his feet found bottom. Her wet hair fanned over his arms, its color like polished cedar. Her gown clung in water-soaked tatters to her delicately curved body. Wolf Heart glanced down at her closed eyelids, remembering her laughter, her maddening questions, her astounding courage. Bursting with effort, he surged ahead, bulling his way through the resisting water. Time and distance crept at a nightmare's pace as he fought his way toward the river's edge.

At last he broke free of the water, lurched onto the bank and rolled Clarissa belly-down onto the grass. With his knees, he straddled her waist, his urgent hands working her ribs, lifting, squeezing to imitate the motion of breath.

Why hadn't he let her go free, back there in the woods? She was such a harmless creature, as fragile and innocent as a fawn. He could just as easily have trailed her back to Fort Pitt, protecting her from a distance until she reached safety. Now, whether she lived or died, it was too late. He had destroyed whatever life she had known, as surely as if he had crushed her skull with a war club.

A sudden shudder passed beneath his hands, a quiver of life that sent a thrill through Wolf Heart's body.

Knowing what must be done, he lifted her by the waist, letting her head hang down. Clarissa choked. Her corseted ribs convulsed as she vomited up a stomach full of dirty brown water.

Wolf Heart steeled himself as he lowered her trembling body to the grass and rolled her onto her back. It would have been easier if she had drowned, he lashed himself. Now, if anything, he was even more deeply torn than before.

She lay with her eyes closed, color flooding her pale cheeks as she breathed. The bodice of her gown, or what was left of it, molded wetly to her small firm breasts, the tatted edging of her camisole stained brown with river mud. The wet tangle of her hair lay pooled on the grass, framing her porcelain features with flame.

Wolf Heart looked down at her for a long moment, then glanced swiftly up at the sky, his fingertips brushing his medicine pouch.

Weshcat-welo k'weshe laweh-Pah. The words of his Shawnee mother, Black Wings, echoed in his memory. *May we be strong by doing what is right.*

His gaze dropped once more to Clarissa's pale face. *Weshemoneto, Master of Life, make me strong,* he breathed in wordless prayer. *Help me remember who I am and what I must do.*

Clarissa opened her eyes to find him crouched over her, his hair dripping, his gaze deeply troubled. A muscle twitched in his cheek as their eyes met. As she stared up at him, the line of his mouth hardened into an angry scowl.

"What did you think you were doing?" he growled, the black tips of his brows almost touching above his nose. "I thought you had at least enough sense to stay in the canoe!"

"What…happened?" She blinked up at him, her mind still emerging from the fog of unconsciousness.

"You almost drowned, that's what! Why did you try such a crazy thing, anyway?"

"I didn't realize it would be so deep." Clarissa's throat felt as if she had swallowed a length of knotted hemp. Her ribs ached with every breath. The sun was a blur of light against the hot blue sky.

"You're saying you don't know how to swim?" He glowered down at her, angry and incredulous.

"Young ladies in Baltimore don't usually take swimming lessons," she retorted coldly.

"So you just jumped into a flooded river and expected to float?"

"Of course not! I meant to wade ashore, not swim. I just underestimated the depth of the water, that's all."

He shook his regal head in disgust. "Did you think it would be that easy to get away from me?" he demanded.

"Not really."

"Then why did you take such a foolish chance?"

Clarissa pushed herself up onto one shaky elbow, her hair tumbling into her water-reddened eyes. "The way I saw it, I had nothing to lose," she said.

"Nothing to lose?" His eyes contained the fury of summer lightning. "That's where you're wrong. You've managed to lose something very important to both of us."

His gaze flickered toward the river. Only then did Clarissa realize that the canoe was nowhere in sight. And only then, as she noticed the water drops glistening on Wolf Heart's coppery skin, did she understand that once more she owed this man her life.

"Not only is the canoe gone," he said with an under-tone of menace, "but also my bow and arrows, my blanket and the corn cakes I was going to feed you as soon as you felt well enough to eat again. Even my parfleche was lost in the river. Now we will both go hungry."

He rose to his full height, looming above her, his face a thundercloud. With one great fist, he caught Clarissa's hand and jerked her upward. She staggered to her feet, her senses reeling dizzily.

"I tried to make this journey easy for you," he said, turning her around and maneuvering her roughly ahead of him. "You chose not to go along. Without the canoe, we have only one way to get to the village. Walk."

It was his voice, rather than any perceived touch, that prodded Clarissa ahead. She willed one leaden foot to move, then the other. Her whole body ached. Her mouth tasted of sickness and river mud. The ground swam like water in her vision. But she would not give Wolf Heart the satisfaction of hearing so much as a whimper from her.

One foot. Then the other. She moved like a sleep-walker, conscious only of the dark presence behind her. Wolf Heart would not let her rest, she knew. He would march her all the way to his village.

She stumbled ahead, forcing each step. Then, abruptly, she blundered into a rain-filled hollow. Her leg buckled beneath her and she collapsed flat on the muddy ground.

Biting back a moan of despair, she braced her arms and worked her weight onto her knees. She would crawl if she had to, Clarissa swore, but she would die before she would beg this arrogant savage for mercy.

She inched forward, fingers clawing the mud. Suddenly the earth seemed to fall away beneath her. She gasped as Wolf Heart's big hands enclosed her waist. His powerful arms swept her upward, turned her deftly in midair, and slung her face-backward over his shoulder. Without a word, he struck out downriver, covering the ground in long, swift-moving strides.

Dazed, Clarissa bobbed limply while the breath returned to her body. Then she began to struggle. Her legs kicked uselessly beneath the clasp of his arm. Her fists pummeled the only part of him they could reach—his muscular buttocks—only to stop abruptly when she realized she was pounding bare flesh.

Her face reddened in spite of her fear. "Put me down!" she sputtered. "Put me down this instant!"

"You're saying you'd rather walk?" Wolf Heart did not break stride. His tone was almost pleasant, but Clarissa did not miss the edge to his question.

"That's not the point! I'm a lady, for your information, and no man has a right to handle me this way!"

"Oh?" Disdain sharpened his voice. "And how would you like me to handle you?"

"With dignity! With respect!" Clarissa's spirits sagged as she realized how ludicrous her demands must sound to him. Here she was, slung over his shoulder like a bag of oats. She was filthy, footsore, and facing a fate so horrible that she could not bear to imagine it. Dignity and respect had long since gone the way of the wind.

"Just let me go," she pleaded, abandoning all pretense. "Turn your back and let me take my chances in the forest with the wild animals. Is that asking so much?"

Wolf Heart did not answer her. When Clarissa twisted her head, she could see that he was gazing upriver, his body tense and expectant.

"Please, Wolf Heart," she persisted. "I'm not your

enemy. I mean your people no harm. Just leave me here. Forget you ever set eyes on me.''

His throat moved against the curve of her body. "It's too late for that," he said softly. "Look."

Stooping, he lowered Clarissa's feet to the ground. The blood rushed out of her head as she stood erect. She swayed dizzily, her vision swimming into darkness. Groping for Wolf Heart's arm, she clung to his solid flesh with both hands. Slowly the world stopped spinning around her. Little by little her vision cleared.

She stared past him, her gaze following the sun-dappled river upstream. A blue heron took flight from the shallows, its long neck folded into its shoulders, its slender legs trailing behind like ribbons. Dazzled, she traced its streaking flight along the curve of the bank.

Only then did she see the three canoes. Still small in the distance, they were bearing swiftly downstream toward the sandbar where she and Wolf Heart stood.

It's too late. His words spun in Clarissa's mind as she stood helplessly, watching the canoes approach. It was too late to run. Too late to hide. Too late to plead for her freedom. She had run out of hope.

Wolf Heart raised an arm and waved. A lone paddler in one of the canoes waved back and, in a moment, the narrow craft had broken away from the others and was angling across the current, moving toward the bank.

Clarissa remained silent, her heart a pulsing knot of dread. Wolf Heart had not spoken to her in minutes— had not, in fact, even looked at her. He was all Shawnee now, every remnant of Seth Johnson buried beneath the visage of a warrior.

The canoe glided into the shallows. Its bow nosed up to the bank and crunched onto the sand. The brave wielding the paddle paused to rest, a grin spreading across his lean, pockmarked face.

"*Tap-a-lot* brother!" He greeted Wolf Heart, but his curious eyes were already devouring Clarissa in fascination. "You told us you were going to hunt bear. Is this a new kind of bear you have taken alive? No, it looks more like a fox! How splendid that red pelt will look on your bed!"

Wolf Heart scowled, his gaze flickering to Clarissa. She could not understand a word of what Cat Follower was saying, of course. But in the hours to come she would be the butt of many such good-natured jokes, and he silently ached for her. Yes, he lashed himself, he should have let her go while there was still time. Now it was too late.

"And what has become of your canoe?" Cat Follower's grin widened, showing the gap of a missing tooth. "You look very wet, brother, as does your fox. Could it be that she spilled you both into the water? What a shame!"

"Never mind that," Wolf Heart retorted a bit sharply. "It's a long walk back to the village. Will your canoe carry all three of us?"

Cat Follower chuckled, one hand indicating the empty hull. "As you see, this was not a good day to go hunting. But my bad luck is your good luck. Since I have no game of my own, there is room for you, and for your white-skinned fox, as well."

"Then I owe you my thanks." Wolf Heart nudged Clarissa toward the canoe. His fingertips brushed her back, feeling the fear in her taut muscles. This time, however, she did not try to fight or run away. She had no strength left.

He seated her in the prow of the canoe, then, pushing

the craft off the sandbar, he slipped into place behind his friend and took up the spare paddle. Clarissa sat in rigid silence as the canoe glided into the current, her hair fluttering like a flame in the afternoon breeze.

Cat Follower's wiry muscles rippled beneath his pockmarked skin as he guided the canoe. Years ago, his family had taken in a French trapper who had stumbled, delirious with fever, into their camp. The white man had recovered and moved on, but the sickness he carried had swept through the small Shawnee village. Only Cat Follower, then a youth of sixteen summers, had survived.

"What do you plan to do with her?" He was staring raptly at the play of sunlight on Clarissa's hair.

"That is not for me to say." Wolf Heart spoke around the painful tightness in his throat. "You know our law as well as I do. It is for the council to decide."

"That will mean the gauntlet." Cat Follower glanced back at Wolf Heart. "The council will demand it."

"Yes, I know."

"This one is not strong, brother. Look at her. She is as thin as a willow."

Wolf Heart heard the note of caution in his friend's voice, and he knew it was meant for him. Even for a man, the gauntlet was a brutal test. He could hardly expect a fragile, city-bred girl like Clarissa to weather such punishment.

Even so, as he watched her lean into the wind, her hair flying like a banner, Wolf Heart knew he could not abandon hope. "A willow bends," he murmured quietly, "but it does not break."

Clarissa heard the low voices behind her, speaking a tongue as alien as the chatter of wild geese or the baying of a wolf pack. The two men were talking about her—

of that much she was certain. But maybe it was just as well she didn't understand what they were saying. She was frightened enough as it was.

Her hands gripped the sides of the canoe as the slim craft sliced through a stretch of white water. The spray was cool on her skin, the canoe's wild, careening plunges strangely exhilarating. Clarissa allowed herself to savor the moment. Soon, perhaps forever, all such pleasures would end.

With two paddlers, the canoe soon gained on its mates. Clarissa sensed the excitement among the other young braves as they turned to gaze at her, staring openly at her russet hair and pale skin. Resolving to be bold, she stared back at them. This, at least, gave her the opportunity to study her captors.

Earlier that day, she had observed that Wolf Heart, with his black hair and sun-burnished skin, could have passed for a full-blooded Shawnee. Now she saw how wrong she had been. He was far too large, for one thing. The Shawnee braves were compact and wiry, without an ounce of extra flesh on their bones. The rich coppery hue of their skins could never have come from the sun alone. The color seemed to glow in them, like light flickering beneath the surfaces of their bodies. For all the terror their sharp gazes struck in her, Clarissa had to admit that these Shawnee were beautiful people.

One of the braves called out, laughing. Wolf Heart's reply was brusque, almost angry. What had the young man said? Had it been something about her?

She risked a glance back at Wolf Heart. He was sitting in the rear of the canoe, the muscles rippling in his arms as he drove the paddle into the water. His hair streamed back in glossy waves from his impassive face. What was he thinking? Why wouldn't he look at her?

Fear tightened its cold grip on Clarissa's throat. Her eyes gazed out at the sun-sparkled water. Her ears heard the laughter of the paddlers and the squawk of a passing crow. It was a sham, all of it, she knew. Death and danger lurked beneath the peace of this golden afternoon. Wolf Heart's face had told her so.

The three canoes had drawn abreast now, and suddenly a shout echoed across the water. The braves leaned vigorously into their paddles. The canoes surged forward with a swiftness that made Clarissa gasp. It was a race! A race to the village!

She strained forward, caught up in spite of her fear. The canoe in which she was riding carried the most weight, and thus rode lowest in the water, but this handicap was balanced by the power of its paddlers. Even Wolf Heart had flung his strength into the contest, his mouth tightened in a grim line as he drove his paddle into the water.

The speed of the canoes became more labored as they turned into a narrow tributary of the Ohio. Now they were moving upstream. The bronze limbs of the young Shawnee gleamed with sweat. Their backs rose and fell with the strain of fighting the powerful current.

Just when it seemed they were all beginning to flag, the pockmarked brave behind her—Wolf Heart's friend—started to sing. Clarissa felt the hair rise on the back of her neck as his thin voice rose to a high-pitched wail then dropped abruptly into a guttural, rhythmic chant that the other paddlers swiftly joined. The canoes surged ahead with renewed vigor, driven by the throbbing beat of the song.

Glancing back over her shoulder, Clarissa saw that even Wolf Heart was singing, although not with any great enthusiasm. She watched him furtively, her own spirit reflecting the blackness that had settled over him with the arrival of the canoes. If only she could talk with him, but that, she knew, would no longer be possible. He had withdrawn into his Shawnee self, and even now he was far beyond her reach.

Turning away from him, she gazed ahead to where the river curved and vanished behind a low, wooded bluff. A fresh breeze cooled her face. She inhaled deeply, flooding her senses with the faint but unmistakable aromas of wood smoke, roasting meat, tobacco and hominy.

Her ribs tightened sharply as if someone had jerked a noose around her. The very smells she was savoring meant that the Shawnee village could not be far. Soon she would know what her fate was to be.

The brightness had faded from the day. The sun lay a finger's breadth above the trees now, blurred by a haze of low-lying clouds. Soon it would be dusk, then nightfall.

Clarissa filled her gaze with the dying light, with the deepening blue of the sky, the pale green of budding trees and the soft earthen red of spring willows. These she would hold in her memory to save for the time when darkness closed around her.

She did not expect to see another sunrise.

Wolf Heart's village was nestled in the lee of the bluff, overlooking the river. Cook fires flickered in the gathering twilight. Smoke curled from the roofs of loaf-shaped bark lodges that ringed from a larger building made of logs.

As the three canoes glided toward shore, Clarissa could see people running down the path to the river—children of all sizes, women, some with babies in their arms, and a few men. They clustered along the bank, pointing and jabbering. She turned to ask Wolf Heart what they were saying, but the coldness in his eyes withered her half-formed words. She would get no answers from him—not in front of his people.

But what did it matter? She needed no interpreter to know that the people clustered along the bank were talking about her, exclaiming over her red hair and pale skin. She held her head high, battling the urge to hide her head beneath her ragged skirts.

Wolf Heart and his pockmarked friend had paddled the canoe in a half circle, rotating it so that when the small craft touched land, Wolf Heart was able to leap out and pull it onto the beach. Clarissa, now in the rear, turned to meet his stony gaze. His head jerked toward the village, an indication, she guessed, that she was to climb out of the canoe and follow him.

Only when she tried to stand did she realize how weak she was. Dark blotches swam before her eyes. Her cramped legs threatened to buckle beneath her—and would have, perhaps, if the pockmarked brave had not caught her arm. She allowed him to steady her as she climbed over the edge of the canoe and stumbled on to the sand. His leathery hand released her cautiously. His curious eyes followed her as she lifted her head and, summoning the last of her strength, tottered up the slope on her blistered, swollen feet.

The Shawnee people were all around her now. Inquisitive fingers caught her hair, tugged her skirts and poked at her strange white skin. Panic tightened its stranglehold around Clarissa's rib cage. She fought back a scream as one wrinkled crone seized a handful of her hair, yanking so hard that Clarissa feared she was about to be scalped.

Terror exploded in her. She spun wildly, flailing at the groping hands and peering faces. She wanted only to get away, to breathe, but they were clawing at her limbs now, their sheer numbers dragging her down. She felt herself stumbling, falling.

"*Wolf Heart!*" The cry tore from her fear-strangled throat. "*Wolf Heart!*"

Suddenly he was there beside her, his arm catching her waist, lifting her as she went down. Clarissa heard his voice speaking quietly but firmly in Shawnee. The people were listening. They were backing away, clearing a path.

She sagged against his shoulder, trembling as they moved forward together. "It's all right," he muttered, leaning close to her ear. "They won't hurt you. They're only curious."

"What's going to happen to me?" She gripped his arm, her broken fingernails pressing anxiously into his flesh.

"That's for the council to decide."

"And when will they do that?"

"Tonight. Maybe tomorrow." He spoke tersely, his voice revealing no trace of emotion. "You're to be given food. Eat it all. Rest tonight while you have the chance."

"And tomorrow?" She swung back to face him, ignoring the pressing crowd as she forced him to meet her gaze. "Tell me! What happens then?"

Something flickered in his eyes as he looked down at her, then his gaze hardened. "It is forbidden to speak of it," he said. "You will know when the time comes."

Clarissa's taut nerves frayed and snapped. "You insolent savage!" she hissed with a fury she had not known she possessed. Her hand went up, and she would have struck him if he had not seized her wrist. Fury blazed in the depths of his cold blue eyes.

"Never do that again," he whispered, his voice a men-

acing rasp. "Now turn around and walk—unless you'd
rather be tied up and dragged!"

Stunned by his ferocity, Clarissa did as she was told.
Anger fueled her strength as she stalked up the slope of
the bank toward the village. She felt his looming presence
behind her, sensed it in the parting of the crowd. Wolf
Heart was clearly a respected man in this savage place.
But it was equally clear that he would never use his in-
fluence to save her. From this point on, she could depend
on no one but herself.

Chapter Five

The sounds, sights and smells of the village were all around her. The acrid scent of wood smoke blended with the savory aroma of simmering beans, corn, squash and wild onion. A wolflike yellow dog sniffed at Clarissa's leg, then backed away, growling at her alien scent. From inside one of the long bark lodges, a woman's voice was crooning what might have been a lullaby.

People seemed to be everywhere—working, eating, resting or simply staring at her in undisguised fascination. The younger children, many of them naked, cavorted around her unafraid, their soft black eyes dancing with excitement. Even the women were lightly dressed, some in long fringed buckskin chemises, others in nothing but beads and short leather aprons. From somewhere beyond the clustered lodges came the nicker of a horse.

"Here." Wolf Heart stopped before a small bark-covered hut. There were several of these, clustered close together in the shadow of the spacious log building she had seen from the river. "For prisoners," he explained curtly. "This one is yours."

She stared at him.

"Go inside," he continued as if he were talking to a

backward child. "You'll be safe as long as you don't try to leave."

"And if I do try?" Clarissa feigned a bravado she did not feel.

"You'll be caught. Your feet and hands will be lashed together behind your back and you'll be forced to lie that way all night." His expression softened, but only for the space of a heartbeat. "Do you want to live, Clarissa?"

Her exhausted body had begun to shake. Her legs quivered beneath her, threatening to buckle. She battled the need to sink against him, to draw strength from his broad, hard chest. "Yes," she whispered, trembling, "I want to live."

"Then you must do exactly what I tell you, when I tell you. Is that clear?"

She stared up into his face, only half-aware of the Shawnee milling around them. Her lips tightened as she swallowed and nodded.

Wolf Heart exhaled raggedly. The fading light cast his features into sharp relief, making them look as if they'd been hacked from rough stone. "Go into the hut," he said. "Eat the food you'll be given. Then try to sleep." His eyes narrowed. "No matter what happens, whatever you hear—or think you hear—stay inside and don't look out. Do you understand?"

Clarissa barely had time to nod again before he shoved her through the low entrance and dropped the deerskin flap behind her. Terror clutched at her as she stumbled into the darkness. She had been fighting fear all day. Now that she was alone, danger and despair finally came crashing in on her.

Clutching her knees like a frightened child, she crouched in the center of the small space, fearful of what might be lurking in the deeper shadows. Her shoulders shook. Her throat jerked in spasms of tearless weeping.

Time passed, how much time Clarissa could not be sure, but all at once she was startled into full alertness by the rustle of the hide that covered the hut's entrance. Firelight glimmered through the narrow opening, silhouetting a low figure that had come inside and was moving toward her.

"Wolf Heart?" The words strangled in her throat. This was not Wolf Heart. It was not anyone she knew.

Clarissa shrank into the darkness, muscles tensed to spring at the first sign of attack. "Don't come any closer!" she hissed at the hunched, shaggy-looking form that was edging toward her. Her broken fingernails clawed at the hut's earthen floor, scraping out a handful of dirt. It wasn't much of a weapon, but tossing it at the intruder's eyes might at least give her the advantage of surprise.

She was reaching back with her arm when she heard a thin cackle of laughter. In the next instant, the mouthwatering aroma of roast meat and vegetables assailed her senses. Her hand unclenched, releasing the dirt back to the floor. Wolf Heart had said she was to be given food. This creeping presence who had frightened her so was nothing more than an elderly woman bringing her a meal.

Still wary, Clarissa edged deeper into the shadows. The crone spoke to her in Shawnee, her ancient voice rasping like the stone wheel of a scissor grinder. *"We-sah,"* she said, thrusting out a bowl made from a hollowed gourd. *"We-sah!"*

The old woman did not appear dangerous, or even unfriendly, but Clarissa had endured a long and dreadful day. Famished as she was, she could not bring herself to reach out and take the food from the gnarled hand. She cringed like a captive animal, refusing to move.

Only when the woman had backed out of the hut and gone, leaving the bowl on the floor, did Clarissa summon the courage to creep forward. The stew, or so it appeared, was still warm. Its fragrance floated into her nostrils, triggering hunger pangs so intense she almost moaned out loud.

Her hands groped for utensils in the dark space. Finding nothing, not even a napkin, Clarissa managed an outraged little sniff. How on earth did these people expect her to eat? With her fingers?

Apparently so.

Salivating in spite of herself, she poked a tentative fingertip into the stew and licked off the juices that clung there. The earthy taste was so rich it made her head swim.

She used her thumb and forefinger to pick out a small chunk of meat and taste it. Venison—she had eaten it before, at the fort. And here was corn, onion and a slice of vegetable that smelled like squash....

Suddenly she was picking up the bowl, tilting her head back and scooping the stew into her eager mouth, making tiny animal noises as she chewed and swallowed. Clarissa had never been so ravenous. Only the fear of getting sick again kept her from bolting it all down at once like a hungry dog.

Within minutes she had finished off every morsel and cleaned the bowl of juices. Abandoning all pretense of manners, she licked her fingers and wiped them dry on the ragged remnants of her skirt. Crawling forward, she pushed the empty bowl under the deerskin flap. She did not want to give the old woman an excuse to come in and startle her again.

What now? Clarissa did not even try to stifle a yawn

as she huddled cross-legged in the center of her prison. It would never do to fall asleep in such a dangerous place. But surely it would do no harm to lie down and rest her trail-worn body for a few minutes.

She explored the dark perimeter of the floor, hoping to find a blanket or sleeping mat. To the right of the entrance, her probing fingers discovered a freshly dug hole which, Clarissa realized with a shock, was meant to serve as a necessity, but there was nothing more in the way of comfort to be found.

Muscles throbbing, she stretched out on her side. The packed earth was hard beneath the bruised contours of her body. She bemoaned the lack of a blanket, but that was just as well, she reminded herself. Any bedding she might find in this place was sure to be crawling with fleas, lice or worse.

She curled her arm under her head and lay staring into the darkness. Through the thin walls of the hut, she could hear the sounds of the Shawnee village—the crackling hiss of blazing pine pitch, the yelp of a dog, the murmured cadence of human voices and, once more, the low half-snorting nicker of a horse. Within the small closed space, the air smelled of stale smoke and the sickly musk of human fear.

How many other prisoners, she wondered, had lain in this miserable hut, chilled, beaten and terrified? How many other wretched souls had spent their last hours on this very spot? Could their spirits be lingering in the shadows, moaning like ghosts on the cold April wind?

But she was being foolish, Clarissa chided herself. To ponder such dark matters would be to lose her courage altogether. If this was to be her last night on earth, she would fill it with pleasant thoughts and happy memories.

She yawned again, willing her mind to drift backward

to another spring, a sunlit time warm with love and laughter. She was six years old, and the apple orchard was in bloom. Clouds of lacy white blossoms seemed to fill the whole sky, their fragrance caressing her as she flew upward on her swing. "Higher, Papa," she sang out, bursting with joy. "Push me higher, higher...."

In the next breath she had fallen into an exhausted sleep.

It was dawn when Clarissa opened her eyes. For a few drowsy moments she lay still, watching the bleak light thrust its gray fingers through chinks in the bark roof. Her body lay wrapped in a thick woolen trade blanket. She nestled deeper into its warmth, only to jerk into full wakefulness.

The blanket had not been here last night. Someone had stolen in while she slept and tucked its clean new warmth around her—someone she had neither seen nor heard.

Heart pounding, she sat bolt upright and rubbed the sleep from her eyes. What did it matter who had brought the blanket? What did it matter that she throbbed in every muscle and probably looked worse than a banshee from an Irish nightmare? This was to be the day of her trial, and if she was not to survive...

A sound caught her ears, a bloodchilling cacophony of voices coming from somewhere beyond the hut. Coming closer.

Whatever you hear—or think you hear—stay inside and don't look out. Wolf Heart's words tugged her back as she strained, quivering toward the sound of the uproar. He would not have spoken without good reason, she knew. But how could she not look? How could she sit here and wait when, for all she knew, the people could already be coming for her? She had to see what was happening.

Lifting the door was out of the question since someone was bound to see her. But there were other ways to look—thin patches in the hut's bark covering, marked by blades of sunlight. Clarissa selected a low spot opposite the door, near to where the commotion seemed loudest. Hunkering in the shadows, she enlarged the tiny hole with her finger, then bent closer and peered cautiously through.

At first she could see nothing but a corner of the log building and a triangle of gray sky above its roof. Then, suddenly, as the clamor grew, a mob of Shawnee women and children, with a scattering of old men, burst into sight around that corner, whooping and screaming as they brandished a veritable forest of sticks, clubs and willows.

Clarissa's throat went dry as they came closer. Her breath caught as she saw, in their midst, two Shawnee warriors half dragging between them a large naked white man.

Feeling ill, she stared at the corpulent figure—the flabby skin as white as a frog's belly except for the head and hands, which the sun had baked red. She stared at the pudgy bewhiskered face, the thinning hair and small porcine eyes.

Even without his grimy clothes, she recognized the man. She had seen him hurtling past her in the storm when the flatboat had capsized and shattered. It was Zeke.

An image of his greasy face leering above her in the rainy darkness flashed through Clarissa's memory as he stumbled past her. Now that face was ashen, the eyes bulging with stark terror. When, she wondered, had they caught him? Had he been here all night in a nearby hut, or had the braves just brought him into the village?

And how soon would they be coming for her?

As the frenzied crowd moved beyond her range of vision, Clarissa scrambled to another small chink and carefully widened it with her finger. She could see an open expanse of ground where the chanting Shawnee were forming two parallel lines, scarcely a pace apart. Her heart contracted as she realized what was about to happen.

The gauntlet—a grizzled veteran at Fort Pitt had described it to her over one of Aunt Margaret's dinners. Prisoners were forced to run between the two lines under a long furious rain of blows. Those who endured bravely were allowed to live as slaves of the Shawnee. Those who did not were dragged off, broken and bleeding, to be put to death.

Clarissa's blood had gone cold. This was the trial Wolf Heart had spoken of so mysteriously. It was to be her trial, as well.

Heart pounding, she pressed closer to the tiny opening to stare out at a living nightmare. The women, children and old ones howled their rage, shrieking like furies as they waved their sticks. Zeke, who had been dragged to the head of the double line, was blubbering like a baby. One of the braves prodded him forward with the point of a spear. From somewhere beyond her vision, Clarissa could hear the savage drumming of tom-toms.

Now would be the time to look away, Clarissa told herself frantically. But she could not tear her horrified gaze from the unfolding tragedy.

Zeke had taken his first tottering steps. He staggered between the lines, bawling like a calf as the stinging blows laid open his thin white skin. Clarissa's stomach lurched as she saw him stumble and go down. Sticks flew and flailed. Then, an agonizing moment later, he was on his feet again, his head streaming blood from a half-dozen wounds.

Clarissa's fists clenched so hard that her ragged nails dug into her flesh. Zeke was an evil man, she reminded herself. He had murdered Tom Ainsworth and, with the vilest intentions, stolen her away from the fort. But did he—or any other human being—deserve to die in such a degrading manner?

She heard him bellow as, nearing the end of the lines, he went down once more. This time he did not rise. Only the frenzied beating of the now-bloodied sticks marked the place where he had fallen. A moment more, and even the screams had stopped.

Sick with dread, Clarissa sagged away from the peep-hole and pressed her cold hands to her face. Soon it would be her turn to run the gauntlet, and she had just watched a man double her size and triple her strength go down. She slumped in the darkness, her shoulders shaking as she imagined the bloody sticks, the crushing blows....

"Now you know why I told you not to look." Wolf Heart's low voice came out of the darkness behind her. She lifted her head, turned and sprang to her feet, suddenly wild with fury.

"Why didn't you just let me drown?" she lashed out, flying at him with her fists. "You knew about this—all the time, you knew about this!"

"Be quiet, Clarissa!" He caught her wrists, whipping her toward him. His blue eyes, struck by a thin beam of light, glittered like a panther's.

"How can I be quiet?" She flung the words at him,

still struggling. "Those people—*your* people, or so you claim! Women and children! The savagery of it—"

"Listen to me!" His arms caught her close, crushing the fight out of her. "There isn't much time! They'll be coming for you soon."

"No thanks to you!" She glared up at him, livid with rage and fear. "Why didn't you prepare me for this?"

"That's exactly what I'm trying to do!" His big hands gripped her arms, almost hurting her in their intensity. "Pay attention, Clarissa. The gauntlet is meant to test you, not to kill you. Do you understand?"

She stared up at him in consternation.

"The Shawnee value courage above all else. Show them you have it!" His clasp tightened. "Whatever happens, no matter how hard they hit you, don't cry out— that's the test! Don't cry out, and you will live with honor!"

With honor? The honor of a slave and prisoner? Clarissa glared at her captor, comprehension feeding her rage. He could have let her go. Instead he had brought her to this.

"I will live!" She wrenched herself out of his arms, quivering with fury. "I'll live through this and more! I'll live to make you curse the day you took me prisoner, Seth Johnson!"

She spun away from him and, impelled by her own anger, flung aside the deerskin and stalked out into the sunlight. She had agonized long enough. She, Clarissa Rogers, would not suffer herself to be dragged outside like a criminal going to the gallows. She would choose the time of her own testing, and it would be now.

Wolf Heart sucked in his breath, aching with worry as he watched her go. He had ignited her anger—that was all to the good. But would it be enough?

He had seen strong men, even seasoned Iroquois warriors, crumble under the punishing blows of the gauntlet. Clarissa was a mere girl, as delicate as she was beautiful. What if he had been wrong about her courage? What if he had saved her from drowning only to deliver her to a more brutal fate?

The uproar outside told him that Clarissa had been seen and taken. Steeling his features and his emotions, Wolf Heart strode out of the hut.

The morning sun was just edging above the trees. In the haze of its golden light, he saw the two young braves escorting her across the grass. She walked between them with a queen's defiant grace, her small head carried high, her dirty, tattered gown fluttering in the breeze.

Did she know that he was also on trial? Had her perceptive mind guessed that even now he was running a gauntlet of his own, a test of his devotion to the Shawnee way?

He had argued well into the night with the council of elders. The girl was not strong, he had pleaded. At least she should be allowed more time to prepare for her ordeal. But Hunts-at-Night, the aging one-eyed chief, had chided him gravely for his concern.

"Many seasons ago we took you into our *wegiwas* and made you one of us. Since that time, you have shown nothing but respect for our ways. You have led many braves on the hunt and won honor in battle. But now, my son, you must examine your own heart. You must ask yourself whether that heart is truly Shawnee, or whether this young white woman has already turned it away from us."

"There is no need for such a question!" Wolf Heart

had argued passionately. "In my heart, my mind and my body, I am Shawnee!"

The old chief's single eye—its mate clawed out long ago by a bear—had glittered in the torchlight. "And when you take a wife—for that time must come soon—will you choose her from among our people?"

Had he hesitated? Certainly not for more than a heartbeat. "I will choose a Shawnee wife," Wolf Heart had answered, his voice ringing with conviction.

The chief's furrowed face had softened into a smile. "*We-sah.* That is good. Tomorrow when the white woman runs the gauntlet, you will stand beside me and watch. Then all who see will know that your tongue has spoken the words of your heart."

Sick with self-reproach, Wolf Heart had left the council, wandered into the night and stared morosely up at the stars. In taking Clarissa prisoner, he had made what he believed to be the only correct choice. But there had been other choices. Had he made them, she would be with her relatives at Fort Pitt. She would be safe and happy, not facing the most fearful morning of her young life.

He had circled the village, then walked lightly past the drowsing guard and approached the prisoner huts. The large white man, taken earlier from the river, was whimpering in the darkness, but no sound came from the hut that sheltered Clarissa.

Pulse quickening, Wolf Heart had dropped to a crouch and raised the deerskin flap that covered the entrance. A pool of blue moonlight had revealed his captive curled on the bare earthen floor, lost in slumber.

For the space of a long breath, he had gazed down at the innocence of her sleeping face, the slender contours of her body and the soft spill of her hair on the ground.

Reminding himself that the night was chilly, he had walked the short distance to his own lodge and returned with the new red blanket.

Kneeling beside her, he had unfolded the blanket and draped it gently over her sleeping form. When she did not stir, he had bent lower and, with careful hands, tucked the edges beneath her hips, shoulders and legs, cushioning her against the hard floor.

Her breathing had been low and even, her body as weightless as a bird's. When she moaned in her sleep, he had battled the urge to lift her in his arms and cradle her against his chest, to soothe and comfort her in the darkness. It would be a false comfort, he had reminded himself harshly. He could not stop what was going to happen. He could offer no promises or kind words. Clarissa Rogers would run the gauntlet in the morning and, if her courage failed, it would be better for her if she had drowned in the river.

A shout from the clearing snapped Wolf Heart's attention back to the present. The lines were forming again, the people shrieking their fervor to the morning sky. There was not one among them who did not have some grievance with the whites—a loved one lost, a home sacked or burned, a season's crops ruined. The gauntlet was the weapon of those who could not go to war, and that weapon was about to fall on Clarissa.

What would he do when the first blow struck her soft white skin? What would he do when she went down, as she surely would? His instincts, he knew, would cry out for him to rush in and save her, but to obey those instincts would mean the end of his life as a Shawnee.

Hunts-at-Night had emerged from his lodge. He stood at the edge of the clearing, leaning lightly on his stick as he waited.

Knowing there was no other choice, Wolf Heart strode across the grass to take his place at the chief's side.

The chief's eye scarcely flickered in his direction, but Wolf Heart knew the shrewd old man had missed nothing. This ordeal was to be a measure of two spirits, Clarissa's and his own.

Clarissa wiped her sweating palms on her skirt and stared the length of the gauntlet. Her gaze moved down the double column of savage faces and quivering weapons to focus on the painted stake hammered into the small open space of ground at the other end. That stake was her goal. All she had to do was reach it.

Fear stirred like a coiled snake in the pit of her stomach. Her legs trembled beneath her as she studied the rage that burned in each pair of eyes. Clarissa swallowed the strangling tightness in her throat. These people were screaming for her blood. Soon they would have it.

The Shawnee value courage above all else.... No matter what happens, no matter how hard they hit you, don't cry out. That is the test.

Wolf Heart's words came back to her as she steeled herself for the run. Clarissa had seen him striding out of the hut to take his place beside the chief. Never mind him, she admonished herself. There was no question where the scoundrel's loyalties lay. She would not think of Wolf Heart now. She would not think of anything except staying alive.

A hush had fallen over the clearing, broken only by the *chuck* of a raven perched in a towering pine. The people seemed to be waiting for something, a signal, perhaps from their chief. Well, then, let them wait! She, for one, had waited long enough!

Lowering her head, Clarissa charged the·lines.

The first few Shawnee were caught off guard by her unexpected rush. But then the cry went up, and the blows began to fall. Clarissa, who had never been struck in her pampered young life, felt each hit as a shock of pain that exploded through every nerve in her body.

She slowed and staggered, biting back a scream as a thorny branch tore through her dress, leaving a bloody welt across her back. Another blow, this one landing squarely along the side of her head, forced her to one knee, enabling more strikes to land, even the lightest of them stinging her face like fiery hail.

Sticks and clubs were everywhere now, beating her down as she crawled forward. Blood from a scalp wound trickled into her eyes, all but blinding her. She could no longer see the stake at the end of the gauntlet.

This was Wolf Heart's doing—and now, though she could not see him, she knew that he stood looking on with his red-skinned brothers, playing the proud Shawnee warrior as he watched her ordeal. If she had a club, she would take pleasure in using it to smash his insolent face!

If she had a club…

Blind rage, terrifying in its intensity, boiled up inside her. Suddenly Clarissa's legs were under her again, pushing her body upward. Her thrusting hands wrenched a stout hickory limb from a screaming Shawnee dowager. With a demon's own strength, she swung it in a wide arc, savoring the resistant crunch of wood on flesh and bone.

First the gauntlet…then that traitorous oaf who called himself Wolf Heart!

She was flailing away like a madwoman now, cutting a swath of bruised heads and limbs as she lunged down the center of the gauntlet. A few paces more and she would be clear of it. She would have him in sight, and then how sweet it would be. The Shawnee could kill her afterward, and likely would, but not before she'd had her taste of vengeance.

All conscious thought dissolved as a heavy club struck her head from behind. Clarissa went down in a swirl of blackness. Her body crumpled on the grass beneath a hail of blows. One finger stirred and reached out to touch the painted stake. Then she quivered and lay still.

Chapter Six

Of the days she lay in a half-conscious stupor, Clarissa would recall but little. There would be the pain-clouded impression of being lifted by powerful arms and carried ever so gently into a place of warm darkness. There would be the leathery softness of tanned robes cradling her battered body and the pungent sting of herbal poultices against her lacerated skin. There would be an overpowering sense of injury—the bruised limbs, the swollen, scab-encrusted face.

And there would be the memory of worried eyes looking down at her—one pair black and sharp, all but buried in a nut-brown maze of wrinkles; the other pair a clear, penetrating blue.

It was to those blue eyes that Clarissa finally awakened on a sunny spring morning, in full possession of her senses. She looked up into Wolf Heart's haggard face and saw the relief etched across his rugged features. She saw the smile that tugged at a corner of his powerful mouth, the warmth that softened his stern gaze as he crouched over her.

And she remembered, at last, all that he had caused to be done to her.

"You!" she rasped, her voice hoarse from lack of use. "I would have killed you if I could have reached you! I would have taken that stick and smashed your arrogant face to a pulp!"

His gaze hardened, the smile turning bitter with irony. "You smashed enough faces as it was. The gauntlet has never come off quite so badly."

"But they let me live...." Her words trailed off as a chilling possibility struck her. Had she survived the gauntlet only to be saved for a more spectacular death by torture or burning?

"Yes, you will live." His words answered her unspoken question. "Your trial is over."

"And I have proven myself worthy?" Her question mocked him.

"Yes."

"To be a Shawnee?" She paused, then plunged ahead, wanting to wound him. "No, thank you kindly! I would rather be a dog!"

"As you like. No one will force you." His voice was cold now, his face a stony mask. Stunned by her own vulnerability, Clarissa glanced away. Her nervous gaze roamed the dark rounded ceiling of the lodge, lingering on the assortment of bundled herbs that hung from the crosspoles.

"Then what's to become of me?" she asked, suddenly afraid she had pushed him too far.

His eyes shifted briefly toward the gray-haired crone who had just tottered in through the doorway, her arms laden with willows. Clarissa recognized her as the old woman who had brought her food in the prisoner hut.

"You have been given to Swan Feather," he said in a low voice. "Her own daughter died in the hunger moon from the white man's coughing sickness. She is old and needs a strong young worker to help her.''

"You mean I'm to be a slave?" Clarissa struggled to rise, but the stabbing pain in her ribs stopped her. She sank back onto the folded robe that pillowed her head.

"A slave or a daughter.'' A shadow flickered in Wolf Heart's grim eyes. ''The choice is yours.''

"I understand.'' She exhaled slowly, closing her eyes as she pondered this new reality. She was not to be released—ever. Unless she proved clever enough to escape, she would never see her aunt and uncle, her brother, or her home again.

Her hand stirred, moving to her face. Her fingertips skimmed one swollen cheek, jerked in shock, then began a frantic groping exploration of her battered features—the smashed nose, the bruised eyes, the half healed welts and cuts, some so deep that she would carry their scars to her grave.

Clarissa's eyes opened wide, as if she were struggling to awaken from a nightmare. ''No,'' she whispered in horror, remembering the chiseled alabaster perfection of her former beauty. *''No!''*

"What is it now?" Wolf Heart scowled down at her, choosing to be puzzled.

"My—face!'' She choked out the words, staring at him through her splayed fingers. ''Don't you understand? My face! It's ruined! What will I do?''

Wolf Heart rose slowly to his feet, towering above the pallet where she lay. From such a distance, Clarissa could not be sure whether it was pity or disgust that glittered in his cobalt eyes. He turned to go, then hesitated.

"You will wear a new face, Clarissa,'' he said softly. ''The face of courage.''

* * *

Wolf Heart strode across the clearing, not knowing whether to laugh, curse or fling himself over a waterfall. Clarissa Rogers was the most maddening woman—no, the most maddening *person*—he had ever known in his life! How could anyone be so heroic one moment and so petty and small-minded another? How could one ordinary woman be so waspish, so stubborn, so vain and, at the same time, so glorious?

By all that was sacred, he should have paddled away and left her in the river to drown!

He had watched over her for the past two days, scarcely leaving her side as she lay half-alive in the darkness of Swan Feather's lodge. He had fed her broth from the venison he'd brought for Swan Feather to cook. He had stroked her hair when she whimpered in her fitful sleep and, with more tenderness than he'd known he could possess, massaged her calves when the strained muscles knotted into cramps.

Through it all, he had felt his long-dormant heart stir and swell like a seed about to take root.

Then she had opened those cat-green eyes of hers and spoken with her sharp little vixen's tongue, reminding him, with the force of a slap, that nothing between them had changed.

Yes, he should have delivered the minx back to Fort Pitt while he had the chance. What a calamity that act would have inflicted on the British!

He reached the river and moved along the bank to where, some days earlier, he had noticed a lone birch, its trunk the perfect length and thickness for a canoe. If no other brave had claimed the tree, he would make it his own. He needed a new canoe to replace the one he'd abandoned to save Clarissa. Maybe the work would even ease his temper.

Finding the birch untouched, he slipped the hatchet out of his belt and laid into the base of the trunk with a flurry of powerful blows. White chips flew under the blade, awakening the scent of the fresh raw wood. Sweat glistened on Wolf Heart's sun-gilded skin as he drove the strength of his anger into the work.

"You're sure that's only a tree you're chopping?"

A laughing voice startled him from the path above the bank. Wolf Heart turned sharply to find Cat Follower perched on a boulder, smirking down at him. "Only a man with woman trouble swings an ax like that!" he said.

"When I want your opinion, wise one, I'll ask for it!" Wolf Heart resumed his chopping, the sound of his friend's laughter mingling with each blow of the ax.

"I was watching when she ran the gauntlet," Cat Follower said. "What a wildcat! But you—I feared I might have to jump in and hold you back myself! You were a bull elk ready to charge! You would have disgraced us all!"

Wolf Heart's next blow buried the hatchet's steel head solidly in the tree trunk. Muttering under his breath, he paused to work it loose.

"No female is worth it, brother." Cat follower vaulted lithely down from the boulder to stand, grinning, on the riverbank. "If one girl frustrates you, go and find another. Now, listen, I have noticed Corn Flower watching you. She has eyes like a doe, and breasts a man could smother between! She—"

"If you like her so much, why not stop yapping and try her yourself?" Wolf Heart interrupted brusquely.

"Too late! I already have!"

Cat Follower whooped with delight as Wolf Heart's last violent hatchet blow sent the tree crashing into the river. "You would like her, too, I think, and she—" His sharp eyes narrowed. "But I see your head is filled with thoughts of the red-tailed fox, and there is room for no other, not even for pleasure. That is not good, my friend."

"Why don't you stop jabbering and help me?" Wolf Heart had leaped into the hip-deep water to haul the tree ashore. The current was so chilly it made him wince. Noticing his discomfort, Cat Follower hooted.

"That water's just what you needed to cool off your hot *passah-tih!* You will be no good to any woman for a moon!" He sank to the ground, weak with hilarity. "Hey—forget women! The village needs meat, and I know of a spot four sleeps upriver by horse where the bucks are as fat as English mules! Let's go hunting!"

"A fine time you pick to ask me!" Wolf Heart had dragged the tree trunk onto the bank and was studying its contours with narrowed eyes, determining where to cut. "This bark has to come off now, while it's soft enough to be rolled and weighted. It will take the rest of the day to do it right."

"Not if I help you." Cat Follower whipped out his own hatchet and began chopping away the leafy crown of the birch. "Come on the hunt with me! The chase will give your mind a rest from thoughts of the red-tailed fox. And if she's like other women, it might even give her a chance to miss you. Come on, it will do you both good! I dare you to say I'm wrong!"

Wolf Heart did his best to scowl at his friend's taunts, but the effort came to nothing and, after a moment of thought, his shoulders sagged in acquiescence. Clarissa's adjustment to Shawnee life would be hard in any case. But it might happen faster without his being there to interfere. Swan Feather, his Shawnee mother's closest

friend, would be the wisest, if not the gentlest, of teach-
ers—and Clarissa, if he knew her at all, would take her
lumps and come up fighting. She would get along well
enough without him.

And if she took a notion to run away?

He forced the worry out of his mind before it could
take root. He could not protect Clarissa Rogers from her
own impetuous nature. If she chose to do a foolish thing,
there was little he could do to stop her.

''Well?''

Cat Follower waited, an expectant grin splitting his
pockmarked face.

''Let it be as you say, brother,'' Wolf Heart muttered
wearily. ''To work, and then to hunting!''

Seven days and nights had come and gone, but Wolf
Heart had not returned to Swan Feather's lodge. For a
time, Clarissa's head had swung toward every sound, ears
straining for the distinctive throaty timbre of his voice—
a deeper pitch than the melodic speech of the men he
called his brothers. She had turned toward every shadow
that passed by the open doorway, hoping, with a surge
of anticipation, that one of them might be his. But it
never was. He had gone and, cut off by the barrier of
language, she could not even ask where.

Clarissa's every thought of Wolf Heart touched off a
war between rage and longing. He had brought her to this
miserable state, and for that she would never forgive him.
But only now that he was gone did she realize how much
she had depended on him. The man who had once been
Seth Johnson was her only link to understanding, her only
connection to the world she had left behind.

The days were lonely but not idle. As soon as Clarissa's swollen eyes could see clearly, Swan Feather put

her to work cleaning the chaff from baskets of beans and peeling the bark from bundles of willow twigs. As soon as she could kneel and use her hands, it was hours over the grinding stone, until her back throbbed and the skin on her fingers cracked and bled. When Clarissa had complained, thrusting out her hands and gesticulating her distress, Swan Feather had simply opened her own workworn palms to reveal an etched maze of scars and thick horny calluses. Clarissa had known better than to complain again.

The old woman was a stern taskmaster. She spoke little and smiled less, communicating her orders with grunts, nudges, gestures and an occasional shove. Clarissa curbed her natural contrariness and did her best to obey. Meekness fostered trust, she reminded herself when her temper began to flare. Only when the Shawnee trusted her would they drop their guard and allow her enough freedom to escape.

That hope of escape was the one thing that kept her spirit alive. As her hands toiled, her mind sifted the means, rejecting some ideas as too impractical, others as too dangerous. Only when she glanced up one day to see two braves ride past her on a pair of handsome geldings—traded, most likely, or stolen—did her plan fall into place.

All she had to do, when the opportunity came, was get her hands on a horse. The rest would be a simple matter of secreting a little food and a weapon for her journey. On horseback, with any luck at all, she could reach Fort Pitt in a few days.

But she'd begun to see that escape would not be easy. She was watched constantly, and so were the precious horses. She would have no choice except to bide her time, waiting for the perfect moment. She would be patient,

Clarissa resolved. And while she waited for a horse, she would explore other means of escape. Sooner or later her chance would come.

Clarissa's days were one long blur of drudgery—so much that she scarcely had time to raise her eyes from her work. Swan Feather kept her busy from early dawn until dusk, grinding corn into meal, sorting herbs, mending moccasins and hoeing the patch of ground where the old woman had planted her garden.

Worse, even, than the tedium was the chilling awareness that, at any moment, the Shawnee could turn on her. That constant, draining fear wore Clarissa's nerves raw, rendering her all the more weary at each day's end.

At night she would collapse on her bed of skins, aching in every bone, joint and muscle. There, while she lay on her back, Swan Feather would smear her face with a smelly concoction of herbs and bear grease. The stuff was so foul that it made Clarissa gag, but at least her face was healing. The hideous scabs were flaking away, leaving smooth but still perceptible ridges of scar tissue.

The face of courage. Wolf Heart's words came back to mock her now. What irony! She would have chosen the unmarked face of cowardice any day! Her only blessing in this accursed place was the absence of mirrors!

Clarissa's dirty, stained gown, which she wore day and night, was growing more and more threadbare. Her sweat-encrusted underthings chafed the tender skin beneath. One by one she had discarded the whalebone stays from her corset as they worked through the worn fabric to jab her flesh like needles.

Swan Feather had brought her a pair of discarded moccasins, which Clarissa fitted to her blistered feet by stuffing the toes with grass, but no one had offered her a change of clothing. No one in fact, aside from Swan

Feather, paid her any attention at all. It was as if she had become invisible.

But then, weren't slaves invisible by nature? How many details could she recall about Jane, the scrawny young black from her own growing-up years in Baltimore? Jane had done the heavy laundry and helped Mrs. Pimm in the kitchen, but her presence had been little more than a shadow in the house, seen little and heard even less. Had Jane been unhappy? Had she cried in the night for the loss of her African homeland, muffling her sobs against her pillow? No one else in the household had known, nor had they cared.

For the first time, she could imagine how Jane must have felt.

On the eighth day of her captivity, Clarissa awakened with an all-too-familiar stickiness between her thighs. The curse, as Mrs. Pimm called it, had struck again!

With a groan of dismay, she sat up and began tearing yet another strip from the ragged hem of her petticoat. Why now, by heaven? Didn't she have enough trouble already? Did her own body have to betray her as well?

She was folding the fabric into a pad, frantically wondering how she would hold it in place, when Swan Feather came in from relieving herself behind the lodge. Clarissa twisted toward the wall, struggling to hide her secret shame, but it was clear that the old woman was not fooled.

The ancient black eyes narrowed. Clarissa braced herself for punishment as Swan Feather descended upon her like an ancient bird of prey. *It's not my fault,* she wanted to shout. *I couldn't keep it from happening! No woman can!*

She gulped back the urge to cringe, knowing that,

above all, she must not show fear. Still the old crone was a daunting sight with her owlish eyes, beaked nose and bristling gray mop of hair. Would she deliver a tirade or even a blow? Curled on the skin bed, thighs pressed tight to contain the crimson flow, Clarissa held her breath and waited.

A half pace from the bed, Swan Feather paused. She shook her grizzled head, then sank down onto haunches, regarding Clarissa with shrewd, knowing eyes.

"We-sah!" she muttered, her ancient face breaking into a toothless smile. *"We-sah!"*

Clarissa stared at her. She knew the Shawnee word meant good, but beyond that it made no sense. There was nothing good about this wretched morning, and certainly nothing good about having the curse.

She was beginning to wonder whether the old woman had lost her mind, when Swan Feather removed all doubt of it. With an exuberant cackle, she seized Clarissa's arm, yanked her to her feet and began tugging her toward the doorway of the lodge.

"No!" Clarissa struggled wildly, but Swan Feather's grip was like an iron clamp. Muttering in Shawnee, the old woman dragged her out into the blinding sunlight where, though it was early, many people were awake and going about their business.

"No—please—" Face flaming, she stumbled along as Swan Feather's voice rose in greeting to her neighbors, almost as if she were making some kind of announcement. Two middle-aged women paused to gaze at Clarissa, both of them chuckling and wagging their heads. Mortified, Clarissa stared fixedly at the ground. This was a bad dream, a nightmare! Why didn't the Shawnee just kill her now and end the torment?

She saw now that Swan Feather was leading her toward a small isolated hut, screened by alders and willow, at the far end of the village—another prisoner hut, perhaps. Clarissa followed now without protest. She did not know what awaited her at the hut, but what did it matter? How could anything be more degrading than what she had just suffered?

The old woman raised the skin flap that covered the doorway of the hut and motioned for Clarissa to enter. Hunkering low, Clarissa crawled into the cool darkness. Anything to escape the humiliating stares, she told herself. Anything.

The space inside the hut was so dim that her sun-dazzled eyes could make out nothing but shadows. Squatting in the entrance, Swan Feather indicated with words and emphatic gestures that Clarissa was to stay. Then abruptly, she lowered the flap and departed.

For a long moment Clarissa remained where she was, clutching her drawn-up knees. She was dirty and bleeding, and the familiar cramps, low in her body, clenched and twisted as if her innards were being squeezed by an invisible fist. But at least she was finally alone.

Or was she?

As Clarissa listened, she became aware of a presence behind her. She heard a rustle of movement, accompanied by the low rush of breathing. The hair on the back of her neck prickled and rose like a cat's. She had no weapon, but if this presence meant her ill, she would kick, scratch and bite for her life!

By now her eyes were adjusting to the darkness. She could make out the feathery seep of light around the doorway and the pale framework of saplings that supported the hut's curved walls and roof. Now, while she had the advantage of surprise, would be the time to strike, Clarissa told herself.

She was crouching low, every muscle tensed to wheel and spring, when the breathiness behind her erupted in an outburst of nervous feminine giggles.

Startled, she jerked around to see two young Shawnee girls, perhaps fourteen or fifteen, sitting bare breasted on the earthen floor of the hut. Clutching each other's arms, they stared at her like a pair of half-grown raccoons, with a mixture of fear, curiosity and mischief.

What in heaven's name was this place?

As Clarissa gaped at the girls in astonishment, a third figure emerged from the shadows of the hut—a strikingly handsome woman of, perhaps, forty, clad in a long buckskin tunic but wearing nothing below. She edged forward on her haunches, speaking softly in a coaxing tone.

"I don't understand!" Clarissa inched backward, less fearful but still uncertain. Why had Swan Feather left her here with these women? What did they mean to do to her?

She inhaled nervously, filling her nostrils with the aromas of hickory smoke, damp earth and something else—an odor so subtle that she was scarcely aware of it, indeed would have been hard-pressed to give it a name. But as it penetrated her senses, suddenly she knew.

These women all had the curse! They had been set apart in this isolated hut to pass the time. And so had she!

The older woman reached into a pouch at her waist and took out a broken yellow corn cake. She held it out toward Clarissa, speaking softly, as if trying to coax a timid animal to eat from her hand. Feeling foolish and awkward, Clarissa accepted the food and settled herself onto the floor an arm's length from the other woman. She'd had no chance to eat breakfast and the fresh, crunchy corn cake was delicious. She chewed slowly, savoring its smoky taste, and she felt a gentle tug at her hair.

The two young girls, still giggling, had moved around behind her. Together they were using a brush made of bundled reeds to comb the mats from her tangled curls.

With a sigh, Clarissa closed her eyes, tilted her head back and let them have their way.

Wolf Heart cantered his mount into the village, leaving Cat Follower to bring up the rear with the heavily laden packhorses. The hunt had been a great success, with enough deer brought down to feed the village for half a moon. Between the stalking, the skinning and the butchering of the meat, he'd had little time to worry about Clarissa. On the long ride home, however, her image had returned to torment his mind until, with the lodges in sight, he found himself almost wild with the need to know she was safe.

"Go on, then!" Cat Follower's laughter echoed in his ears as Wolf Heart kneed his mount and broke away from the train of horses. "See if your red-tailed fox still waits! I will tell everybody I shot all this fine meat myself!"

Ignoring his friend's good-natured taunts, Wolf Heart surged ahead on his spotted horse. What if something had happened to Clarissa while he was away? What if she had met with some accident, or tried to escape and lost herself in the forest? He would never forgive himself for leaving her.

Women, children and dogs scattered at his approach. Mindful of their safety, he slowed the horse to a trot. Ahead he could see Swan Feather's lodge, with its overhanging willows. Would Clarissa be there? Would she still be angry?

Dropping the horse's reins over a bush, he slid off its

back and strode toward the lodge, quelling the urge to run like a fool. His spirits sank as he saw that the door-yard was empty. Worry gnawed at the pit of his stomach as he raised the skin flap and saw that there was no sign of life inside the lodge. Only the coals of the fire, banked with ashes, winked like small red eyes in the darkness.

It was too soon to panic, he cautioned himself. The two women could be fetching water or digging roots at the edge of the forest. All the same, his heart dropped like a stone when he glanced up and saw Swan Feather hurrying toward him alone.

"Good hunting!" Her broad smile and cheerful greeting left Wolf Heart confused, but he knew it would be rude to ask about Clarissa right away. "I saw the meat in front of the council house," Swan Feather chatted on, "and I said to myself, 'That rascal, Cat Follower could not bring so much game in by himself! The son of my friend has returned!'"

"Cat Follower did well enough." He cleared his throat. "We set aside the haunch and skin of a fine buck for you. I will go and get it now."

"*We-sah!*" The leathery brown fingers squeezed his forearm. "You are better to me than ten sons of my own blood!"

Wolf Heart hesitated still. "Do you have enough firewood for smoking the meat?" he asked, feeling as awkward as a boy of sixteen winters.

"Is it really the firewood that troubles you?" Swan Feather's wise old eyes danced knowingly. "She has been in the moon lodge these past four days. It was her time, and so I sent her. She will learn many good things there, I believe."

Relief sang inside him. "Then she is well?" he asked, feigning disinterest.

"Well and strong. A good worker, too. But angry. Very angry inside."

"Her anger has given her the strength to stay alive."

"That may be. But anger for too many sleeps is not good." The old woman released her grip on Wolf Heart's arm. "Soon, perhaps today, she will finish her moon. Then you will see her again."

Before Wolf Heart could respond, she reached out and clasped his wrist with her rough old hand. "Listen to me, son of my friend. In my life, I have seen more than a few white captives come among our people. Some, like you, forget their old lives and become Shawnee in their very hearts. Others—" A strange sadness crossed her face. "Others never do. They pine away and die of sorrow, or they spend their days making plans to escape and go back to their people. Do you hear what I am saying?"

Wolf Heart gazed down into the hawklike ferocity of her eyes. She was so small and shriveled that he could have lifted her like a child between his two hands. But she was not small in courage or in wisdom.

"I hear," he murmured, knowing all too well what she meant to tell him.

"But does your heart hear? Does it want to hear?"

The piping melody of a wood thrush filled Wolf Heart's silent pause. In the northern sky, a long vee of geese winged toward their summer mating grounds, their hoarse cries echoing behind them.

"You are a brave warrior and a leader of men." Swan Feather continued when he did not answer. "Our people will need a strong war chief in the times ahead." Her ancient eyes narrowed. "A war chief needs a loyal wife at his side."

"When the time comes, I will choose a Shawnee woman. I gave my word to the council."

"And you, above all, are a man who keeps his word."
Swan Feather nodded in grave approval, but something
flickered in her dark eyes, something she swiftly concealed.

Wolf Heart shifted uncomfortably, wary of what she
might say next. "I will get the meat for you," he said,
half turning to go. "And the deerskin."

"Two skins if you can spare them," Swan Feather
said. "I expect I will have need of them."

"Then the two skins will be yours if I have to wrestle
Cat Follower to get them." Wolf Heart forced a smile as
he took leave of her and walked back toward the place
where he had tied his horse.

"Wolf Heart."

He turned again to see, from a greater distance now,
the old woman standing alone in the shadow of her lodge,
looking so ancient and frail that he was seized by a sudden premonition that he would not have the blessing of
Swan Feather's wisdom for many more moons.

"Do not judge me too harshly, son of my friend, until
you understand why I speak as I do," she said gently.
"I have already begun to love the girl as I would love
my own daughter. But I love you even more, and I see
sorrow ahead for you both. Do not let your heart cloud
your judgment."

"I am not a fool," Wolf Heart protested as color
heated his face, making lies of his words.

"*We-sah.*" She turned to go inside her lodge. "Then
by all that is sacred, do not let yourself become one."

Chapter Seven

On the morning of the fifth day, Clarissa emerged from the warm darkness of the moon lodge like a butterfly unfolding from its cocoon. She had slept to her heart's content on the soft skins and blankets. She had feasted on the savory stews and corn cakes Swan Feather and other women left every evening outside the door of the lodge. She had sat patiently for hours while the two young Shawnee girls made a plaything of her hair, combing it, braiding it, adorning it with beads and feathers from the bundles they had brought, the two of them laughing in delight at each new effect.

She had learned and played a half-dozen games with string, bones and sticks. She had learned so many new words that the conversations around her were starting to make sense. And she had learned that in the world of the Shawnee, the natural cycle of a woman's body was viewed not as a curse but as a blessing.

"*Peh-eh-wah!* Come with us!" The prettier of the young girls tugged at her arm, pulling her downhill in the direction of the river. The two of them had ended their cycles on the same day as Clarissa, and now they frolicked like puppies, happy to be in the open once more.

When Clarissa hesitated, blinking in the bright sunlight, the other girl caught her left wrist and joined in the tugging. *"Peh-eh-wah!"* she urged. "We bathe now!" She made a swimming motion with her free hand. "Come!"

Clarissa remembered the cold muddy water of the river. She remembered the awful sensation of drowning, the helplessness, the burning want of air, and for a moment she almost lost heart. Only the thought of being clean once more kept her moccasined feet moving down the slope. Drowning, she resolved, would be preferable to spending her days in her present state of abject filth!

The girls had turned onto a narrow trail, worn smooth by the passage of many moccasins. Their tiny breasts jiggled as they trotted along single file, the patterns of leaf and shadow beautiful on their coppery young torsos. Clarissa stumbled along behind them, clutching her ragged skirts. What would it be like, she wondered, to run free in such a manner, with the morning breeze caressing her naked skin?

The very idea! She brought herself up with a sharp mental slap. She was a civilized woman, not a savage, and as soon as she could find a way to escape, she would put this barbarous place behind her for good! Meanwhile, she owed it to herself to maintain some semblance of dignity—and that most certainly did not include cavorting bare breasted in public!

Looking down through the budding trees, she could see the place where they were going to bathe. It was not the river at all, but a deep transparent pool cradled by rocky ledges and fed by a frothy spring that gushed from an overhanging cliff. The cliff was festooned with ferns and dotted with mossy clusters of deep blue flowers that looked, for all the world, like forget-me-nots. It was as beautiful a spot as Clarissa had ever seen.

Squealing with abandon, the two girls raced down the trail toward the pool. At the crest of a high ledge, they kicked off their moccasins, flung aside their little leather aprons and vanished, whooping gleefully, over the brink.

Clarissa, who had fallen behind, heard the double splash. Half out of breath, she raced to the top of the ledge and peered cautiously over. A sheer twenty feet below, she saw the girls swimming in circles like sleek young otters.

"Peh-eh-wah," they called, waving to her. "Come! Take off your clothes and jump!"

Clarissa hesitated, feeling foolish and frightened. The water looked cold. Worse, it looked deep. Jumping was out of the question. But there was a trail, she swiftly noticed, winding among the ledges, leading to a narrow sandy bank at the water's edge. The girls splashed and played, ignoring her as she picked her way downward and, at last, stood on the sand at the rim of the pool.

Still hesitant, she poked at the water's surface with one tentative toe. A chill flashed through her body, eliciting a tiny gasp. The pool was even colder than the river had been, and the very notion of that icy water against her skin...

But what was she thinking? Clarissa upbraided herself. She, Clarissa Rogers, who had survived the terrors of the gauntlet, was not about to be daunted by a little cold water!

She would rinse out her gown first, she resolved, attacking what was left of her buttons. Then, wearing her underclothes for modesty, she would ease herself into the pool for a nice cold bath.

The girls turned to watch her as she slipped out of the threadbare gown and, crouching at the water's edge, began to scrub it on a rock. They paddled lightly as they floated above the crystal depths, showing no fear at all. How easy they made it look, as if they'd been born in the water!

Clarissa spread her gown over the boulders to dry, then, bracing her senses, she stepped carefully into the pool.

The girls giggled as she waded forward, her teeth chattering as the icy water inched up her bare calves. Clarissa saw their darting, mischievous glances but thought nothing of it until, without warning, the two Shawnee imps lunged at her. Shrieking with laughter, they seized her arms and yanked her headlong off the shallow edge into the deep water.

Clarissa went down fighting. Anger battled panic as she touched the rocky bottom, pushed off with all her strength and came up kicking, clawing and sputtering for air. Luckily, as she went down a second time, the girls seemed to realize she was in trouble. Grabbing her on each side, they propelled her back into the shallows where she staggered, coughing and gasping, toward the bank.

She was safe, praise be! But what a fool she had made of herself in front of these young Shawnee! It would never happen again, Clarissa vowed as she crawled, dripping, onto the sand: Whatever it cost her in effort and courage, she would learn to swim. She would learn or drown trying!

Her thoughts scattered like milkweed fluff as her eyes came level with a pair of large fringed moccasins planted firmly on the sand.

Her pulse lurched then broke into a rampant gallop

while her gaze crept upward along the length of two long leather-clad legs, over the subtly bulging leather breech-cloth, over the broad tan chest and muscular shoulders, to fix at last on Wolf Heart's amused face.

"Does this sort of thing always happen when you get near water?" he teased her without so much as a word of greeting. "Maybe Swan Feather should name you Drowning Rat."

"My name is Clarissa Rogers." She pushed herself onto her elbows, glaring up at him, unable to read any emotion in his enigmatic blue eyes. He had gone away without warning and now, at the worst possible moment, he had come back to taunt her. She wanted to fly at him, to lash him with furious words for leaving her alone. But she had been so lost without Wolf Heart that now the very sight of him almost caused her to weep with relief.

"Are you all right?" he asked, dropping to an easy crouch beside her.

Clarissa shook her hair out of her eyes, passionately wishing she could call him a whole string of angry names but knowing it would be foolish. Her best chance of escape depended on what she could learn from this man and whether, however unwittingly, she could lure him into helping her.

"Teach me to swim!" she demanded, forcing the words through her chattering teeth. "I want to learn—I must—the sooner the better!"

She expected Wolf Heart to laugh at her again, but he gave her little more than a curt nod. Clarissa became aware of the two girls, watching them avidly from the center of the pool. "Tonight," he said in a low voice, "I will come for you at Swan Feather's lodge when the moon is up. Be ready."

"I can't imagine Swan Feather will allow me to go!"

Clarissa snapped, her spirits sinking as she thought of the tasks that would have piled up during her time in the moon lodge. "The old slave driver is probably just waiting for me to come back so she can put me to work!"

His eyes flashed like wings of a blue jay. "She will allow it if I ask her," he answered, then hesitated, as if weighing the words he was about to speak. His gaze searched her face, arousing in Clarissa a scathing awareness of her scars.

"Speak gently of Swan Feather," he said in a low voice. "I know you think of her as a hard old woman, but there's more to her than what you see. Swan Feather is one of the *mekoche* people, the healers of the Shawnee. As a young woman she married a man of the Kispoko— the warrior sept—and came to live in this village. Even after her husband died, then her sons, and then last winter her daughter, she chose to stay among us and bless us with the gift of her healing."

"That's all well and good for you," Clarissa retorted. "The only gifts she's blessed me with are blistered hands and aching muscles!"

A bitter smile twitched a corner of Wolf Heart's mouth. "I wasn't going to mention this," he said, "but yesterday Swan Feather told me something that should have surprised me but didn't."

"What was that?" She met his hard, direct gaze, struggling against the urge to lower her face.

"She said she had already begun to love you."

His expression had not changed. Clarissa's lips parted in denial, but he cut her off before she could speak.

"I meant to say nothing. But Swan Feather has had enough sadness in her life. I wouldn't want you to be the cause of hurting her again."

Clarissa gulped back the tightness that had crept into

her throat. Swan Feather loved her? That cantankerous old slave driver? No, it had to be some kind of Shawnee joke! Wolf Heart was toying with her emotions, running her through a gauntlet of his own design. But she would not be manipulated. She would not let herself believe his deceitful words.

As if he had sensed her resistance, Wolf Heart's expressive eyes dulled to the hardness of slate. A mask seemed to slide across his features, pleasant but impersonal, hiding all traces of his former earnestness.

Clarissa's fingers pressed hollows in the sand as she groped for something to say, anything to bridge the void that had opened between them. Her scrambling mind invented one inanity after another, only to reject them all as foolish and artificial.

A whoop from the center of the pool put a merciful end to the silence. The two Shawnee girls had kept still long enough. Now they wanted attention.

The prettier of the two hooted at Wolf Heart, giggled and executed a graceful surface dive that flashed the sleek little moons of her bare buttocks. Clarissa stared, openmouthed, as the second girl did the same. Seconds later their glossy heads broke into the sunlight. They laughed, squealed and splashed each other, clearly for the benefit of their warrior audience.

"Are you thinking you'd like to learn that trick?" Wolf Heart glanced down at Clarissa, a sardonic smile tugging at his mouth. "I could ask the girls to teach you."

"Oh!" She glared up at him in sudden outrage.

"You didn't like my offer?" The pupils of his eyes glittered dangerously.

"How can you say such a thing to me?" She clambered to her feet, snatched up her dress and moccasins from the rocks and wadded them into a hasty bundle beneath her arm. "For your information, I happen to be a lady! And even in this place, I expect to be spoken to as such!"

With an indignant huff, she spun away from him and stalked up the path. Behind her, Wolf Heart's sharp-edged laughter echoed off the cliffs. Was he following her, or had he decided to stay behind? She paused beyond the second bend, ears straining for the pantherlike cadence of his footsteps behind her. Only the distant gush of water and the too-cheerful whistle of a chickadee disturbed the morning stillness.

Let him stay, she lashed herself angrily. Let him watch the girls bathe, or even jump into the pool and join them. He could drown, for all she cared! If this was typical sport, no wonder the wretch liked being a Shawnee!

At the top of the ledge she slipped behind a screen of elderberry bushes to tug on her dripping gown and shove her sandy feet into her moccasins. It was time she returned to Swan Feather's lodge. Otherwise the old woman was bound to scold her for staying away so long.

She said she had already begun to love you.

Wolf Heart's words burned into Clarissa's mind as she zigzagged her way up the slope. The whole notion was nonsense, of course. No one had loved her in the years since her father's death—certainly not Junius or the coolly efficient Mrs. Pimm. Even the young officers who'd flocked around her at Fort Pitt had only been drawn to her gaiety. None of them had loved her. How could they? They had scarcely known her!

So why should a smelly, disheveled old Shawnee woman, who had shown her no regard at all, be any different?

Clarissa mounted the crest of the bluff, the morning

breeze chilling through her wet clothes. The answer to
that question didn't matter, she reminded herself. No one
in this savage place mattered. At the first opportunity,
she would be gone. She would never see the old
woman—or the man who had once been Seth Johnson—
again in this life.

Her pulse quickened as she thought of her escape plan.
Yes, she could accomplish it! All she needed was a few
supplies, a weapon, a horse and an unguarded moment
to slip away. Then she could ride all the way back to
Fort Pitt, and in a few weeks' time, this whole nightmare
would be behind her.

Only her scarred face would remain, a grim souvenir
that she would carry to her grave. The briefest glimpse
of her reflection in a glass would rouse memories of the
gauntlet and Wolf Heart. And always, with those memories, would come the same scalding surge of anger she
was feeling now.

When she reached Swan Feather's lodge, Clarissa
found the old woman outside, wrestling a large fresh deer
hide on to a frame made of lashed poles. Sweat glistened
on her wrinkled face as she struggled to position the hide,
still heavy with its own moisture, over the frame's edges.
Her gaunt ribs heaved with effort. Clearly the task was
too much for her stooped, arthritic body.

She has already begun to love you.

Bracing her senses against the dead animal odor, Clarissa hurried forward to help. The old woman scarcely
glanced up as she dropped to her knees beside the frame,
seized a corner of the hide and began pulling it outward.

The hide's texture was as repulsive as its smell. The
stiff, dull brown hair that covered the outside was flecked
with blood and already drawing flies. The inner surface
was so slippery that her fingers could barely get a grip

on it. Its slimy coating left the smell of rot on her fingers, and it took all of Clarissa's self-control to keep from retching. But this was no time to indulge the delicacy of her senses. Not when Swan Feather was so much in need of help.

As Clarissa stretched each corner of the hide to its limit, Swan Feather used rawhide laces to fasten it to the frame. When the fourth corner was at last secured, the two of them lifted the frame and leaned it against the side of the lodge. Clarissa's head swam with the stench. As Swan Feather disappeared into the lodge, she collapsed against the trunk of a stout hickory, her stomach lurching. It was all right, she soothed herself. The grisly task was done. She could scrub the filth from her hands, fill her lungs with fresh air, and then—

Clarissa's thoughts ended in a silent groan. Her spirits sank beneath a flood of dismay as she saw Swan Feather coming out of the lodge again, carrying four stout poles and yet another saggy, reeking deerskin.

Wolf Heart had not meant to walk home by way of Swan Feather's lodge. All the same, his unbidden feet had carried him there, and now he stood at a careful distance, screening himself behind a thicket of budding alders as he paused to watch the two women at work.

They were bent over the two deer hides he had given Swan Feather, each of them using a sharp-edged bone scraper to clean every trace of flesh, fat and blood from the shiny inside surface. The task was one that every Shawnee girl learned in childhood, and Swan Feather, who had flensed hundreds of such skins in her lifetime, worked with quiet efficiency, her gnarled hands never missing a stroke.

Clarissa hacked away at her deerskin as if it were a

hated enemy. Her russet curls clung to her cheeks and
forehead in sweaty tendrils. Her small shapely breasts,
barely hidden by the threadbare bodice of her gown,
bounced and swung with the force of her motion.

Did she know, Wolf Heart wondered, what Swan
Feather was planning to make from the two deerskins?

As he watched, she paused to fling back her hair and
wipe away the sweat that drizzled into her eyes. For the
space of a long breath, her hands massaged the small of
her aching back, straining the tenuous fabric over her taut
little nipples. The artless pose triggered a rush of heat to
Wolf Heart's loins, the urge so compelling that decency
forced him to avert his eyes. When he glanced back a
moment later, he was relieved to see her bent dutifully
over her work again.

A bemused smile teased at his mouth as he walked
away. Clarissa was being uncharacteristically docile, he
thought. And judging from what he knew of her, that
could mean only one thing: she was up to no good.

He remembered her passionate demand that he teach
her to swim. Only a fool would fail to wonder what lay
behind it—and whatever Swan Feather might think of
him, he was no fool.

So what could it be? Had those half-grown girl-puppies
wounded Clarissa's pride at the pool? Was she set on
holding her own against them? For most women, that
would be cause enough, and it may well have entered
into her reasoning. But no, Wolf Heart conceded after a
moment's thought, Clarissa's motives would not be that
simple. There could be only one possible explanation for
her demand. She was planning to escape.

Swimming was vital to survival in the wilderness. After three near-drownings, no one would know that better
than she did. She would be an eager pupil—too eager,

perhaps. To gain every possible advantage, the sly minx would not be above using her wiles to throw her teacher off guard. When he was under her spell, then she would make her escape.

Not that he was surprised. How could he have expected anything less of her? She had fought him from the first moment of their meeting. In her own determinedly devious way, she was fighting him still.

At the crest of the bluff, he paused and stood gazing out at the river. Ohio-se-pe, the beautiful river, the Shawnee had named it long ago. And the French had echoed the meaning, calling it *la belle rivière*. But it was Clarissa, not the scene before him, that glimmered like a ghost spirit in his thoughts.

He remembered her face as he had seen it that morning, sunlit water beads glistening on the faint scars that lent strength of character to her beauty. He remembered the thrust of her chin, the stubborn spirit that had flamed in her cat-green eyes as she spoke.

"Teach me to swim!"

A bitter smile flickered across Wolf Heart's face as he swung away from the bluff and strode back toward his own lodge on the outskirts of the village. Yes, he resolved, he would keep his promise and teach Clarissa to swim.

He would teach her well.

From late afternoon through twilight, the venison haunch had roasted over the fire pit in Swan Feather's lodge. The sizzling juices ignited spurts of blue-tipped flame where they dripped onto the hot coals. Mouthwatering aromas curled through the smoke hole to drift on the evening breeze, inviting friends, neighbors and passersby to wander in and partake.

Clarissa huddled outside in the shadow of the wood-pile, her knees clasped tightly against her chest. Her belly growled with hunger, but after so many hours of working those foul-smelling hides, the very last thing she wanted was deer meat!

She closed her eyes for a moment, too weary to think. Her back and shoulders throbbed from bending over the hides all day. Her fingers were raw from gripping the rough bone scraper. Worst of all, she reeked of moldering deer hide from head to toe.

Reaching down, Clarissa gathered up a fistful of sandy earth and rubbed it between her hands in a vain effort to absorb the stench. Washing in dirt! She shook her head at the very idea. What she wouldn't give for a warm soapy bath and a night between clean muslin sheets!

With a restless sigh, she brushed her hands clean and wiped them on the hem of her skirt. It was getting dark now. A cricket had begun to chirp beneath the woodpile, its song echoed by another in the brush. Glancing up, Clarissa saw that a golden sliver of moon had edged above the treetops.

''I'll come for you at Swan Feather's lodge when the moon is up. Be ready.'' The memory of Wolf Heart's rich voice speaking those words sent a gush of antici-pation through Clarissa's body. Not that he would be coming, of course. Her show of temper at the pool had taken care of that possibility.

Given time to think, she might have held her tongue. But when he had ogled those two girls showing off their lithe young bodies, and even suggested, however jok-ingly, that she learn to do the same...

Her hand clenched into a fist at his remembered in-solence. No, she had been in the right! She would not waste another minute thinking about the wretched man! She would learn to swim some other time!

From her hiding place, she could see Swan Feather's guests wandering in and out of the lodge. She recognized the one-eyed chief, Hunts-at-Night, walking beside the pretty middle-aged woman from the moon lodge—praise be, could those two be husband and wife? And there was Wolf Heart's friend Cat Follower, grinning impishly as he ducked to enter the doorway.

As far as Clarissa could tell, there were no invitations to Shawnee social events. Anyone who smelled a feast cooking was welcome to come and share. She had seen no beggars among the Shawnee.

The same open spirit, in fact, seemed to apply to Shawnee children. From the time they left their mothers' breasts and began to toddle among the lodges, they were watched over by all the villagers, who saw that no little one went without what was needed, be it feeding, cleaning or a bit of gentle discipline. There were no foundlings in the Shawnee world, no orphanages, no small children hired out as spit turners, wool pickers or powder monkeys. Instead, they—

Clarissa's thoughts cartwheeled into oblivion as she saw Wolf Heart striding up the path.

She shrank into the shadows as he came closer. Tonight he looked every inch a Shawnee warrior—tall, stately and savage as a panther. His blue-black hair streamed over his muscular shoulders. The twin eagle feathers fluttered from his scalp lock, as if challenging some unseen enemy to claim them. His silver earrings glittered in the moonlight, opulent treasure against the golden bronze of his skin.

Clarissa waited in an agony of silence, expecting him to look for her, but he did not even glance in her direc-

tion. His purposeful steps carried him straight to the door
of the lodge, where he ducked beneath the frame of the
doorway and vanished inside.

Bewildered and chagrined, she stared after him. Then,
as curiosity quenched her welling anger, she pressed her
ear against the lodge's rough bark covering. From inside,
she could hear the deep rumble of Wolf Heart's voice
mingling with the conversation of the other guests.
Straining her ears and mind to their limits, she could
catch a word here, a phrase there, but it was no use trying
further. The Shawnee tongue was still beyond her understanding.

All the same, there was no mistaking the warm, con-
vivial spirit that radiated from around Swan Feather's fire
circle. Listening to the cheerful tones and intimate laughter, Clarissa was overcome by a deep sense of loneliness.
She curled tightly into herself, her arms hugging her
knees, her eyes stinging with unshed tears. The moon was
a yellow blur in the eastern sky, the cricket songs like
the small, shrill inner cries of her own anguish.

She could get up and walk away right now, she
thought. Why not? No one would see her go. She would
almost surely die in the wilderness, but what did it matter? No one would miss her. Junius would gladly inherit
her dowry. Swan Feather would find another captive to
boss and scold. And as for Wolf Heart—

"So, there you are." His voice shattered her reverie.
Clarissa gasped as she looked up to see him towering
over her, his fierce black silhouette outlined by the newly
risen moon. She gazed up at him, her emotions a whirlpool of anger and longing.

"Are you ready to go?" he asked pleasantly enough.

"I've changed my mind. It's too cold." She hugged
her knees, feeling wretched and contrary. Didn't he know

that she was sick with exhaustion, that her once soft hands were raw and sore, that she reeked like the inside of a tannery? Didn't he know that, for reasons she could not even pretend to understand, she wanted to be beautiful for him, more beautiful than she could ever be again?

"Come on." His hand settled firmly onto her shoulder.

"Why should I?" she challenged him perversely.

"Because if I have to throw you over my shoulder, carry you all the way to the pool and toss you in, we're going to be the talk of the whole village."

"You wouldn't!"

"Don't try me." His grip tightened, and she knew that if she did not move under her own power, he would do exactly as he'd threatened. Clinging to the last remnants of her dignity, Clarissa struggled to rise on legs that were numb from sitting. One knee came up straight, but the other, tingling unbearably, buckled beneath her.

His big hand caught her waist as she stumbled, pulling her up against him. As her palm braced against his chest, the feel of his hard, cool flesh jolted through her with the force of summer lightning. Clarissa stifled a moan. "Please," she whispered, wishing she could drop into the ground and vanish. "Just let me go."

"You asked me for a swimming lesson. That's what you're going to get." His hand, firm against the small of her back, propelled her away from the lodge and onto the shadowy path.

Clarissa dragged along beside him in silence, too tired to make conversation, let alone think of learning to swim. Maybe she would just sink into the water and drown, or even better, maybe she would succeed in drowning *him!* Now there was something to anticipate! She squared her shoulders, feeling better but still out of sorts.

"You didn't have to sit outside alone," Wolf Heart was saying. "You would have been welcome in Swan Feather's lodge with the others."

"I'm afraid I wasn't feeling very sociable."

"There were some good people there," he continued as if she hadn't spoken. "Some of them would like to be your friends. White Moon, the women's chief—"

"The women have a chief?" Clarissa asked, her interest suddenly piqued.

"Is that so strange?"

"Well, we certainly don't have such a thing in Baltimore! The men would never stand for it!"

Wolf Heart chuckled under his breath. "Shawnee women have more power than you can imagine."

"Power!" Clarissa exploded. "Yes, I've seen that power! They work like mules!"

"They work hard," Wolf Heart agreed calmly. "But they have a voice in the council, and they can even keep the men from going to war. They own their *wegiwas*— their lodges—and all the things in them. In all things, Shawnee women are equal to men."

Clarissa stared down at the moon-dappled path, thinking of Junius and the comfortable town house and prosperous business he'd inherited as a matter of course— because he was male. Wolf Heart walked beside her in silence, the low, even sound of his breath mingling with the whisper of newborn leaves.

"Tell me about your women's chief," she said, struggling against the overpowering sense of his nearness. "What did you say her name was?"

"White Moon, the wife of Hunts-at-Night. She mentioned that she had met you."

"Oh." The things he had told her earlier were beginning to make more sense now. "Yes, we met in the, uh—"

"The moon lodge. I know."

"You know about the moon lodge?" Clarissa choked, too shocked, even, to blush. She was doing her best to understand Shawnee ways, but the idea that a man, especially this man, would know where she had gone and why was so embarrassing that she wanted to hide.

"The women's chief is most often a chief's wife, or perhaps his mother or sister," Wolf Heart continued, ignoring her agitation. "She speaks for the women in the council, and when—"

"Look!" Clarissa seized his arm, transfixed by wonder. The trail had emerged from the trees to wander along the crest of the bluff. Far below the spot where they stood, the darkened river glittered with rings of golden light. It was a magical scene, so beautiful that, for a moment, she forgot her misery, her anger and all she had suffered in this place. "What is it?" she whispered in awe.

"Fishing." He stood behind her now, his voice a velvety rasp in her ear. "The first fishing night of the season. The lights down there are torches set on poles in the water. The fish are drawn to the light. They come—"

"And then they're caught. Poor foolish fish!"

Fearing that she might have moved too close to the sheer ledge, Clarissa took a step backward and came into full contact with the hard wall of his body. Her breath caught in a little gasp, and she might have moved forward again but there was no safe place to go. She stood trembling like a leaf, her back tightly pressed into his lean, solid warmth.

Wolf Heart tensed slightly. Without a word, his arms slid around her, holding her against him with a gentleness that made her ache. His long hands cradled her ribs, the fingertips not quite touching the tender swell of her breasts. Could he feel her heart? Clarissa wondered. Could he feel it leaping and pounding like one of the trapped fish in the water below? Could he feel the jerky cadence of her breathing and the waves of heat that shimmered downward to pool in the dark pulsing center of her womanhood?

Her whirling mind had all but ceased to think, but she remembered, like a dream of some long-ago world, the revelations of her married cousin. She remembered gasping in disbelief when Jenny had told her what happened to a man when he was ready to make love. Only now did she realize how true those words had been. The rockhard ridge was unmistakable against the curve of her back—warm, real and large beyond her wildest imaginings. The idea of all that engorged maleness fitting so precisely inside her...

Clarissa's face flamed as she swept the image furiously from her mind. This was no time to lose her head, when she was in clear danger of ruin. Perhaps she should say something, ease away from him, even scream or struggle.

But Wolf Heart had not moved. He continued to hold her tenderly in front of him. His hands were still, but the pulse throbbed in his arms and chest, encircling her with a cadence as deep and wild as the savage beat of a war drum. The lights on the river below had begun to blur in the soft night mist.

She closed her eyes. The liquid weight that stirred in her own loins was so compelling, so dizzyingly sweet, that if she were to turn in his arms, she knew she would be lost beyond all hope of escape.

And she could never allow that to happen.

She stirred, marshaling her resistance as Wolf Heart's

throat moved against her temple. "We should go," he said huskily, his breath ruffling her hair. "You'll never learn to swim this way."

"Yes." She found her voice as he released her, then stepped back to give her more room. Her pulse was ragged, her throat dry. She felt as if she were running a very different kind of gauntlet, and this race was far from over.

"It's too cold for swimming," she stammered. "You should take me back to Swan Feather's."

"The water feels warmer at night. You'll see." His hand clasped her elbow, its pressure firmly insistent. Clarissa stumbled along beside him, her body still aching for fulfillment. It could not happen, she warned herself again. She had made her plans. She was going to escape at the first opportunity. She was going back to her old life, and the very last thing she needed was to return to Baltimore a ruined woman!

The moon had risen above the treetops. It hung like a great coin in the sky, flooding the land with the riches of its light. Clarissa steeled herself against the softness of the night and the magnetic power of the man who walked beside her. She would be as cold as winter ice, she vowed. She would learn from Wolf Heart. She would even use him, if she had to.

But whatever happened, she would not—could not—allow herself to fall in love with him.

Chapter Eight

As he followed Clarissa down the hill, Wolf Heart cursed the betraying response of his own body. This was not what he'd had in mind when he'd resolved to teach Clarissa to swim. Quite the opposite—he'd only meant to insure that if she did, in fact, try to escape, she would not end her life at the bottom of the river. The last thing he'd planned on tonight was seduction.

But then, who was seducing whom? he mused, his eyes tracing the fluid sway of her hips in the darkness. Clarissa had known—she *must* have known—what she was doing to him there on that moonlit ledge. Yet she had been as cool as the first autumn frost, standing there with his achingly aroused *passah-tih* risen hard against her hips. The memory of that moment seared his face and his conscience. He should have moved back at once, easing them both away from the danger of the precipice. So, why hadn't he? What had he been thinking when he stood fixed to the ground, cradling her against him? Was he blundering into moon-madness?

Still visible below, the lights on the river glimmered through the evening mist. The night was warm for spring, the wind whispering like the breathy voice of a woman in love. Wolf Heart's arousal had dwindled to the hollow ache of unfulfillment. And that, he vowed, was all he would allow himself to feel for this woman. Swan Feather had spoken wisely. Some white captives never embraced the Shawnee way of life. It was time he faced the fact that Clarissa was one of them. Sooner or later she would escape, or she would die trying.

She glanced back over her shoulder, her wild russet mane fluttering in the nighttime breeze. When would she make her move? Would it be an impulsive plunge as her last attempt had been? Or would she act with patience and cunning this time, waiting until everything she needed was in place?

And what would he do if he had a chance to stop her?

"Are you coming?" she demanded, tossing her splendid head. "If you don't mind, I'd just as soon get this swimming lesson over with!"

A wry smile tugged at a corner of Wolf Heart's mouth. "Don't be too impatient. Some things take time and practice. Swimming is one of them."

"I plan to learn fast!" She raced down the trail ahead of him, feet flying in her oversize moccasins. She was as fluttery as a killdeer luring a mink away from its nest, Wolf Heart observed darkly. And her eagerness was all show. He hung back, waiting to see what she would do.

He didn't have to wait long. Clarissa gave a little yelp as she stumbled and went down. When he caught up with her, still taking his time, she was crumpled beside the trail examining her bare foot, the moccasin lying beside her in the grass.

"I...think something may be broken," she said, looking up at him as plaintively as an injured puppy. "You'd best take me back to—"

"Let me see." He cut her off brusquely as he sank to

a crouch. She did not protest as he lifted her foot and cradled it between his hands, but he caught the nervous shift of her pupils in the moonlight. Her body stiffened uneasily as his thumbs began a careful exploration of her bones, starting with the toes and working upward.

"Does that hurt?" His fingers manipulated the ball of her foot. Her bones were as delicate as a crane's. She shook her head, her lips pressed tightly together.

"Higher?"

She nodded. "I think it's my ankle. I—must have sprained it."

"Then it's a good thing we're going for a swim," he said, his voice betraying nothing. "Cold water is the best thing for sprains."

"It may be more than a sprain," she said, correcting herself swiftly. "One of my bones may be broken. In any case, I'm certainly in no condition to swim!"

"We'll see." His fingers worked their way around her slender ankle. No heat. No swelling. She was fine. "Does this hurt?" He pressed lightly against the hazelnut-size outer knob of her anklebone. The sharp intake of her breath was worthy of an accomplished actress.

"Yes! Yes—there!" she whispered.

"I see." He glanced up, scowling. Her face was as blandly innocent as a baby's. "Well, then, there's only one thing to do."

Before she could speak, he had caught her behind the knees and shoulders, sweeping her up in his arms as he jerked to his feet. Too startled to protest, she stared up at him as he turned and strode on down the trail.

"Where are you taking me?" He had covered a dozen long steps by the time she found her voice.

"You'll see."

"But this isn't the way back to the village! It's—"

Her words dissolved in an outraged gasp as she realized what he was up to. For an instant, her whole body went rigid. Then she began to wriggle furiously. Her feet kicked wildly at the air, tossing her remaining moccasin onto the trail. Her angry fists pummeled his chest hard enough to leave bruises. "Put me down!" she rasped, all wild motion. "Put me down this instant, you beastly, unprincipled...*Indian!*"

Wolf Heart's only answer was a raw-edged laugh as he tightened his grip, swung off the trail and stalked decisively toward the ledge that overlooked the pool.

Clarissa had been fighting to escape. Suddenly she clung to him for dear life, her arms clutching his neck in an unbreakable stranglehold. "No!" she gasped in horror. "You wouldn't dare throw me off! You mustn't! I'll drown!"

"*Throw* you off?" He laughed again, a rough, savage sound that sent a chill through her body. "*Throw* you off? Why, you've sadly misjudged me, dear lady! I would never do such a thing! Throw you off, indeed!"

Still holding her in his arms, he took two running strides and leaped off the ledge.

Clarissa screamed in rage and terror all the way down. Then the water closed around her like an icy shroud, shutting out the world as her senses had known it.

She gripped Wolf Heart's shoulders, fighting panic as they sank together. *He would not let her drown*—again and again she forced herself to remember that one truth. A wretched Shawnee turncoat he might be, and an unrefined brute, as well, but she knew, with sudden surety, that she could trust him with her life.

Realizing that her weight would only pull him down, she willed herself not to struggle as his powerful legs kicked for the surface. Her bursting lungs told her that they had gone deep, so deep that an eternity seemed to pass before they broke at last into the night-chilled air. She pushed upward, spitting, choking, gulping life back into her body. Wolf Heart's arms supported her in the water. She sagged against his chest, her ribs seized by racking spasms.

"How's your ankle now?"

The playful question with its mocking edge rumbled in Clarissa's ear. Startled, she looked up into his grinning face. "You—" she sputtered, her fear congealing into white-hot rage. "You insolent, unsufferable—"

He let her go.

She gasped, swallowing water as she went down again. This time anger gave her strength. Her legs began to kick furiously, driving her upward until she broke the surface. Murder glittered in her eyes.

"I should have drowned you!" Her feet and hands paddled furiously. "I should have pulled you under and kept you there!"

"You would never have done it." Water drops glistened like jewels on his straight black eyebrows. "You're a fighter, Clarissa. Your own urge to survive would have been too strong. See, look at you now! You're swimming!"

"Oh!" She blinked, so startled that she stopped paddling. Her head promptly went under, but this time a series of confident kicks brought her to the surface again. The water, which had seemed so cold at first, was deliciously cool now. "*This* is swimming?" She laughed, her anger forgotten in the delight of her discovery. "But it's easy! There's nothing to it!"

"Well, there's more than you might think." His critical frown could not quite hide his pleasure. "You've

learned the first lesson. But there's more. Do you f[...]
strong enough to go on?''

''Yes!'' Clarissa was all eagerness now, thrilled by her
new accomplishment.

''Come on, then. I'll need a place where I can stand.''
He hooked her waist with his free arm and kicked for the
shallows. A stone's toss from the bank he found bottom
and stood erect, the silky black water lapping at his tautly
puckered nipples. The thumb-size, fringed pouch he always wore dangled just below the surface of the water,
held down by its own weight. Someday, when she knew
Wolf Heart better, she would ask him what was inside—
but there would be no someday, Clarissa swiftly reminded herself. At the first opportunity, whenever it
might come, she would be on her way back to Fort Pitt.

''Are you ready?'' He took her hands and swung her
around to face him.

Clarissa gripped his big rough fingers, her feet kicking
frantically behind her. By now she was beginning to tire.
Her breath came in gasps, and her side had developed a
sharp stitch, but she forced a smile, determined not to let
Wolf Heart see that she was flagging.

''Did *you* have to...learn to swim when you...became
a Shawnee?'' she asked, panting between words.

''Yes and no. I could swim well enough before. But I
had a lot to learn.'' He scowled momentarily, then lowered himself neck deep into the water. ''For this, you'll
have to trust me,'' he said.

''Trust you? Ha!'' She blew across the glassy surface,
spraying his stony face with water. ''Why, you're the
very last person on earth I'd trust!''

His eyes flickered as if he'd been stung, and for an
instant he hesitated. Suddenly realizing how much she

wanted this lesson to continue, Clarissa swiftly reversed her course.

"All right, but no tricks," she said. "Do you promise?"

"Why should I promise if you don't trust me?" It was his turn to tease her now.

"Because otherwise I'm climbing out of this pool right now! So, do you promise?"

"All right, I promise." He eased her away from him, pushing her farther out into the water. "Now let go of my hands."

Clarissa released his fingers, keeping her eyes locked with his. The water was over her head here, and for all her newfound paddling skill, she was uneasy.

"Just relax." His hands reached underneath her to support her waist. The motion brought his face within a finger's breadth of hers. A bead of water, holding its own tiny gold moon, glittered on his lower lip. What if she were to lean forward the slightest bit and flick away that shining drop with the tip of her tongue? What would Wolf Heart do to her?

What a deliciously wicked thought!

"I'm going to turn you over," he said, gently rotating her body until she faced upward. "Now straighten your legs, put your head down and arch your back a little—that's it—as if you were lying on a bed. How does it feel?"

"Oh." Clarissa gave a little moan of wonder. She was floating languorously in the cool dark water, Wolf Heart's hand lightly supporting the small of her back. Her hair flowed outward like sea moss, fanning in slow ripples around her head. She managed a nervous little laugh. "It feels magical! Like nothing I've ever experienced in my life! But, oh, for heaven's sake, don't let go of me!"

His laugh was like the rumbling purr of a great sleek-muscled cat. "It wouldn't make any difference if I did let go. The water would hold you up. All you need to do is let it. Trust the water, Clarissa, and trust yourself. That's the whole secret of swimming."

Clarissa stretched her bare toes. She closed her eyes, giving in, for the moment, to the sheer sensuality of lying suspended in liquid coolness. Her senses unfolded like night-blooming blossoms, opening to the sigh of the wind and the crystalline tinkle of the spring, to the far-off cry of a loon and the fresh aromas of wet moss, wood and flowers, to the feel and taste of water on her wind-chapped lips.

Now and again, at night, she had dreamed of floating in the sky like a cloud. This was even more wonderful. This was real.

"Open your eyes." Wolf Heart's throaty whisper caressed her like the stroke of fingers on a harp. "Look up."

Clarissa's mouth formed a silent "Oh" as her eyelids fluttered open. She was gazing upward at the ring of cliffs that surrounded the pool. Cascading ferns and mosses, beaded with moisture, festooned the rocky ledges. Sprays of tiny white flowers nestled among them like bunched lace. High above, the great golden orb of the moon glowed against the inky velvet of the sky.

"The Shawnee believe the moon is the home of Kokomthena, our grandmother, who made all living things." Wolf Heart's voice, blending with the sounds of darkness, had taken on a mystical quality. "She made the deer and the bear and the panther. She made fish and birds and insects—and people. First the Delaware, then, when she'd had more practice, the Shawnee."

"And do *you* believe that, too?" Clarissa asked, still lost in floating.

"Why not? It makes as much sense as anything I ever heard in church."

"But do you really *believe* it?" she persisted, suddenly aware that his hand was no longer supporting her back.

"I choose to believe it, as I choose to be Shawnee."

Clarissa struggled to keep her calm balance in the water even as she struggled with the paradox of this man who so stubbornly declared himself to be what he was not.

"And did your grandmother make white people, too?" she asked, chipping away at the edges of his maddening logic.

Wolf Heart's pensive silence darkened as the seconds passed. "Our grandmother was wise," he said at last. "She knew the Shawnee would need enemies to fight. Otherwise they would grow weak and lazy. So she made the Iroquois. But the whites came from far away, long after the old stories were set for telling."

"So your grandmother didn't make them?"

"Kokomthena's grandchildren follow her laws." A bitter edge had crept into his voice. "They don't ravage the land or claim to own it as white people do. Why would she make such selfish, wasteful creatures?"

"But *you* are white!" Clarissa was becoming agitated now, losing her equilibrium in the water. "You're no more Shawnee than I am Chinese—"

She went under, righted herself and came up facing him, thrashing and spitting. "I know what you're trying to do!" She flung the words at him. "But it won't work, Seth Johnson, so you may as well give up! You'll never succeed in making me over into a hide-scraping, buckskin-wearing, moon-worshiping Shawnee squaw!"

His eyes narrowed sharply. Then, with a suddenness that made her gasp, his powerful hands caught her elbows and snatched her out of the water, lifting her up until her gaze was level with his own. His face was a stone-cold mask, devoid of expression. Only his cobalt eyes, striking flinty sparks that turned moonlight to fire, betrayed the heat of his fury. At that moment he looked all savage in his terrible beauty. He looked, she thought, as if he could kill her.

Wolf Heart! Clarissa's throat moved, but no sound emerged. She hung suspended between his massive arms, her heart pounding like thunder.

"Don't, Clarissa," he said in a low, flat voice. "Don't—"

"Wolf Heart." She found her voice, the name emerging in labored syllables. Tears welled in her eyes, one salty drop spilling over to trickle down her scarred cheek. "Please," she whispered, not even sure of what she wanted from him. "Please…"

A shudder passed through his body as he caught her hard against him. She felt the crush of his enfolding arms. Then his cool, firm lips covered hers, devouring, possessing, sweeping away her resistance as a flooded river sweeps away a child's dam of twigs.

In an explosion of long-denied hunger, Clarissa's mouth molded to his. Her jaw slackened, leaving her open to the thrusting ravishment of his tongue. The taste of him was smoke and wild honey, laced with the mossy freshness of the pool. She could not get enough. She licked and nibbled wantonly, needing more, needing all she could take, all he could give her.

He groaned as her arms slid around him, locking their bodies together. His hands ranged over her back, skimming the boundaries of her aching breasts, then moving downward to cup her buttocks, curling her inward against the thick, sweet hardness of his aroused manhood.

The moon and stars seemed to burst like rockets in Clarissa's head. Heaven help her, she wanted him! She wanted the unthinkable act her cousin had described to her, wanted his touch in the burning places that had known nothing but her own tentative fingertips, wanted the press of his lean coppery weight upon her and that great swollen hardness filling her with its heat, burning away her innocence, making her, at long last, a woman.

Her skirt floated around her like the petals of a ragged flower, exposing legs that were bare except for the tattered remnants of her muslin drawers. Wolf Heart groaned, only half in protest, as she slid an exploring knee between his thighs. The satin stroke of flesh against flesh rippled through her, stirring a well of molten heat in the depths of her body. She arched against him, head flung back as his feral, nipping kisses moved down the damp slope of her throat.

Take me, Wolf Heart. Had she spoken the words or only imagined them? *Take me here, now. It's what I want, all I want....*

She was drifting into a long spiral of ecstasy when she felt him tense against her. He froze, head up, listening, then suddenly pushed her away from him. Clarissa reeled with hurt bewilderment. Then she too heard the sound of voices from the path above the ledge—laughing voices, a man's and a woman's. She stood gazing toward the sound, only half-comprehending what it might mean.

"Blast—it's Cat Follower!" Wolf Heart whispered, yanking her into the shadows. "This way!"

"Do you think they saw us?" Clarissa's cheeks burned as if they'd been painted with fire.

"I'd wager they weren't looking all that carefully!"

He guided her into the blackness under the mossy lip of a lodge-size boulder. She huddled beside him, teeth chattering, as the voices atop the ledge grew louder, peals of laughter echoing off the cliffs.

Suddenly, amid resounding whoops, two lean bronze bodies clothed only in moonlight plummeted headfirst from the top of the ledge and splashed together into the pool. Cat Follower surfaced first, flashing his familiar grin. An instant later, a pretty young woman, dark and sinewy, broke into the air with a squeal of delight and flung herself on top of him.

"Are they in love?" Clarissa whispered as the two wrestled joyously, giggling and grabbing boldly at any part of each other's bodies they could get their hands on.

"More likely they're just having a good time." Wolf Heart's wry chuckle sounded forced. "Come on. While they're busy, we can sneak around behind this rock. The trail goes up to the ledge from there."

Clarissa trudged after him, the wind biting through her water-soaked gown. The chill, if nothing else, had shocked her back to full reality. Her raw nerves twitched. Her face smarted with shame as she realized how close she had come to utter ruin.

Never, she vowed with each ragged breath. Never again.

Wolf Heart was a renegade savage who could offer her nothing but hardship, privation and danger. To give herself to such a man, as she had so nearly done, would be to abandon any claim to virtue and gentility. True, she might still escape and return to Baltimore, but she would return a tainted woman, an outcast to the end of her days.

Above her on the winding path, Wolf Heart's looming silhouette blocked out the moon. Clarissa picked her way along in his shadow, the rocky ground bruising her tender feet. He had not spoken since leaving the pool, and the silence that hung between them now was as dark and heavy as the river.

By the time they neared the top of the long trail, the stars were out. Below the ledges, the lusty whoops and giggles had faded to breathy moans. It didn't take a vivid imagination to picture what was happening.

Clarissa blotted the forbidden image from her mind, her heart lurching as a new possibility struck. The rocky pool was a natural spot for dalliance. And Wolf Heart seemed to know the place well, perhaps too well. How many young women had *he* taken here for the very same purpose? she wondered. How many before her?

The rage that boiled up in Clarissa was sudden, hot and dangerous. What a silly little fool she had been! He had brought her here with intentions that were no better than a common knave's, and she had all but succumbed!

Too indignant to hold her tongue, she charged up the path to where he waited, his torso glistening, his arms folded across his broad chest. "You!" She hurled the word at him like an epithet. "You knew exactly what you were doing down there, didn't you? You arranged it all, from the very beginning!"

His craggy features might as well have been cast in stone. "You were the one who wanted to learn to swim," he said in a taut voice.

"Oh, but I got more than I bargained for, didn't I? You had more than a swimming lesson in mind! You were planning to—to have your way with me!"

"Have my way with you?" he echoed her words incredulously. "Have my way with you?" His throat made a little half-choking sound. Then he burst into raw-edged laughter.

"I don't see what's so funny!" Clarissa stormed, her

outrage growing by the minute. "Just because I wasn't inclined to become one more notch on your lodge pole, or however it is you keep track of your conquests—"

"*My* conquests!" He was struggling for composure now, his long cheek muscles determinedly rigid. "Give yourself some credit, Clarissa Rogers. You wrapped yourself around me like a she-lynx in heat!"

"Oh!" She glowered at him, a vein throbbing in her temple. A freshet of hot tears stung her eyes as she pushed her way around him and veered off the path. "Get out of my way, Wolf Heart or Seth Johnson, or whoever you are! I don't care how many Shawnee girls you take to that pool or what you do with them there! Just don't you come near me—not ever again!"

Wolf Heart stood rigid on the crest of the bluff as Clarissa's stumbling footsteps faded into darkness. She would be safe enough, he told himself. The village was not far, and there was no one in it who had any reason to harm her. All the same, he worried. Clarissa was as unpredictable as a half-grown wildcat. On her own, there was no telling what kind of devilry she might stir up.

A shadowed object at the side of the path caught his eye. Dropping to a crouch, he picked up one of the over-size moccasins Swan Feather had given Clarissa to wear. For the space of a breath he cradled it in his hand, remembering the scent and feel of her in his arms and the taste of her lovely wanton mouth on his. He should have known better than to get so close to her. The sensual explosion had only made things more awkward and painful between them.

Walking back the way they'd come earlier, he found the mate to the moccasin. Clarissa had no other shoes. He would need to find her before she came back looking for them, or perhaps injured a bare foot on the treacherous ground.

Bracing himself for another confrontation, Wolf Heart strode off in the direction she had gone. The full moon cast the landscape into hues of old silver and tarnished gold. Hickory and alder, their branches fuzzy with newborn leaves, whispered in the night wind. Although Clarissa could not have gotten far in such a short time, the fact that she had left the path would make finding her more difficult. He thought of calling out, then remembered that in her stubborn pique, she would not be likely to answer him.

Guided by instinct, he wound his way among thickets of willow and blackberry. Just ahead, cast into stark light and shadow by the moon, was an outcrop of rocks, some of them half again as high as a man's head. From the top of the formation, Wolf Heart reasoned, he might be able to look out over the patchy wood and see the way she had gone.

Climbing the rocks, however, proved unnecessary. As he neared the outcrop, Wolf Heart's ears caught a primitive, wounded sound through the high bushes. For a moment he stood stock-still, listening tensely. Then his shoulders sagged in relief and dismay as he recognized Clarissa's wrenching, hiccuping sobs.

He approached on stealthy feet, not wanting to startle her into flight. Had she lost her way? Was she frightened? In pain? Or was this just a womanly response to their encounter on the ledge—and if such was the case, would he be wiser to leave well enough alone?

Moments later, still at war with himself, he emerged from the thicket on the near side of the outcrop. He could see Clarissa now, a stone's throw away, huddled on a low boulder with her back toward him. Her hands were pressed against her face. Her thin hunched shoulders shook in racking spasms of emotion.

He took a cautious step toward her, then froze in horror when he saw that she was not alone. Flattened above her on the topmost rock, its sleek form gleaming like a spill of molten gold, lay an enormous puma.

Wolf Heart's stomach clenched as he realized he had brought no weapon with him, not even a club or knife. It was too late to grope for a rock on the ground or snap a limb off a tree. There was nothing in his hands except a pair of limp, worn-out moccasins.

Should he shout? Try to warn her? Not yet, he swiftly resolved. Any sudden move on Clarissa's part could trigger a lightning attack of fangs and slashing claws. Only when he was close enough to leap in and protect her would he dare to take such a risk.

Eyes never leaving the huge cat, he edged closer to the rocks. The puma was straining forward on its rocky perch, ears pricked in curiosity. In all likelihood, it had never heard anything like the noises this human female was making. Under different conditions, the scene might have been amusing. But there was nothing funny about the danger to Clarissa. Wolf Heart crept closer, praying for enough time to reach her.

The long tawny tail hung down the side of the rock, its dark tip twitching in the moonlight. Watching, Wolf Heart sensed the deliberation in the shadowy feline mind. Would it attack? Would it slink away unseen and unheard? Or would it remain, listening in perplexity to those alien, oddly compelling sounds?

The great head lowered slightly, neck extending. The massive shoulders and hindquarters tensed, tail quivering like a bowstring along its elegant length, and Wolf Heart knew he was out of time.

"Ha!" He charged across the clearing, hurling one moccasin, then the other, at the lithe golden form. The missiles bounced off the tawny hide, doing no damage, but the distraction was enough to throw the huge cat's leap off balance. Veering sideways, it lost its footing and slid down the face of the rock, a spitting, clawing ball of fury. By the time it struck the earth, almost at Clarissa's feet, Wolf Heart was beside her.

"Ha!" he shouted again, bracing himself, half-crouched, feet apart, to meet the deadly spring. But there would be no attack. The startled animal had had enough. It wheeled and streaked away to vanish like lightning into the black night.

Clarissa stood blinking as Wolf Heart exhaled and straightened to his full height. A moment ago she had believed herself alone, free to give vent to the rage, pain and homesickness that was threatening to crush her soul. Then Wolf Heart had shouted in the darkness, and a great yellow ball of fury had crashed at her feet and bounded away.

Still grappling with what had happened, she stared at the huge pug marks on the moonlit ground. Her face stung with the remnants of dried salt and humiliation. It appeared that Wolf Heart had saved her life again. But even for this, she would not have chosen to let him see her private tears.

"I know I should thank you," she said in a cold trembling voice. "But I didn't ask you to follow me here. What did you think you were doing?"

In answer, he bent from the waist and picked up two limp objects that lay in the weeds at the base of the rock. Without a word, he thrust the moccasins into her hands.

Only then, as he turned and began to walk away, did

the clear recollection of what had happened strike her like a dash of ice water. She saw him now, pounding into the clearing, yelling like a berserker as he waved those ridiculous shoes above his head. She saw him flinging the moccasins toward the rocks, saw the huge tawny cat come skidding down the sheer face, clawing wildly for a foothold.

Inexplicably, perhaps hysterically, she began to giggle.

Wolf Heart had reached the edge of the clearing. He paused, then glanced back over his shoulder, his face obscured by shadows. The laughter died in her throat as he turned and walked slowly back toward her.

Clarissa stood still and let him come. Suddenly she was tired of games. She was tired of verbal and emotional fencing matches. She wanted only to rest.

She slumped against him as he gathered her into his arms, savoring the solid strength of his big hard-muscled chest. He held her tenderly, making no effort to push things beyond the moment, and she realized that he too was tired. They had battled, parried and argued to an exhausted draw.

"I want to go home," she whispered, not fully understanding what "home" meant anymore. Was it the cold, lonely house in Baltimore, ruled by Junius and the straitlaced Mrs. Pimm? Was it Fort Pitt, where her harrowing journey had begun? Was it Swan Feather's crude lodge? Or was "home" a place she had known only in unremembered dreams?

Wolf Heart did not speak, but Clarissa felt his arms scooping her up as if she were a tired child drifting into slumber at the end of a long day's outing. She lay unresisting as he carried her back toward the village, her head pillowed in the musk-scented hollow between his shoulder and chest, his heartbeat a low and steady throb in her ear.

The wind had warmed and softened. It whispered in the low grasses, making them sing against Wolf Heart's legs as he walked. The hooting cry of an owl from the deep woods blended with the low chirr of crickets and the faraway nicker of a horse. Somewhere in the darkness, the great golden puma would be running free, grateful—if such a beast could feel gratitude—for its harrowing escape.

Warm and sleepy, Clarissa nestled deeper into the cradle of Wolf Heart's embrace. Images blurred as she recounted the long day—her emergence from the moon lodge, her chagrin at the pool, the odorous deer hides—and Wolf Heart. Wolf Heart most of all—his return, his laughter, his maddening pride, and the long, searing kisses that had left her limp with need. It had been a terrible day. A wrenchingly glorious day. And now it was over.

Tomorrow morning she would wake up levelheaded and sensible. She would start planning her escape, every precious detail of it, from gathering and stashing her supplies to stealing a horse and covering her tracks. Tomorrow, Clarissa vowed, she would do it all. But not tonight. Tonight she needed Wolf Heart's supporting arms around her. She needed the deep cadence of his breathing and the clean, musky aroma of his skin sweeping through her senses like forbidden wine.

Through a blur of sleep-weighted lashes, she could see the high-riding moon and, around its pale ring of light, the glimmering stars. One star fell, leaving a long white streak across her darkening range of vision, and that was the last of the night she would remember.

* * *

Wolf Heart glided through the thicket with long careful steps, trying not to disturb the precious burden in his arms. Clarissa slumbered like a child, her head lolling against his chest, her fingers resting lightly on the medicine pouch that hung there. Her empty moccasins nested in the curve of her body. Her lashes lay on her pale cheeks like shadowy golden fans. Maddening as a bee sting, erratic as the darting flight of a hummingbird, she had finally settled into rest.

When had he first realized he loved her?

Had it happened in the pool, when she'd gazed up at him, transfixed with delight at her mastery of water? Had it happened when she'd melted against him, blazing with all the fire of her innocent need? Or had there been no clear moment at all, only a slow unfolding, like a flower's change from bud to blossom?

Where had it come from, this aching tenderness? He had not nurtured it, not wanted it. And even now, he did not welcome it. In loving Clarissa, he had opened the door to disaster and placed his own Shawnee spirit in peril.

Through the trees, he could see the flickering amber glow of the village fires. Clarissa stirred as they moved nearer. She whimpered like a little cat, her head butting his chest before she sighed and sank even deeper into sleep. How tempting it would be to carry her to the seclusion of his own lodge and there, by firelight, to settle her on the deerskin bed and lose himself in her sweet young body for the rest of the night. No one in the village would question what had occurred. There would be no judgment, no condemnation, as one might expect in the white world. The Shawnee would view the new union as they viewed all natural events—with the serene acceptance of a quiet pond that reflects what is held above it.

Wolf Heart hesitated for an instant, then set his feet resolutely on the trail to Swan Feather's lodge. Nothing was going to happen. Not tonight, not ever. Possessing Clarissa would be like possessing a flame. She would sear him with her heat, but he could never bind her to him. A part of her would always be yearning toward the world she had left behind.

"I want to go home." The memory of her poignant whisper echoed in his mind, and he knew that Swan Feather's advice had been wisely given. But how could he set Clarissa free and send her back? She belonged to the village and to the old woman whose daughter she had replaced. He had no right to defy Shawnee law.

Through the trees he could see the dark outline of the lodge, the last embers of firelight flickering through the open doorway. The smell of roast venison lingered on the night air, recalling Swan Feather's generous celebration of his gift.

From somewhere beyond the village, the fierce, lonely call of a wolf quivered on the darkening wind. Wolf Heart listened, a strange restlessness stirring inside him. The wolf was his *unsoma,* the creature that had appeared in his boyhood vision to become his guide and personal sign. He had taken his name from that long-ago vision and promised, for always, to follow the path of the wolf in courage, resourcefulness and loyalty to his clan.

It was a promise he had never broken.

Clarissa's body lay lightly against him, her legs and her impossibly long, thin feet dangling over his arm. He recalled seeing her outside Swan Feather's lodge that morning, hunched awkwardly over the deer hide, sweating and muttering as she scraped the slimy surface. Her battered courage tore at his heart. She was as out of place in his chosen world as a jewel-colored songbird in a nest of eagles.

Once his path had seemed so clear. Where was it now?

As if in answer to his unspoken question, the wolf howled again. Its call came from deep in the woods now, growing fainter with distance. Wolf Heart's inner sight glimpsed the animal running full out through the moon-shadowed forest, hot on the scent of prey, baying a signal to its kin. A shiver of response passed through his body, and he sensed suddenly that the wolf was calling to *him.*

Was it a sign? Had he ventured too far from the promise of his vision? Wolf Heart gathered Clarissa close as the blood-chilling call rang again in his ears, and he knew beyond certainty that he must follow it this very night. He would endure the boyhood ordeal of fasting and cold. He would open his mind, his heart and his spirit. And he would not return to the village—or to Clarissa—until he had learned all the wolf had to teach him.

The old woman was sitting alone in her lodge, the coals in the fire pit casting her walnut face into black and amber furrows. She glanced up at him, her gaze sad and knowing, and he realized there was no need to speak. She too had heard the call of the wolf, and she knew what it meant.

Swan Feather's ancient eyes watched him as he crossed the open floor and gently lowered the sleeping Clarissa to the skin bed. Her stern gaze softened as it rested briefly on the exhausted girl, then shifted back to Wolf Heart.

"Go," she whispered. "I will watch over her as best I can, but I am an old woman, and her spirit is free."

Wolf Heart nodded, understanding all too well the caution in her voice. His eyes lingered on Clarissa's face, knowing it might be for the last time. Then, forcing himself to move, he slipped out through the door of the lodge and into the night. There would be no need to return to his own lodge. A vision-quest required no food, water or weapons, only a weakened body and an open spirit.

Without a backward glance, he began to run. The dark wind swirled around him, cooling his skin and sweeping through his long, black hair. As he plunged ahead, he felt the forest close around him, felt the power of the night and heard, in the distance, the wild, compelling cry of the wolf.

Chapter Nine

Early the next morning, Swan Feather woke Clarissa with a none-too-gentle shake. *"Peh-eh-wah!"* the old woman demanded, tugging at her arm. "Come!"

Biting back a groan, Clarissa rubbed the sleep from her eyes, fumbled for her moccasins and tottered outside into the crisp dawn air. The sun was no more than a pale blur above the treetops, and the breeze puckered her skin into gooseflesh beneath her damp gown.

On the near side of the lodge the two deer hides, still lashed to their pole frames, gleamed with morning dew. For a sinking moment, Clarissa braced herself for another session with the scraper, but Swan Feather clearly had other plans.

"Eat." She thrust a fist-sized hunk of last night's roast venison into Clarissa's hands. The meat was cold and streaked with congealed fat, but when she tasted a sliver, she discovered she was ravenous. Forgetting all she'd learned of proper manners from Mrs. Pimm, she ripped off a larger piece and stuffed it hungrily into her mouth.

She had scarcely begun chewing in earnest when the old woman tugged at her elbow, motioning her toward an overgrown trail that led off through the thicket beyond the lodge. Only then did Clarissa notice the empty reed basket clutched under her ropy arm.

Giving up on the urge to eat more, she followed the dwarfish figure into the thicket. For all her arthritic old bones, Swan Feather could scurry through the underbrush like a rabbit. Clarissa found herself stretching her own long legs to keep pace as the trail wound beneath mossy deadfalls and around clumps of lichen-encrusted rock.

The sun, by now, had crept above the horizon, flooding the forest with daylight. Birds trilled in the morning brightness. Squirrels barked, chattered and scolded from the trees.

As her sleep-drugged mind stirred into wakefulness, Clarissa remembered last night's swimming lesson and Wolf Heart's soul-searing kiss. She recalled their quarrel, the squalling puma dropping almost at her feet and, less sharply, the long walk home, drifting off in the security of his strong arms while the stars danced in her head. The sensation of being lowered to her bed lingered in the fog of memory, and she realized that Wolf Heart must have returned her to Swan Feather's lodge.

Returned her, when he could have just as easily taken her to his own.

Furious color flooded her cheeks as the implications of last night's behavior sank home. She had thrown herself at him like a wanton, with no regard for her own virtue or status as a lady. If Wolf Heart had been a different sort of man—

"Peh-eh-wah!" Swan Feather had gained a good twenty paces on her. She stood at the next bend in the trail, motioning impatiently with her free arm. Clarissa broke into a lope that carried her swiftly to the old woman's side.

"Where...is Wolf Heart?" She struggled with the

Shawnee words she had learned in the moon lodge. More than anything she wanted to find him and put things right after last night's angry accusations.

"Gone." Swan Feather's face was as inscrutable as her answer. When Clarissa gazed at her, bewildered, she turned and pointed northward, away from the village and the river. "Gone," she said again in Shawnee. "Gone a long time."

"Where? How—how many days?" Clarissa asked, holding up her fingers, but the old woman was already moving ahead, shuffling along the trail at her ground-burning pace. Still reeling with surprise, Clarissa stumbled along behind her. Wolf Heart had given no hint about leaving last night. How could he just vanish like this? What right did he have to go without telling her?

Every right, Clarissa reminded herself miserably. She had no more claim on him than he had on her.

"Look." Swan Feather had stopped at the edge of the trees. Before them lay an open meadow, knee-high in lush spring grass and dotted with budding wildflowers. A grazing doe, her belly swollen with fawn, raised her graceful head at their approach, then flicked her white-ruffed tail and bounded into the trees. A flock of gold-finches, feeding on last year's dry sunflower seeds, exploded into fluttering wing.

"Come." The old woman walked into the open, looking cautiously in all directions. This could be a dangerous place, Clarissa realized with a shiver. The two of them, alone and weaponless, were as vulnerable here as the deer and birds.

Clutching her basket, Swan Feather pushed into the thick wet grass. An air of wildness had come over her, as if she had shed her old woman skin and left it behind her in the village. Here she was alert, her senses sharp, her movements quick and light.

Steel flashed in the sun, and Clarissa realized Swan Feather had drawn a small sharp knife from beneath her buckskin tunic. With a little grunt, she pounced on something in the grass, hacking and jabbing so fiercely that dirt erupted from beneath the blade. Had she trapped some kind of animal? A ground squirrel or woodchuck? Clarissa waited tensely and was wondering whether she should move in and help when Swan Feather yanked a fat scraggly root out of the ground. Jabbing it into the air, she spoke in Shawnee, uttering what sounded like a name.

When Clarissa only stared, she barked the word again, less patiently this time, and shook the knife in her direction. Guessing at what she wanted, Clarissa repeated the meaningless syllables once, then again. Swan Feather nodded and tossed the root into her hands. Ginger—Clarissa recognized the sharp smell from Mrs. Pimm's kitchen. This wild variety was more delicate, more subtle in its pungency, but there was no mistaking it.

She repeated the name once again for good measure and was about to pass the root back to Swan Feather when the old woman suddenly doubled over, clutching her stomach in a show of agony.

"What is it?" Clarissa sprang to Swan Feather's side, only half-aware that she was speaking in English. "Are you ill? Can I take you back to the village?"

Ignoring her concern, Swan Feather seized the root again and shook it emphatically in Clarissa's face. *"Wesah!"* She pointed to her stomach. "Good for this!"

Only then did Clarissa realize that the old woman was trying to teach her Shawnee medicine.

Her first reaction—laughter—was swiftly replaced by

a bittersweet swelling in her throat. This was the most precious gift that gruff old Swan Feather had to offer— her skills as a healer. She had offered it freely. And all she asked in return was that her gift be accepted and valued.

She has already begun to love you. Wolf Heart's words echoed in her memory. At the time, she'd refused to believe them. Now she understood that love could be expressed in many ways.

But as she fought back a softening rush of tears, Clarissa forced her mind toward reality. She meant to escape, and no human attachment was going to hold her back. In this transient world, she could not allow herself to love or to be loved. The price—her own freedom—was far too high.

She would learn as much as she could from Swan Feather, she resolved, feeling crass and ungrateful. The knowledge would serve her well in the wilderness. But she would keep an iron rein on her emotions. And she would be neither loving nor lovable in the process. To do so would only cause pain.

The old woman dropped the ginger root into the basket and thrust the whole thing toward Clarissa, indicating she was supposed to carry it. Then, catching sight of another medicinal treasure, she strode off in that direction, as fast as her arthritic old legs would carry her. Clarissa hurried along behind her, clutching the basket with one hand and her dew-heavy skirts with the other.

The morning passed swiftly as the basket filled. Some of the herbs Clarissa recognized—bayberry, dandelion, milkweed and chicory. But memorizing their Shawnee names was a challenge, especially when Swan Feather would stop in midstride, whip one of the wilting plants from the basket and demand to hear its name. As for their uses, it was all Clarissa could do to bite back a smile when the old woman went into one of her wild pantomimes. How else, after all, could she demonstrate that dandelion root worked as a laxative, that bayberry eased coughing spells, or that curly dock was a fine treatment for itching?

But then again, today's lesson went far beyond grunts and gestures. Clarissa was learning more of the Shawnee language than she would ever have believed possible the first time she'd heard it. Her ears were quick to catch familiar words and phrases, even when combined into new meanings. What was more, she remembered nearly all of what she heard.

The discovery astonished and pleased her. Like so many girls, her formal education had ended with dame school, and when she'd begged to continue, as Junius had, he had brusquely informed her that the female mind was too weak and fragile to bear the strain of higher learning, especially such pursuits as mathematics, Latin and Greek. Now Clarissa found herself amazed at her own mental alacrity. Could it be that Junius was wrong—that she was bright, even intelligent?

By the time she and Swan Feather had worked their way across the meadow, the sun was halfway to noon and the basket was overflowing with herbs. In spite of herself, Clarissa looked forward to the sorting and drying of each plant and to watching the old woman use them in her cures. Her footsteps were light and quick as they recrossed the grassy open. If only Swan Feather would teach her more, she might even be content here for the time that remained until her escape.

The two of them had barely reached the trees when Swan Feather's shaggy head jerked upward. Motioning for Clarissa to stop, she stood as still as a gnarled stump, listening intently.

Clarissa strained her own ears, a shadow of fear darkening her sunny mood. She herself could hear nothing more than the rustle of leaves and the wistful call of a mourning dove, but Swan Feather's manner was enough to tell her that something was wrong.

"Down!" The old woman whispered the word in Shawnee as she pulled Clarissa behind a thick clump of blackberry bushes. Only then did Clarissa see the danger. Fear jerked its noose around her heart as three strange Indians emerged from the woods on the far side of the meadow.

The first impression that entered her mind was that they were not Shawnee. They were as lean and slick as weasels, their oiled bodies bare except for leggings and breechcloths, their scalps shaved except for bristling roaches along the midline. They moved like shadows, like prowling beasts of prey.

"*Mingwe*—Iroquois." Swan Feather's contemptuous whisper confirmed her own guess. "Don't move."

Clarissa pressed deeper into the thorny bushes, wishing fervently that Wolf Heart had not chosen this time to be away from the village. What if there were more of these Indians in the trees, perhaps a whole war party?

Her scrambling mind groped to remember what she had heard about the Iroquois at Fort Pitt. A federation rather than a single tribe, they were the most powerful group of Indians in the region. Her heart jumped as she remembered that, unlike the Shawnee, the Iroquois were allies of the English—*friends!* She had only to speak out, show herself, and chances were good they would take her with them to the nearest British outpost in the hope of a reward.

But what would they do to Swan Feather? What would they do to the people in the Shawnee village?

Two more Indians had come out of the woods to join the first three in the meadow. From her hiding place, she could see them clearly now, their faces hideously streaked with war paint. Most likely a raiding party, counting on surprise for a slashing attack and a swift retreat with whatever they could carry off. They would kill anyone who got in their way.

The five melted into the trees once more and began to move stealthily around the fringe of the meadow, drawing ever closer. Clarissa's gaze flickered to Swan Feather. The old woman's stringy gray hair and weathered buckskins blended with the mottled hues of the bramble patch, rendering her as well camouflaged as a nesting grouse. But Clarissa's own faded gown and fiery hair stood out like a flag. Only a blind man would fail to see her, and the Iroquois would have eyes like hawks. When they found her, they would find Swan Feather, as well, and there would be no reason to leave an old Shawnee woman alive when a single blow from a war club could silence her for good.

There was no time to lose. Clarissa's instincts took over as she edged away from Swan Feather, answering the old woman's startled gaze with a furtive motion to keep still and stay put. By now the five braves were well within arrow range and closing in rapidly. Brambles clawed at Clarissa's clothes and skin as she crawled, her body flattened against the ground. She would put as much distance as possible between herself and Swan Feather. Then, when she could no longer hide, she would break and run.

But run where? If she threw herself on the mercy of the Iroquois, they would likely keep her tied while they raided the village. And if she raced to warn the villagers, she would risk an arrow between her shoulder blades, or worse.

A magpie squawked from its scraggly nest in the top of a dying hickory tree. Startled by the sound, Clarissa jerked upward. The sudden movement of her bright hair was enough to alert the brave in the lead. In a flash all five of them were plunging after her like hounds after a doe.

Struggling to her feet, Clarissa wheeled and ran without another thought, straight toward the village.

An arrow whined past her ear to thud, quivering, into the trunk of a tree. Had the shot been a miss or a warning? Now, surely, would be the time to turn around, raise her hands and shout *"English! English! Friend!"* But Clarissa's feet would not stop running. She had to reach the village. She had to warn the people.

Her heart threatened to explode out of her chest as she pounded, ducking and dodging, along the brushy trail. The braves were gaining fast, and when they caught her, there would be no mercy. English or not, she had clearly shown where her loyalties lay.

One of her moccasins caught on a root, and she stumbled forward, righting herself just in time to avoid a headlong sprawl. When running with one shoe proved impossible, she kicked off the mate and stumbled on barefoot over the rocks and brambles. The Iroquois had not uttered a sound, but they were so close that Clarissa could hear them breathing behind her. Only the fact that she was English, she suspected, had kept them from impaling her outright with an arrow or knife.

The five were almost upon her when she burst into a clearing near the village and found three Shawnee braves, Cat Follower among them, working on a canoe.

"Mingwe!" She screamed out the word Swan Feather had spoken. *"Mingwe!"*

The enemy burst out of the trees before the Shawnee had time to gather their wits and seize their weapons. But the Iroquois, too, had been caught off guard by the chase. Pandemonium erupted in the clearing as the warriors closed and clashed in a wild scramble. The Shawnee were outnumbered five to three—no, five to *four,* Clarissa amended blindly as she seized a stray hatchet and waded into the fray, swinging it with a fury that, even to her, was startling.

Her strength was not a warrior's. Her wild blows glanced off the enemy, inflicting no worse than a few shallow gashes, but she did manage to distract one of the Iroquois long enough for Cat Follower to strike him solidly in the side of the head with a rawhide mallet. Cat Follower's impish grin flashed as the brave went down, bleeding and unconscious. "Run and bring help, little sister!" He laughed, crouching low for another leap into the melee. "If I let you come to harm, Wolf Heart will skin me alive!"

Clarissa, who had understood much of what he said, felt the rush of color to her cheeks as she spun away. But there was no need to race for the village. Alerted by the uproar, a band of half-grown boys armed with sticks, knives and arrows burst out of the trees and charged, screaming, into the fight. Swift on their heels ran a half-dozen women, shrilling like banshees as they brandished their hoes and digging sticks. Among them Clarissa recognized White Moon, the women's chief.

The Iroquois had had enough. Bruised and bloody, they seized their fallen cohort and fled for the trees, pursued by more than a score of shrieking, cursing Shawnee. Dizzy with relief, Clarissa sagged against the felled birch that the braves had been stripping for their canoe. Through a blur of sweat, she saw Swan Feather stumble into the clearing, armed with a huge broken tree branch. The sight of the fierce old woman was so laughable and so endearing that Clarissa began to giggle uncontrollably. Tears streamed down her face as pent-up fear and tension dissolved into laughter. They had come so close—she and the Shawnee—to an awful, bloody tragedy. Now it was over. But beneath her giddy relief lay a strange unease, as if fate were drawing her where she had never meant to venture.

White Moon, her handsome face beaming, strode up to Clarissa, clasped her shoulders and squeezed her with warm, strong hands. "My sister," she said in Shawnee. "My good, brave friend."

Following White Moon's lead, the other women surrounded Clarissa, babbling, touching her hair, embracing her. Through the tangle of their arms and heads, Clarissa could see Swan Feather's gap-toothed mouth spread wide in an approving grin. These were the same women who had jabbed and taunted her on her arrival here, Clarissa reminded herself harshly. These were the women who had beaten her senseless and scarred her face in the running of the gauntlet. She could not forget that fact when they offered their friendship. She could not forget who she was and what she had resolved to do.

She would learn from the Shawnee and make use of their newfound trust in her. But no human tie, no matter how compelling, she vowed, would ever bind her to these savage people—least of all to Wolf Heart.

Willing her heart to harden, Clarissa lifted her chin and smiled.

The sky and woodland swam before Wolf Heart's eyes as he slumped cross-legged in the mouth of the cave. For four days he had neither eaten nor drunk, and his perception had begun to drift. Through the mirror of his heightened senses, sunlight flowed like water, glittering with the hues of a hundred shattered rainbows. Trees loomed like monsters, gesticulating with spidery arms. The wind on his naked skin cut like the flint-honed edge of a knife.

He had long since ceased to feel hunger, or even thirst. His stomach had shrunk to the hardness of a clenched fist, and the inside of his mouth had shriveled like rawhide in the sun. He felt, at times, as if his physical body had died, leaving nothing but the essence of his spirit—and even that had begun to gutter like a spent candle.

He had done all that was required. Still the wolf had not come to him. Instead it was Clarissa he had seen—her fiery hair weaving like a ribbon among the spring willows, her sharp features captured for an instant along the bright edge of a cloud, her arms reaching out of the night to hold him in his dreams.

Was she standing in the way of his true vision, or was she a part of it? Wolf Heart no longer knew. Crushed by his own failure, he could only stare at the black circle on the rock where he had burned tobacco as an offering to Kokomthena. There was no shame cast if the vision did not come, he reminded himself. He could always try again at a later time. But the thought of returning empty to the village was more than his pride could bear.

Was that the stumbling block to his vision? His own stubborn, self-serving pride?

With an effort that made his head swim, Wolf Heart pushed himself to his feet and staggered to the lip of the cave. Bracing his arm against the opening, he stood looking down beyond the ledges, across a carpet of alders and willow, to where the broad expanse of the Ohio-se-pe curved like the body of a great undulating serpent, its waves glittering like scales in the golden slant of afternoon sunlight.

Four days was the customary time allowed for a vision-quest. He could stagger down to the river and replenish his body with clear, fresh water. He could return to the village—to Clarissa, whose remembered image, even in his weakened state, filled his body with yearning.

But no, he would not go back, Wolf Heart vowed, repenting of the very thought. He would stay in this sacred place, denying the demands of his body until the vision came.

The vision that would, once more, seal his identity as a Shawnee.

Turning from the entrance, he stumbled back toward the cave's shadowed interior. He had heard stories in the council house, ancient tales of vision-seekers who had sacrificed fingers to Weshemoneto, leaving, after the price of the vision, only the two digits needed to draw a bowstring. The floor of the cave was littered with sharp-edged pieces of flint. Transfixed with sudden horror, Wolf Heart stared down at his own fingers. Did he have the awful strength? Did he want the vision so badly that he would lay his hand on the bare rock, raise one flinty blade and—

He recoiled with a shudder, fearful that in his half-crazed state, even the thought might lead to action. Seeking refuge now, his thoughts fled to Clarissa—the flash of her moss-green eyes, the night-cooled sweetness of her body against his burning loins, her moist, eager mouth, the softness of her breast in the cup of his palm....

But this was leading him nowhere! Wolf Heart's hand clenched into a ball of frustration. Where was the simple faith of his boyhood, when he had asked for the vision and it had come? Why was it so much harder this time?

Head swimming, he braced himself once more in the mouth of the cave, leaning outward above the steep, brushy slope. He should lie down, he thought, maybe try to sleep and hope for the vision in a dream. But he knew that his churning mind would not release him to slumber—or to anything else of worth. A vision-quest demanded a disciplined spirit and an open heart. He had left the village in a raging turmoil that had not abated in four days of fasting. Was his failure a sign in itself? Did he need to go back to the village and resolve this madness with Clarissa? Was that the price of the wolf spirit's guidance?

Weshemoneto, Master of Life, help me! He breathed the unspoken plea, eyes closed, and at that instant Wolf Heart felt the ground drop away as if he had been jerked off the face of the earth. The rain-weakened lip of the cave had begun to crumble beneath his weight. With a sucking groan, it gave way entirely and plunged down the near-vertical slope, carrying him with it.

Dazed by hunger and shock, he scrambled desperately to stay upright, but the weight and speed of the collapsing earth was too much for him, and he was swept off his feet. A sea of mud and rocks closed around him as he fell, crushing out life and breath. Fighting all the way, he careened into darkness—and then into the darkness beneath darkness where time and space lose all meaning. Deeper he spiraled. Endlessly deeper.

The vision came, then, with a shattering clarity that Wolf Heart would remember to the end of his days.

It began with water. Pure, crystal bright and teeming with life. Wolf Heart saw it first as a rivulet, sparkling its way over stones and trickling among emerald grass blades. Then, as if soaring to an eagle's height, he saw it from far above, winding and curving, joining other streams, other rivers, all of them flowing together until at last, as his gaze took in the amazing length and breadth of it, he knew he was looking down at the Beautiful River, the Ohio-se-pe.

But even as he caught his breath at the river's beauty, a shadow fell across the woodland. His throat constricted as he saw the dark tide of blood seeping down the watercourse, flowing from the east, spreading downward and outward like a foul-fingered hand. Startled birds exploded into flight, only to drop like feathered stones as the murky horror filled the air around them. Dead and dying fish circled belly-up in the slow eddies of the river. Deer, bears and bounding pumas fled for their lives as the darkness closed like a hungry beast, and now Wolf Heart saw that the land itself was smoldering. Yellow tongues of flame snaked upward, dancing and twisting over the charred ground. Smoke clogged the air. The acrid fumes seared Wolf Heart's lungs. He choked, fighting for breath.

Then far below, from the western reaches of the land, he saw a solid figure rise up. Blurred by smoke, the figure became a young man, tall and well formed, his hair long and black, his handsome face pure Shawnee. And as he strode into the burning, unafraid, the wind whispered a name. It was a name that blazed through Wolf Heart's mind, then vanished like a flame—a name he would not remember until he heard it again, years later, as a silver-haired elder.

Tecumseh…

As the lithe young man forged through the destruction, others rose up and followed him—streams of Shawnee, Creek, Delaware, and warriors of other tribes that Wolf

Heart did not recognize. But he knew their purpose, and he knew the dismal odds against them. As they flowed like water across the land, the burning blackness engulfed them. One after the other, Wolf Heart saw the warriors fall until, at last, even the stalwart young man, the last hope of the Shawnee, staggered, sank and disappeared into darkness.

What followed was yet blacker than what had gone before. Slowly, like the ebb of autumn, waters shrank and retreated across the wilderness, flowing backward against their own natural paths, leaving nothing behind but their dry rocky beds. Wolf Heart saw the shadows of the Shawnee, the Delaware, the Cherokee, the Creek, even the Iroquois moving with the water, in the water, as part of it, and he knew that he was seeing the future. He knew that the people of his spirit would battle the people of his blood, and that there would be no question of the way it would end.

Sick with despair, he turned away from the spectacle and found himself just above the ground once more, at the place where the ledge had fallen. He saw his own body, lying bloodied and still, half-crushed by earth and rocks, and he knew that if his spirit chose to return to the lifeless flesh, he would see all that had come to pass in his vision. Only by choosing death now would he be spared the heartbreak of what was to come.

As Wolf Heart hesitated, still staggered by what he had seen, a new question struck him. Where was his guiding spirit? No wolf had appeared in his vision or shown itself during the quest. Even the wolf voice that had drawn him to this place was silent. He had not heard the call since the night he had carried Clarissa in his arms.

He had undertaken the quest in search of a personal answer. Why had he been given a vision so immense and so terrible that he would give anything to blot it from his memory? And why did his own question remain unanswered?

And then suddenly he knew.

The vision *was* the answer—a glimpse of what he would face if he chose to share the fate of the Shawnee nation. And Wolf Heart knew what his choice must be, even as he knew he could not ask Clarissa to share that choice. He was a Shawnee warrior, and whatever the future might hold, his place was with his people.

His people. That was Wolf Heart's last conscious thought before he rejoined his battered body and sank into oblivion.

Clarissa sat bolt upright in the darkness of the lodge. The pewter light seeping through chinks in the bark roof told her it was dawn but barely so. Swan Feather, always an early riser, lay curled like a child beneath her worn bearskin robe, her breathy snores misting the cold morning air. Last night's coals glowed faintly in the blackened hollow of the fire pit.

Nothing was amiss—Clarissa could see that. So why was her pulse racing like the heart of a hunted doe? She had been sound asleep, exhausted past all dreams after a backbreaking day toiling over the hated deer hides, which had been buried in the ground to loosen the hair, then stretched on their racks for more scraping. By rights, she should have slept until the old woman nudged her awake at sunrise. Something had startled her. What was it?

Too restless to go back to sleep, Clarissa groped for her moccasins, stole across the lodge and slipped outside into the shadowed dawn. The sky was dark, with a pale rind of moon hanging low in the western sky. The birds were silent, waiting for first light to begin their morning song burst. Today would be the fifth day of Wolf Heart's absence.

It was Cat Follower who had, at last, explained the vision-quest. Taking pains to use the simplest possible words, he had described the ordeal of fasting and isolation—the loneliness of it worse, even, than the hunger because of the Shawnee ties to family, clan and tribe. Four days, he said, and the seeker could return in honor.

Four days. Clarissa had counted every heartbeat of that time, and suddenly she knew what had awakened her.

Wheeling in her tracks, she plunged onto the trail that led to Wolf Heart's solitary lodge. As she ran, she imagined reaching it, pausing outside the entrance to catch her ragged breath, then nudging aside the edge of the flap to let a finger of light fall across his bed—and seeing him there, sprawled in exhausted sleep, broad of chest and long of limb, gaunt from his four-day fast. She imagined holding her breath as he slept, willing herself not to awaken him as she filled her eyes for as long as she dared. Against all logic, her heart danced with anticipation.

But when she reached it, the lodge sat silent in the dawn. No thread of smoke curled from the roof hole. No object had been moved since Wolf Heart's departure.

A coil of dread tightened in her stomach as she crept closer and lifted the deerskin flap that covered the entrance. She knew now he would not be there. No sound of breathing came from the dark space, and there was no sense of the raw energy that quivered around Wolf Heart's presence wherever he went. Clarissa raised the flap all the way, moving aside to let dawn's silver light shine fully into the lodge.

Her curious gaze took in the rumpled bed, the long hickory bow and the fringed buckskin quiver that hung from a roof pole, the gleaming flintlock musket leaning in a shadowed corner, an empty parfleche and the bridle for his horse, flung down as if in haste beside the lifeless fire pit. His familiar scent lingered in the darkness of the lodge—clean, lightly pungent, and so masculine that it triggered an odd tightening in the warm depths of her body. Her breath caught in a small suppressed gasp as the sensation quivered upward. She wanted Wolf Heart, wanted his touch, wanted his deep caressing voice. She wanted him here. Now.

Torn between emotion and common sense, she lowered the flap and forced herself to turn away. It was too soon to worry, she told herself. Wolf Heart was a warrior, strong and resourceful. And it was only the fifth day of his quest.

But something had awakened her in the silent gray dawn. Something dark and fearful, something Clarissa knew she could no longer ignore.

She had to find Cat Follower.

The young brave's bachelor lodge was on the far side of the village. Clarissa broke into a pounding run, skirting the council house and the horse corral, startling a mangy brown dog that began to bark, setting off the voice of every cur in the village. Ignoring the commotion, she hurled herself toward Cat Follower's lodge and flung aside the skin door.

A shaft of light illuminated two figures beneath the rumpled furs. The girl, her face veiled by her straight black hair, groaned and burrowed deeper into the bed, but Cat Follower, sensing Clarissa's agitation, rose up on one elbow, rubbing the sleep from his eyes.

"My brother has not returned?" he guessed at once.

"Something's wrong—bad. I feel it here." Clarissa

touched the spot over her heart, underscoring the words she spoke in halting Shawnee.

For a moment she feared Wolf Heart's friend would laugh at her. But Cat Follower, to his credit, blinked himself fully awake, sat up and slid his beanpole legs from beneath the robes. "A moment." His gesture showed the smallness of the time. "Wait outside. I will come."

Realizing that he was naked, she flushed, backed awkwardly out of the lodge and lowered the flap. Seconds later he appeared, still adjusting his loincloth. A musket, similar to Wolf Heart's, was slung over his shoulder by a leather strap. A knife hung at his hip, sheathed by a beaded scabbard.

"Do you know where he is?" she asked.

"I know the place. A cave above the river. I will go there now."

"I'm going with you," Clarissa insisted. "I must."

She saw him hesitate, frowning at her as if weighing her courage. Then slowly he nodded. "Come, then. But prepare yourself—" He turned away, leaving the rest of the words unspoken. The silence was more dreadful than anything he might have said.

Clarissa struggled to match his storklike strides as they moved into the woods, swiftly leaving the village behind. The brush was high and thick on both sides of the narrow trail. Leaves dripped with dew, soaking Clarissa's hair and gown as she swept past them. She bit back the urge to ask Cat Follower more questions. The young brave was so grim and silent that she feared what his answers might be.

The cave was no more than an hour from the village. It was Cat Follower, striding in the lead, who first saw the fresh, wet fan of earth and rocks below the broken mouth of the cave. He froze, staring in horror. Clarissa gasped as she came up from behind and saw it, too.

"Wait here." He thrust out an arm to hold her back. Clarissa burst past him, heedless of the danger or the thought of what she might find. "Wolf Heart!" The cry tore from her throat as she ran. *"Wolf Heart!"*

Chapter Ten

It was Clarissa who saw him first. Wolf Heart lay nearly buried in mud and rocks with only one leg, one arm and shoulder, and the left side of his face showing above the debris. His eyes were closed, his face gray and lifeless.

"Wait!" Cat Follower tried to hold her back, but Clarissa would have none of it. With a cry, she flung herself down beside Wolf Heart. Her trembling fingers explored his face and hair, then began to claw frantically at the earth that held him.

"Is he alive?" Cat Follower clasped one of the boulders that anchored his friend's body, heaved it to one side, then seized another and began to pry it loose.

"I don't know!" Clarissa groped along Wolf Heart's cool throat for a pulse. *Be alive,* she prayed silently. *Please, please be alive.*

Her fingers fluttered urgently down along the hollow between his windpipe and the muscular cords that supported his neck. Nothing—she felt nothing. Why couldn't she have stopped him from going off on this ridiculous vision-quest? Why hadn't she forced him to take her to his lodge that night and kept him there any way she could with her arms, her lips, her body?

Why hadn't she told him that she loved him?

Her fingers moved lower, pressed harder against the hollow of his throat. *Please,* she prayed silently. *I'll do anything. Give anything.*

"Is he alive?" Cat Follower demanded again, pausing to catch his breath and wipe the sweat from his pock-marked face.

"I can't tell, not until we get more of him uncovered!" Clarissa had felt no pulse, but she could not admit defeat until all hope was gone. Desperately she began to scrape at the stubborn earth, pawing with her bare hands while Cat Follower moved the heavier rocks. By the time they freed his chest and face her palms and fingers were bloody, but she scarcely noticed.

Please! She groped for his pulse again, more carefully this time. A little sob broke from her throat as she felt a light tick of movement beneath her fingertips. "Hurry!" she urged Cat Follower as she slipped supporting hands under Wolf Heart's head. *"Hurry!"*

Wolf Heart groaned as his shoulders came free—a miraculous sound to Clarissa's ears. But even as his eyelids fluttered open, she could not help wondering how badly hurt he was. The landslide could have broken his legs, crushed his ribs, his spine. He could be crippled, or paralyzed, and trying to move him might only make his injuries worse.

"Get help!" she ordered Cat Follower. "Men with poles to carry!" She knew no other way to describe a stretcher in Shawnee, but the young brave seemed to understand. Without a backward glance, he was off, racing back toward the village, leaving her alone with Wolf Heart.

His eyes were fully open now. They stared up at her in dazed confusion, like a lost child's. Aching with tenderness, Clarissa cradled his head in her arms. "It's all right," she murmured over and over, wanting desperately to believe it was so. "It's all right."

His lips were dry and cracked. They moved awkwardly as he tried to speak, but no sound emerged except a hoarse breathy croak. His obvious thirst tore at Clarissa's heart. Though the river was scarcely two hundred paces away, she had nothing for carrying water and, in any case, she dared not leave him to fetch it.

"Hush." She bent low, kissing his forehead, his eyes, his cheeks, wetting his lips with her own tongue. He moaned, struggling to speak. "Lie still," she whispered. "It won't be long now. Cat Follower is bringing help."

His throat moved in a paroxysm of effort. "The vision..." he whispered.

"You found what you were looking for?"

"No." His face was ashen beneath its sun-burnished surface. His blue eyes held a haunted look, as if his soul had passed through the portals of hell. "No," he rasped again. His lips closed. He shuddered convulsively. Clarissa held him close, suddenly as much afraid for his mind as for his body. What had it done to him, this barbaric ordeal of fasting and isolation? What kind of savage society would require such things of a man?

Before she could ponder these questions, Cat Follower burst out of the trees, followed by three braves all running hard. One brave balanced a pair of long stout poles and a fistful of leather lashings. Another carried a blanket. Cat Follower gripped the neck of a calabash—*water*. She slumped in relief at the sight of it, her tears blurring the sight of Wolf Heart's tortured face.

Their pace slowed as they mounted the treacherous fan of the slide. For Clarissa, a small eternity seemed to pass before they reached the spot where Wolf Heart lay with his head pillowed in her lap. Cat Follower thrust the calabash into her hands, then swiftly joined the other braves in digging the debris from around Wolf Heart's body.

"Careful now." She raised Wolf Heart's head, tipped the calabash to his lips and was gratified when he gulped it thirstily. "Not too fast, or you'll make yourself sick," she warned, aching with tenderness. "How do you feel? Can you tell me how badly you're hurt?"

"I...don't know. The vision...Hunts-at-Night...bring him..." He spoke with less strain now that he had moistened his throat, but nothing he said made any sense to Clarissa. He was clearly out of his head.

"It's all right." She cradled his head against her breast, passionately wishing she could believe her own words. "Don't try to talk. Not yet."

Cat Follower and the other braves had him fully uncovered now. His limbs appeared straight and unbroken, but who could say what horrendous injuries lay beneath the scrapes, bruises and mud that covered his battered flesh.

Two of the braves had rigged the poles and blankets into a makeshift stretcher. Clarissa kept her eyes fixed on Wolf Heart's face as they laid the poles parallel to his body. His eyes were open, the pupils gazing upward as if staring at something no one else could see. "Be careful," she whispered as they eased the stretcher beneath him. "Don't hurt—"

Her own words ended in a gasp as Wolf Heart's face contorted in sudden pain. Cat Follower had clasped his rib cage to slide him onto the blanket, and the pain had all but undone him. Only his tightly clenched jaw had kept him from crying out. Crushed ribs, Clarissa surmised worriedly. How many and how badly they were broken remained to be seen.

Cat Follower's second effort was more carefully made. Sweat beads formed on Wolf Heart's pale face as his friends eased him onto the stretcher, but he did not flinch or cry out. The four braves lifted the poles, two on each side. Then, almost too swiftly for Clarissa to follow, they took off at a trot for the village.

"Not so fast—you'll hurt him!" She sprinted after the stretcher, a stitch jabbing her side as she ran. Wolf Heart's eyes were tightly closed, his teeth clenched against the jarring pain. Tiny specks of whisker stubble, black against his ashen skin, sprinkled his upper lip and the long square line of his jaw.

Ahead, in the village, word of Wolf Heart's accident had spread. More than a score of people had swarmed out to meet the stretcher. In their lead, snapping orders like a diminutive general, was Swan Feather.

"Bring him into my lodge!" She kept pace with the stretcher in spite of her arthritic legs. "Be careful! Don't bounce him like that! He's an injured man, not a dead buck! And the rest of you, out of the way!"

The crowd parted in deference to the disheveled old woman. This was Swan Feather's arena, and she was master here. Sides heaving from the run, Clarissa hurried after the growing procession. Nothing mattered to her now except staying close to Wolf Heart.

With Swan Feather barking directions, the four braves carried him inside her lodge, laid him, stretcher and all, beside the small crackling fire where water was already heating in two clay pots. Clarissa squeezed in through the crowded entrance. She struggled to reach the spot where he lay pale and still, the amber firelight gleaming on his bruised skin.

"Go!" Swan Feather dismissed the braves with a wave

of her hand, then looked sharply at Clarissa. ''Only you are to stay. I will need your help.''

As the lodge cleared, Clarissa flew to Wolf Heart's side. His eyes opened as she flung herself down beside him. His cracked lips twisted, moved. ''Hunts-at-Night...get him for me!''

''There's no time for that now,'' Swan Feather cut in. ''Listen to me, son of my friend. I am brewing some leaves to make you sleep. When you awaken—''

''No!'' Wolf Heart struggled to sit up but was stopped by the stabbing agony of his cracked ribs. He fell back onto the stretcher, his eyes agitated, insistent. ''I must speak with him—alone. Get him! Get him now!''

''I'll go!'' Clarissa was on her feet before the old woman could argue. If the one-eyed chief could do anything to ease Wolf Heart's troubled mind, she wanted him here.

''Hurry, then!'' Swan Feather's impatient voice echoed behind Clarissa as she ducked out of the lodge and raced toward the council house. ''Hurry!''

Hunts-at-Night listened intently as Wolf Heart recounted, in labored whispers, the horror of his vision. They were alone in the lodge, the chief having sent everyone else outside to wait. Swan Feather's herbs simmered in their pots on the fire, the redolent steam filling the darkness around them.

''I saw it all.'' Wolf Heart spoke through a red blur of pain. ''The end of our world, the end of all we hold sacred, at the hands of those whose blood I share.'' The words ended in a grimace as a shaft of agony stabbed upward from his ribs.

''Not so, my son.'' A thread of warmth wove subtly into the chief's voice. ''Your blood is Shawnee, as is your heart. You are as much a part of us as if you had been born in one of our *wegiwas*.'' He stared into the flames. ''Would it surprise you to know that my own dreams have been the same as your vision?''

Wolf Heart gaped up at him in surprise.

''I know what is going to happen to our people,'' Hunts-at-Night said softly. ''And now you know it, too.''

''But what can we do to prevent it?'' Wolf Heart demanded, stunned by the chief's fatalism. ''There must be a way! We have to think—we have to plan—''

''And we will do all of those things.'' Hunts-at-Night's scar-streaked face reflected the dancing shadows. His single eye glowed like a fiery coal. ''We will fight like the warriors we are. We will lose in the end, but we will lose honorably. That is all we ask of Weshemoneto, and all that he asks of us.''

''The others, the council—'' Wolf Heart struggled to rise, but an explosion of pain lanced his side and he fell back onto the stretcher, gasping. ''We have to warn them! We have to prepare everyone!''

The chief shook his head. ''What you have seen will take many years to happen. Would you bring fear and sorrow down on our people so soon? I, for one, would not make such a cruel choice.''

Wolf Heart closed his eyes, fighting the pain that gripped his ribs like the talons of a great eagle. His ears heard the laughter of the people—the women singing as they tended their patches of corn and squash, the children shouting happily as they played hoop and pole or chased each other among the lodges—and he knew that Hunts-at-Night was right. The terrible vision was not meant to be shared, perhaps not for years to come. Perhaps never.

''When the dark time comes, our people will need a strong war chief,'' the old man said. ''You were given the vision as a blessing, not as a curse. Use it wisely, and you will guide our people on the path of wisdom and courage.''

''There are times…when it is more than I can do to follow that path myself.'' Wolf Heart felt a bloodred fog welling in his mind, clouding his reason. He struggled to stay conscious.

''You are young and still learning,'' the chief said. ''Be true to yourself and your people. When the black days come, you will be ready.'' He straightened from his crouched position next to the fire. ''Rest now. Give your body and spirit time to mend. We will talk more when you are well.''

Wolf Heart's mouth worked in an effort to speak, but no words would cross the bridge from his brain to his tongue. He watched the chief turn away and drift out of his range of vision. Then the fog swirled around him, and he began sinking slowly into it. He heard distant voices, the sound of light, running footsteps, and then Clarissa was bending over him, her moss-green eyes as tender as springtime, her russet hair glowing like flame in the firelight. Her tough, slim hand caught his own, her fingers interweaving with his as she pressed his bruised knuckles to her lips.

''It's all right,'' she murmured in English, her tears cool and sweet on his skin. ''Rest. We'll take care of you.''

Wolf Heart's hand tightened around hers. Then he closed his eyes and, at last, let the deepening fog enfold him and carry him away.

For Clarissa, the days passed like a whirlwind. Wolf Heart's strong body was swift to heal, but Swan Feather would not hear of his being moved from the lodge until he was well on the way to recovery. By day he reclined against a pile of skins and baskets, his torso lashed to a frame of woven willows to immobilize his broken ribs. Though his gaze darted about the confined space with the ferocity of a hawk's, he clearly realized that mending bones took time, and, because he wanted that time to be as short as possible, he forced himself to keep still.

At night he lay restlessly in the darkness of the lodge, too impatient for sleep. From her place near the snoring Swan Feather, Clarissa would hear him shifting on his bed and hear the sharp exhalations of his breath like the *whuff* of a captive puma pacing the bounds of its cage. She felt his frustration in the darkness, his longing to be back in action. Sometimes it was all she could do to keep from creeping across the open floor, slipping her arms around him to nestle close as she whispered words of comfort in the privacy of the language that only the two of them shared.

Would he welcome her? Clarissa had no way of knowing. Wolf Heart had closed himself off since the vision, refusing to talk about what he had seen. Clarissa had teased, cajoled and wheedled, but he had resisted her every effort to draw him out. Never easy to know, he had closed himself within a tight fortress of silence, leaving her outside, hurt, angry and alone.

Clarissa had long since come to realize that she loved Wolf Heart—loved him with all the power of her young, giving heart. She loved the lithe bronze grace of his body, and the glimpse of white skin where the leather cord that held his breechcloth shifted up or down on his lean flanks. She loved the wavy fall of his blue-black hair over his sinewy shoulders, the sudden flash of his cobalt eyes when he was amused, intrigued or irritated. She loved the sight, scent and sound of him. But even love was not enough to bind her to the world of the Shawnee, Clarissa reminded herself sternly, especially when Wolf Heart shut her out of his thoughts like an unwelcome visitor.

Once more she took up the planning of her escape.

Although Clarissa was expected to be in attendance, it was Swan Feather who served as Wolf Heart's chief nurse. Her arthritic hands ground the herbs between stones, mixed them into poultices and shaped them to Wolf Heart's purpled flesh. Her knotted fingers wrapped the buckskin strips around his ribs, binding him tightly to the willow frame. He submitted quietly to her care. Only the subdued rage that smoldered in his eyes told Clarissa how much he hated being so helpless.

As Swan Feather worked, she also taught. Her ancient voice droned in the smoky darkness of the lodge, describing each herb, how it was mixed, how it was used. Clarissa listened eagerly, welcoming any diversion from the strain of being so close to Wolf Heart. Her command of the Shawnee language was growing by the day, as was her understanding of the healing medicine. Often she found herself anticipating Swan Feather's questions, her mind forming answers as the questions were asked. When, Clarissa had dared to wonder aloud, would she be allowed to practice what she was so avidly learning? Swan Feather's only response had been a shrug of her shoulders.

More and more the old woman had begun to rely on Clarissa to gather the herbs she needed. Clarissa had become adept at finding freshly sprouted yarrow among the meadow grass and coaxing thistle root from the earth without pricking her fingers. She was learning where to find the strongest willow bark and when to pick the sprigs of wintergreen that wound their way beneath the shadowy pines.

She enjoyed these forays and the freedom they gave her. She had even entertained the idea of disappearing into the forest and heading upriver toward Fort Pitt. But the risks of such a venture always made her hesitate. To beat the odds against her survival, she would need two things—a horse and a cache of supplies. So far, she had neither.

On this day, as she strode through the village with her empty basket, the people she passed nodded and spoke in greeting. Children, laughing and unafraid, scampered past her ragged skirts. Dogs that had once barked and growled lifted their heads and wagged their tails at the sight of her.

White Moon, the women's chief, was coming out of the council house. Her face crinkled in a smile as she saw Clarissa. "I was just coming to talk with you," she said. "The young women want you to join their ball team for the spring bread dance."

"The spring bread dance?" Clarissa blinked as the absurd image of Shawnee dancing around a loaf of bread shaped like a braided Maypole flashed through her mind. There was no image at all to go with the idea of a Shawnee ball team.

"It's great fun," White Moon reassured her. "The women play against the men, and the losing side has to gather firewood for the big bonfire we'll be having the following night. There'll be dancing, singing, feasting— ah, but you look surprised. Why?"

"I—didn't know—" Clarissa stammered, her face reddening as she groped for the right words.

"You didn't know our people liked to have fun?" White Moon laughed. "Kokomthena, our grandmother, made men and women to enjoy themselves, and to enjoy each other's bodies. When she looks down from the moon and sees feasting, dancing and lovemaking, she is pleased.''

Clarissa gulped. "It's just that I've never played your kind of ball before," she hedged. "I wouldn't know what to do. I'd be no good to the team at all."

Again White Moon laughed. "Any woman who shows your courage in the gauntlet will do well in our game. As for your learning, the game is half a moon away. There will be plenty of time to practice."

"But I have to help Swan Feather!" Clarissa blurted, seizing on the first excuse that came to mind. "She needs me!"

"Swan Feather will spare you to practice for the game. It will be to her honor if you play." White Moon smiled over her shoulder as she turned to go. "The women's team meets in the clearing most days, when the sun stands above that tall pine. Everyone will be happy to see you there."

Dismayed, Clarissa gazed after White Moon's graceful retreating figure. Where she came from, ladies did not play rough, rowdy games, especially against teams of men! What had she gotten herself into? More to the point, how was she going to get out of it?

Swinging her basket like the tail of an annoyed cat, she stalked through the outskirts of the village and into the forest. As her moccasined feet found the path to the meadow, the woodland stillness fell around her. The breeze whispered in the soft spring leaves. A thrush piped its song from a blackberry thicket, calming her turbulent spirit.

She was being a goose, Clarissa chided herself. She had faced far worse than this silly game, where she would have nothing to lose but her dignity. All she had to do was grit her teeth and get through it. Then she could crawl off and nurse her bruises while the Shawnee enjoyed their feasting and dancing.

Feasting and dancing.

Clarissa froze in midstep, eyes wide, heart pounding. Why hadn't she thought of it sooner? The coming festival, with everyone distracted by merrymaking, would be the perfect time for her escape.

She hurried down the meadow path, her mind churning with plans. With so much food being prepared for the feast, she would have no trouble slipping some corn cakes and venison into a parfleche and concealing it in the woods to be picked up later. As for getting her hands on a horse—Clarissa shivered with anticipation. No one would be eager to guard the animals during the celebration. With any luck at all, she would be able to slip into the enclosure, choose her mount and lead it quietly into the trees. By the time the reveling Shawnee missed her, she would be mounted and well on her way back to Fort Pitt.

Half a moon away, the women's chief had said. As civilized people counted time, that would mean the frolic was about two weeks off. That would give her ample time to prepare.

The sight of the sun-flecked meadow through the trees hushed the wild milling of her thoughts for a moment. Each time she came to this place, she was stunned by the ever-changing beauty of its waving grasses and flowers. She would miss that beauty when she was safely back in Baltimore, she realized with a sharp tightening of her throat. She would miss many things.

Most of all, she would miss Wolf Heart.

But this was no time for sentiment, Clarissa upbraided herself. In the days ahead she would need a clear head and an uninvolved heart. Anything less, and she would be lost.

Struggling to remember Swan Feather's instructions, she gathered pokeweed, thistle, plantain and wood sorrel from among the long grasses. Cattails were sprouting around a pond at the meadow's far boundary. Those too might prove useful, Clarissa reasoned, and she set out to get them.

The morning breeze toyed with her hair, its touch so tantalizing that she reached behind her head, loosened the leather thong that held back her curls and let them stream in the wind as she ran. Red-winged blackbirds called from the rushes that rimmed the pond. Their harsh whistles scolded her cheerfully as she bent to the task of cutting spring cattails with the small sharp knife she'd brought along.

Glancing up, she caught sight of something else growing along one of the cold streams that fed the pond. Watercress! She loved watercress—and its tangy leaves would make a fine spring tonic for Swan Feather, whose usual energy had begun to flag of late.

She circled the pond, taking care to watch for snakes in the swampy morass of weeds. She could still see the watercress, but the stream on this side was walled off by brambles and stinging nettle. Approaching from the other side might be easier, or at least not so painful.

Impatient but determined, Clarissa raced back around the pond. By now the sun was high, her skin warm and flushed as she flung herself down beside the joining of pond and stream. The watercress was on the far side now, still out of reach, but perhaps if she leaned out over the calm crystal water she just might be able to—

Clarissa's heart lurched as she glanced down and

caught sight of her own image, perfectly mirrored in the pool's quiet surface.

Since the day of the gauntlet, she had avoided looking directly at anything that might reflect her own face—a polished knife or hatchet blade, a glassy trade bead, an open bowl of water. She'd had no wish to see what her fingers told her was there—the long slanting scars, the misshapen nose. Now for the first time she confronted her own changed features.

A gasp escaped her lips as she stared down at the water. The face that stared back at her was not the flawless porcelain oval she remembered. But its features were far less grotesque than she'd imagined them to be. It was, in fact, an interesting face. A striking face.

She tilted her head, noting how the broken nose and slightly lopsided upper lip lent her an air of raw sensuality that she had never possessed before. And the skin above her left eyebrow was slightly puckered, giving her eyes a questioning look. As for the scar across her chin that she'd imagined to be so hideous, it was little more than a shadow, like an elongated dimple.

"You will wear a new face—the face of courage."

Wolf Heart's words echoed in Clarissa's memory as she blew on the watery surface, shattering the image into a hundred rippling fragments. How much courage lay behind her intriguing new face remained to be seen. But for now she had better things to do than sit here admiring herself like a flame-haired Narcissus!

Stretching to her limits, she caught a fistful of watercress from the wet green tangle at the stream's mouth, yanked it loose and tossed it into her basket. The leaves gleamed like tiny cabochons of Chinese jade where they lay against the drying meadow herbs. When she sampled a sprig, its fresh peppery taste burned lightly on her tongue. Swan Feather would enjoy it, too, she reminded herself as she reached for more. And perhaps Wolf Heart, as well.

Wolf Heart.

Something tightened in her chest as she thought of him waiting in the darkness of the lodge, glowering like a tethered eagle, seething with boredom. In that other, distant world, she might have brought him books to read or set up a chessboard and challenged him to a game. She might have entertained him with a tune on the clavier, which she played prettily if not brilliantly. She might have even invited friends over for a discussion of philosophy or mathematics. But here, in this wilderness, there was nothing of light or learning, nothing to challenge the mind of an intelligent man like Wolf Heart. He was wasting his life here among the Shawnee. But that was his choice, Clarissa reminded herself.

Her own choice would be different.

At the meadow's edge, she paused to fill the folds of her skirt with fresh green grass. She would be wise to make friends with the horses. If they knew her and expected food, the nervous animals would not be so skittish when the time came to lead one away.

With purposeful steps, she strode back along the trail toward the village. Two braves rolling bark for a canoe greeted her with good-natured grins. From the doorway of a lodge, a tiny dark-eyed girl smiled shyly as she clutched her puppy in her arms. The world of the Shawnee was not all bad, Clarissa conceded. But it was not her world. Soon she would leave it all behind.

She swallowed the hardness in her throat as she approached the clearing where the horses were tethered. One distant day all of this would be like a dream. The river and the forest. The village and the people—Swan

Feather and White Moon, Cat Follower and the battle-scarred Hunts-at-Night. The women and the children. And Wolf Heart.

Clarissa choked back a little cry as the truth sank home.

When she left the Shawnee world, it would be forever. There would be no letters, no returning for visits. To these simple people, her going would be as final as if she had died.

Her own memory, she knew, would dim as well. In the long years to come—years filled with the trials of living—the faces so clear to her now would fade like portraits drawn in sand.

She would lose them all.

Wolf Heart eased his bruise-mottled torso upright along the willow frame, gritting his teeth against the urge to groan aloud. He was alone in the smoky darkness of the lodge. Swan Feather had hobbled off to tend her corn patch and Clarissa had left on one of her many errands. No one was here to fuss over him or cajole him to a show of cheerfulness. For once he could act as miserable as he felt!

A rivulet of sweat dripped from his armpit to trickle down his side. He had not bathed fully since before the vision-quest, and he smelled like a white man. The musky odor, which he had disliked all his adult life, had spawned his habit of swimming daily in some pool or river. Now the smell lay on his unwashed skin, rising like a miasma into the stale air around him. He felt dirty, prickly, sore and mean.

And Clarissa had just appeared in the doorway of the lodge.

"How are you feeling?" She still spoke to him in En-

glish when they were alone. As a result, his own memory
of the language had sharpened, and he found himself
speaking fluently, using words and phrases he had not
heard since boyhood.

"How do you think I feel?" He glared at her and was
wryly amused when she bridled in response.

"I was only being polite. You didn't have to snap at
me!" She set down the herb basket to brush away the
grass blades that clung to her pathetic rag of a skirt. Why
would she bother with such a small vanity? Wolf Heart
found himself wondering. And why would there be torn
grass on the front of her skirt, when there appeared to be
none on the back? What was Clarissa up to now?

"Are you hungry?" She bent to the herb basket to
inspect her gatherings. A finger of sunlight, probing
through the bark roof, ignited the blaze of her hair. Wolf
Heart watched the quick sure movements of her hands,
aching suddenly with the urge to reach out, catch those
hands in his own and feel the roughness of her small
chapped knuckles against his skin.

These past days and nights in the lodge, seeing her,
hearing the velvet rasp of her breathing in the night,
catching the essence of her woman-scent as she passed
him in the small space had been sheer torment. He knew
what the vision had told him. He knew that he and Clarissa could cause each other nothing but grief. But that
did not stop him from wanting her.

It did not stop him from lying awake in the darkness,
his loins feverish with the memory of holding her close.
It did not stop his hungry gaze from following her about
the lodge, lingering on the graceful sway of a hip or the
exquisite bud of a nipple pressing against the threadbare
fabric of her bodice. Only his injury and Swan Feather's
nearly constant presence had kept him from reaching out

to catch Clarissa's waist, pulling her against him and letting their arms, hands and frantic, eager mouths bridge the chasm that had opened between them.

That, and the fear that she would not welcome him.

"I asked whether you were hungry." Her voice was low and taut as she knelt beside the basket, her sun-flecked green eyes on a level with his own.

"Swan Feather gave me something before she left," he said, feeling the tension that crackled between them like the prelude to summer lightning. "You don't have to stay, Clarissa," he added softly.

"Did Swan Feather change your poultices?" Her fingers quivered as she sorted the herbs, spreading them in a fan on the packed earth floor.

"The poultices can wait." He studied her from where he sat, painfully braced by the frame of willows. Her hands had slowed in their motion. When she raised her eyes to look at him, her face was flushed. Beautiful, he thought.

"I can change the poultices," she ventured impulsively. "I've watched Swan Feather do it. I know what she uses. Here, let me—"

She reached out to touch his wrappings, but he checked her motion with a dangerous flash of his eyes. At any other time he might have welcomed her touch, but the idea that she would be repulsed by his filthy condition was more than he could bear.

"What's the matter?" Her green eyes blazed like a bobcat's. "You don't think I can do the job? I've a mind to tie you down and show you I can, Seth Johnson!"

The use of Wolf Heart's Christian name was meant to irritate him, and it did. "Then save one hand to hold your nose," he snapped, "because that's what you'll need!"

She stared at him then, sitting on her haunches, biting

back suppressed laughter. "By heaven, you do smell like a sheep pen on an August afternoon, don't you? We can't have that!"

She scrambled to her feet and began rummaging through Swan Feather's stash of bowls, calabashes and odd scraps of buckskin. "What do you think you're doing?" he asked, suddenly uneasy.

Her tangled hair swung as she glanced back over her shoulder. "You need a bath," she announced, her eyes sparking with determination and mischief. "And I'm going to give you one!"

Chapter Eleven

What in heaven's name had possessed her?

Clarissa shook her head in disbelief as she dropped a heated stone into a large calabash of water to warm it. Offering to give Wolf Heart a bath had been the last thing on her mind when she'd walked into the lodge and found him alone. But his words and manner had challenged her, triggering her calamitous temper. She had blundered into her own trap, and now there was no way out.

He watched her in silence, glowering from under his thick black eyebrows as she selected a soft scrap of tanned buckskin, rough on its inner side, to serve as a washcloth. Scrubbing down a wounded bear would be less daunting, she thought. For all his white blood, there were times when Wolf Heart appeared savage to the core. This was one of them.

"You'll thank me when this is over," she said, approaching him with the heavy calabash balanced between her hands. "I hope you'll have the good sense not to struggle. It wouldn't take much strain to undo the healing of those ribs."

He glared at her as the words sank home, but he did

not move. Wolf Heart was no fool. "You don't have to do this," he growled.

"Oh?" Clarissa knelt beside him, dipped the buckskin into the calabash and left it for a moment to soak up the warm water. "And what, pray tell, are my other choices? Listen to you grumble all day because you're so filthy you can't stand yourself? Put up with the smell of you night after night until you're well enough to leave? No, thank you!"

She wrung out the buckskin and started on his face. At the touch of the pleasantly warm water she felt the resistance easing out of him. He closed his eyes as she wiped down his forehead, his temples, his nose and cheeks, tracing each contour of his powerful jutting bones. His lashes lay as black as the barbs of a crow feather against his golden skin.

Clarissa willed her emotions to freeze, her mind to focus on her task, but his nearness was already doing disturbing things to her. She could feel the quickening of her pulse and the small, warm, jerky flutters low in her body, like an itch in desperate need of scratching. She should try to talk, she thought. Chat about the weather, about the coming ball game, anything. But no words would form in her mind.

Abruptly surprise came to her rescue. Her hand paused. She leaned closer, gazing at his chin in astonishment.

His eyes shot open. "What is it now?" he demanded gruffly.

"You have...whiskers!" she gasped, staring at the minuscule dots of black stubble.

"Of course I do."

"But I've never seen—" She groped for the rest of the phrase, thinking how ridiculous she must sound. "I've never seen you shave!"

"I don't," he answered calmly. "Most Shawnee men have no hair on their faces. Those few who do—" he gave her a sharp sidelong glance "—usually have it pulled out."

"And you?" She stared at him, flabbergasted.

"Years ago, when my beard started to come in, my Shawnee mother began pulling it out one hair at a time because she wanted me to look like one of her people. I fought like a young bear at first, but with time I got used to it."

"And who does this for you now?"

"The children in the village have sharp eyes and small fingers. As these whiskers grow long enough to be pulled, they will do it for me and have great fun at my expense."

"All that so you'll look Shawnee!" Clarissa exploded. "Good heavens, doesn't it hurt?"

He scowled at her as if she were a backward child who had asked too many questions. "As I told you, I've grown used to the pain," he said. "And, yes, I do it to look Shawnee. To *be* Shawnee."

Clarissa restrained the urge to fling the wet buckskin in his exasperating face and stalk out of the lodge. That a man would go to such lengths to forsake his own blood was beyond her understanding. Thank heaven, she was planning her escape! The sooner she left this maddening man and his adopted tribe of savages behind her, the better off she would be!

Resolutely she dipped the buckskin into the warm water, lifted the dripping mass and squeezed the excess from its folds. "Lean forward if you can, and I'll scrub your back," she said.

He strained against the woven willow brace, allowing her to reach behind him. His back was rock hard, the rows of muscle like buttresses of coiled stone. They tightened at her touch, quivering subtly along the curve of his spine.

Steeling herself against his nearness, she reached lower to find the inward slope at the small of his back and, still lower, the thumb-sized hollows above his buttocks. "Let me know if I hurt you," she murmured, her voice rasping in her tight throat.

His only answer was a low, almost inaudible groan.

Clarissa's thoughts blurred as she rubbed the buckskin in slow circles over his satiny skin. Drifting in a whirlpool of sensation, she inhaled the damp musky scent of him. Her breast pressed the muscled curve of his neck where she leaned past his shoulder, the contact igniting small shimmering waves inside her, the sensation so delicious that she could not will herself to pull away. She closed her eyes.

The brush of her knuckles against the leather thong of his loincloth—quite by accident—jolted her with sudden awareness. She paused, her eyes wide and startled, her breath catching in her throat. Wolf Heart's body was too close, his masculine aura too threatening to the fragile barrier of her innocence. Her own desire was drawing her toward a precipice, and once she stepped over its edge there could be no going back.

Was that what she wanted—the precipice? That spiral of wild abandon that would end her girlhood forever? All she had to do was let her fingers venture lower. If it didn't happen now, it would happen soon. That much she knew.

"That…should take care of your back," she muttered, slipping out of the awkward position and plunging the buckskin into the water again. Her gaze darted from her hands to the floor, then to the empty doorway. She had never been a shy person, but she could not look at him now. Her eyes would tell him everything. "Lean back."

She pieced the words together like beads from a broken string. "I'll do your shoulders next. And your arms. And when I'm finished, I'll change your poultices, unless, of course, you think I'm not able."

"Clarissa." His massive hand seized her wrist, yanking her around, forcing her to face him. "You can quit playacting," he said in a thick voice. "We both know where this rubdown is going. The only question is, how far will we get before you slap my face and go flouncing out of here?"

"How dare you?" Clarissa would have drawn away in a show of outrage, but his grip on her arm held her prisoner, half-crouching above him, her eyes mere inches from his own. "I was doing you a kindness," she hissed, "a simple act of Christian charity, and if you choose to interpret that as anything but—"

He kissed her then, his free hand catching the nape of her neck and twisting her head down toward him. His lips were fierce in their taking, raw and hard; and as his naked need met her own, Clarissa whimpered like a small lost animal. Her flailing fingers tangled in his hair. Her mouth softened like hot tallow, molding to his hardness, opening as if she could drink him into her.

"You little wanton," he muttered, his chapped lips rasping hers. "All that show of being a proper lady…this is what you are, Clarissa. This is *who* you are!"

He kissed her again, a savage, bruising kiss that blazed through her body, igniting tiny rivers of flame that surged through every part of her. Her free hand fluttered over his chest, brushing the tiny hard beads of his nipples, ranging down over the buckskin wrappings that held him to the willow brace, skimming his navel, then venturing lower, lower still to explore the contours of the solid shaft that thrust upward, straining the confines of his loincloth. Dear heaven, the size of him…

She pulled back abruptly, her heart pounding like the hooves of a runaway mare.

"I won't hurt you, Clarissa," he murmured, drawing her back into his arms. "There's no part of me that would ever hurt you."

"I—know." She twisted away from him, flinging herself backward with a force that almost sent her sprawling. "It's not that! It's not that at all!"

"Then what's the matter?" His eyes glittered sardonically, turning cold as he leaned back into his willow brace. "Did your prim side win out after all? Or is it that you can't stomach the idea of being touched by a dirty savage?"

"Oh—" Clarissa stared at him, rage and frustration exploding inside her. How could she explain her reason for pulling away? How could she tell Wolf Heart that loving him would bind her to this place in a way she had no wish to be bound, making escape impossible? It could not be done.

"I hope you're not waiting for an apology," he said in a flinty voice. "If you are, you'll be waiting a long, long time. I'm no gentleman, Clarissa. And you, for all your fine airs, are no lady."

If he'd aimed his words at inciting her, they had hit their mark. "You!" She shot his cold anger back at him. "You are the most arrogant, self-righteous, contemptible—"

She could not finish the sentence. As the tears came, she could only wheel away from him and stumble blindly out the lodge, upsetting the calabash of water and almost colliding with Swan Feather, who was just coming home. The old woman shot her a concerned glance as Clarissa veered out of her path. Clarissa knew that out of respect, if nothing else, she should stop and explain. But her throat was so choked with emotion that she could not trust herself to speak. She could only hope Swan Feather would understand and forgive her.

The forest loomed in her tear-blurred vision, its shadowy depths offering a place to hide. She plunged onto the meadow path, running blindly, wanting only escape and the release of exhaustion. She ran until her ribs heaved and her chest ached and her gait had slowed to a stumble. She ran until one dragging toe caught in a tree root, sending her into a headlong sprawl.

She landed hard, but a hundred seasons of rotting leaves cushioned her fall. She lay there, facedown on the damp forest floor, too tired to get up and too humiliated to go home—wherever home might be. Nothing seemed solid or certain anymore, least of all who she was and where she belonged.

Wolf Heart gazed at Swan Feather through the drifting haze of smoke. There was no need to explain what had happened between himself and Clarissa. The old woman had seen both their hot flushed faces. She knew.

He spoke formally, choosing his words with care. "My bones are mending swiftly. You have cared well for me, friend of my mother, and I am grateful, but it is time for me to return to my own lodge."

"You know you are welcome to stay." Her own speech too was guarded and deliberate, allowing him to save face. "But perhaps you would sleep better alone, without the snores of an old woman to trouble you."

"I have slept very well here, but I have wearied you. You are the one who needs to rest." He studied her through the smoky haze. Her eyes, of late, appeared shadowed, sunk deeply into the wrinkled pits of their sockets.

"You may sleep in your own lodge, then," she conceded as if it were her decision. "But you must let me bring your meals and change your wrappings, unless..." She let the words trail off as she stared into the smoke. Then, as if picking up a dropped thread, she finished. "Unless, of course, you would rather have the girl do it. She has learned well and is quite capable of caring for your needs."

There it was. Behind his own stoic facade, Wolf Heart felt his pulse skitter like a youth's. Swan Feather's words had opened the door to his asking for Clarissa in marriage. He had only to make the next move.

He was searching for words to explain his dilemma when she spoke again.

"You promised the council you would take a Shawnee woman. Once, as I told you, I believed that she could never become Shawnee. But she has proven herself many times over. She is strong and brave and not afraid of hard work. She is worthy in every respect."

"Worthy, yes. Willing, no," Wolf Heart said. "She has no wish to become Shawnee or to become my wife. These things she has told me."

"Naturally she has." A wistful smile flickered in Swan Feather's ancient eyes. "Before he took me in marriage, I told my husband much the same thing—that I had no wish to live with a Kispoko warrior, among his people. But even as I spoke the words, my heart was straining to go with him."

"At least you were Shawnee," Wolf Heart said, warmed by her manner in spite of himself. "That made things simpler."

"True. But the girl cares for you, I know. The day you

were carried here, so badly hurt, she never left your side. I have seen the way she watches you when you aren't aware of it. I have seen the softness in her eyes.''

"And I have felt the sharpness of her claws.''

"Would you choose a woman without passion? Without spirit?''

Wolf Heart shifted his weight against the willow brace, remembering how Clarissa had gone molten in his arms—and remembering the contempt in her eyes when she had pulled away from him.

"Enough. We're talking in circles,'' he growled, pushing to a crouch, then rising unsteadily to his feet. His legs quivered as he started toward the door, waving away the old woman's efforts to help him.

"It's too soon for you to leave,'' she argued. "Surely you can stay a few more days.''

"I have already stayed too long, friend of my mother. A man should sleep in his own lodge.'' He moved toward the doorway, steeled against explosions of pain that ricocheted like musket fire around his ribs. Pride and his status as a warrior demanded that he walk home under his own power, showing a stoic face to the world. It would demand all the strength he possessed.

"I will make your fire and bring your food,'' Swan Feather called after him as he bent to clear the low doorway.

"When my ribs are mended I will shoot and dress a buck just for you,'' he answered, his jaw tightening with each movement.

"And I will make you a fine pair of leggings from the hide,'' Swan Feather shouted after him, not to be outdone. "They will be finished in time for your wedding!''

Wolf Heart walked through the village, greeting those he passed as if nothing were amiss. Only after he had entered the solitude of his own *wegiwa* did he slump to the floor and allow himself a long, low grunt of agony.

Small as it was, the bachelor lodge seemed spacious after the crowded clutter of Swan Feather's dwelling. His possessions lay exactly as he had left them, the musket resting stock down with its long barrel leaning against a wall, the hastily discarded bow and quiver, the rumpled bed and the lifeless black hole of the fire pit. How silent it was, this private place of his. How cold and lonely the nights would be without the whisper of Clarissa's breathing to warm the darkness.

Clarissa wheeled on the slippery grass, her fingers clawing at the leather ball. She feinted to the left, then raced to the right, but she was not fast enough. Three lithe brown bodies slammed into her at once, knocking her off balance. As she went down, the ball spun out of her grip, to be snatched up by other hands and swept off in the opposite direction with the shrieking players in pursuit.

For the space of a long breath she lay on the trampled green, feeling the pain of every bruise, twist and jolt. This crude Shawnee sport was as rough as the gauntlet, she groused, and today's skirmish was only a practice game between two teams of women. What would it be like playing against the men tomorrow?

The Shawnee women, most of them naked except for small leather aprons front and back, hooted as the ball shot between two goalposts at the far end of the field. Any adult female who judged herself physically able was allowed to play, and teenage girls bounced along beside hobbling white-haired crones. Clarissa, who'd insisted on playing fully clothed, had been made to understand that she was representing Swan Feather, who had grown too arthritic to compete. Her presence in the game would bring honor to Swan Feather's lodge.

She struggled to her feet as the players stampeded back in her direction. Aside from her time in the moon lodge, she had practiced with the team every afternoon. The women, she had learned, could carry the ball with their hands. The men would only be allowed to bat or kick it toward the goal. Aside from that, there seemed to be no rules at all. Kicking, gouging, trampling a downed player and other such forms of mayhem were not only acceptable but roundly cheered. All to the good, Clarissa reminded herself. The wilder the game, the better the chances for her escape.

As she hurried to rejoin the play, she caught sight of a tall familiar figure standing on the far side of the field, talking with Hunts-at-Night. Wolf Heart was nearing full recovery from his injuries. He moved freely about the village now and no longer needed help with fire-making or meals. It was well-known, however, that he did not plan to take part in the ball game. The rough play would present too much of a risk to his healing ribs.

Thrusting his unsettling presence from her mind, she waded full bore into the melee of shrieking, charging women. The ball had flown loose, eluding a score of grabbing sweat-slicked hands. Seeing a sudden opening, Clarissa flung herself toward it. She felt her outstretched fingers close around the ball. Her fingernails dug hard into the wet leather, and in the next instant she was breaking free, streaking across the grass toward the opposing team's goal.

What she lacked in weight and strength, Clarissa made up in speed. Her long legs ate up the ground, putting more and more distance between herself and her howling pursuers. Exhilaration welled up inside her, bursting out of her throat as a savage, whooping cry.

Just ahead she could see the two goalposts. Fixing her attention on them, she brought her arm back for the throw. So intent was she on an accurate aim that she did not see the two willowy forms darting at her from the side. Only when their hands seized her flying skirts did she become aware of the girls who had shared her first time in the moon lodge. By then it was too late. The drag on her gown threw her off stride, causing her feet to tangle. Her own momentum sent her pitching forward, and she landed facedown on the grass.

The ball popped from her grasp as she fell. One of the girls snatched it up and the two of them raced shrieking in the other direction. Dazed by the impact, Clarissa rose shakily to her knees. Stars spun in her vision. She blinked them away, her cheeks flaming with humiliation as she imagined Wolf Heart laughing at her.

"That was a good run." White Moon stopped beside her and extended a hand to help her up. Even with her sweat-tousled hair and her pear-shaped breasts dangling over her ribs, she managed to look dignified. "Run like that in tomorrow's game, and the men will be gathering firewood!"

Clarissa massaged a bruised hip as the women's chief signaled the end of the day's practice. "I couldn't outrun Red Fawn and Laughing Bird," she said ruefully. "They seemed to come at me from nowhere!"

"So they did!" White Moon laughed as they walked together. "Those two little minxes were waiting on the side of the field, and they dashed in and grabbed you as you ran past them! But don't worry, they'll be playing on your side tomorrow."

"Do you really think we have a chance of winning?"

Clarissa looked straight ahead, avoiding White Moon's open, friendly gaze. This pretended interest in the game was necessary, she knew. But she could not help disliking herself for it.

"We have an excellent chance!" The women's chief responded with enthusiasm. "Especially with Wolf Heart out of the game!"

"Is Wolf Heart a good player?" Clarissa asked, her interest no longer feigned.

"Oh, yes!" White Moon laughed. "Wolf Heart is the best player in the village. For five years he has led the men's team against us, and we have gathered firewood after every game." Her eyes narrowed slightly. "What a shame you will not be playing against him. You would enjoy it, I think, even if we lost."

Color flashed in Clarissa's cheeks as White Moon's gentle teasing sank home. She imagined the gossip in the moon lodge and the village garden patches. What were people saying about her and Wolf Heart?

Before she could frame a response, White Moon touched her arm. "Wait here," she said. "I have something for you."

She trotted to the edge of the clearing. When she returned she was carrying a small rolled object made of leather. "For you," she said, pressing it into Clarissa's hand.

Clarissa's heart sank as she shook out White Moon's gift to its true shape. It was a small leather apron, fashioned with a thong and two flaps, identical to the brief garments the other women wore in the game.

She dangled the scanty garment between her thumb and forefinger as gingerly as if White Moon had presented her with a dead squirrel. Color flamed hot in her face as she imagined wearing it even in private. "I thank the giver," she said, struggling to be gracious and honest at the same time, "even though I question the wisdom of the gift."

"It is not required that you wear it," White Moon assured her gently. "I understand that among white people it is shameful for a woman to show her body. But we have no such shame here. We dress as we do so we can move freely in the game and so our clothing can't be seized by other players, as yours was today."

"I'm s-sorry," Clarissa stammered, feeling foolish. "I wouldn't offend you for the world, but I can't—I truly can't—" She rolled up the tiny apron with unsteady fingers and would have returned it if White Moon had not laid a light hand on her wrist.

"No offense is taken. Keep my small gift. If you change your mind, it will be there for you. If not, I will understand."

"You are too kind to me. Everyone here is too kind to me." Clarissa thrust the rolled leather awkwardly into her pocket, meaning the words in a deeper sense than White Moon could possibly have known. If the Shawnee were cruel to her, everything would be easier. She would not be constantly torn. She would simply be able to hate them.

"If you are given more kindness than you can hold, pass some of it on. That, my daughter, is as much as our grandmother expects of us." For the space of a heartbeat, White Moon's strong fingers tightened around Clarissa's wrist. Then she smiled and strode across the field toward the place where her husband stood with Wolf Heart beside him.

After the first few steps she paused to glance back over her shoulder, and Clarissa knew she was being invited to come along. Swiftly she shook her head and turned away in the opposite direction. Her relationship with Wolf Heart had been strained since his departure from Swan Feather's lodge. Clarissa had found herself avoiding him on her errands through the village—and aching to see him although she stayed out of his path. The memory of his searing kisses haunted every hour of her existence, waking and sleeping. Sometimes the longing to be near him was so strong that she almost cried out with the pain of it. But she knew she could not give in to her desires. She could not allow her love for Wolf Heart to hold her prisoner.

The afternoon sun blazed hot, drying the sweat that soaked her hair and clothes to a salty crust. While the other women were still milling about the playing field would be a good time for a solitary swim, Clarissa resolved as she strode into the trees and set her moccasins on the path to the pool. Over the past moon, she had taken every opportunity to practice her swimming. Although she might never match the otterlike grace of the young Shawnee, and she had yet to dive from the ledge on her own, she handled herself with confidence in the water. She would never fear it again.

As she passed the berry thicket at the top of the ledge, Clarissa hesitated. White Moon's gift lay rolled in her pocket, a slight but provocative bulge. She would never wear such a scanty garment, of course, but curiosity buzzed like a pesky insect in her brain. How would she look wearing the little leather apron? How would it feel against her bare skin?

Privacy was rare in the Shawnee village. Even Swan Feather's lodge was no refuge from inquisitive eyes. If she truly wanted to try on the apron, there would be no more secluded place than here, no better time than now.

After checking carefully in every direction, she slipped

into the bushes where a small open space formed a natural bower that served handily as a dressing room. She had always swum in her clothes, or at least in her chemise and drawers. This time would be no different. She would try the apron, then get dressed again before following the zigzag path down to the water's edge.

Feeling more than a little wicked, she hung the leather apron on a twig, then began removing her sweaty clothes. Her dress and undergarments, which she had worn night and day for nearly two months, were so frayed and matted that they no longer seemed to be made of cloth. Clarissa peeled them away like a snake shedding its skin—and like skin, the fabric held the shape of her body for an instant before slumping into a lifeless ring around her feet. She stood as naked as Eve in the circle of thorny bushes that were just beginning to flower. Her mauve nipples puckered tautly as a stray breeze slipped over her skin. The russet nest at the joining of her thighs glistened in a beam of sunlight.

Trembling, she reached for the apron, adjusted it around her hips and double-knotted the ends of the leather thong. The flaps covered the essentials front and back, but little more. How strange it seemed, to be wearing so little.

She raised her arms, feeling the lightness of sun and air on her skin as she had never felt them before. A giddy sense of freedom swept over her as she turned one way, then the other in the prickly confines of the blackberry patch. How would it feel to run through a windswept meadow like this, unhindered by skirts and corseting? How reckless it would be! How glorious!

How unthinkable!

A blue jay, perched smartly on an overhanging hickory limb, cocked its crested head at her. Its black eyes, bright with interest, seemed to follow every move of her nearly naked body. "Shoo!" Clarissa waved her hands at the troublesome bird, but it only fluttered to a higher branch, where it sat wagging its head and scolding her in its raucous voice. *Shame,* it seemed to say. *Shame, shame, shame!*

"Oh, hush!" Clarissa tossed her moccasin at the jay— a move that was as unwise as it was impulsive. The shoe caught on a low branch of the hickory tree and hung there, just out of reach. When she stretched on tiptoe, straining to retrieve it, the vicious blackberry thorns jabbed into her tender flesh.

Biting back a whimper of pain, she glared up at the dangling shoe and at the bird, which had fluttered to a higher limb and seemed to be laughing at her now. She was frustrated and annoyed with herself, but she had to get her shoe back, and standing here fussing wasn't going to do the job.

Putting her temper aside, Clarissa forced herself to think. Retrieving the shoe would be simple if she had a long stick. All she needed to do was find a broken branch on the ground or snap one off a tree. The only trouble was, there was nothing usable here in the middle of the blackberry thicket. She would need to look outside.

She reached for her gown, only to find its frayed bodice hopelessly enmeshed in the thorns. She struggled with it for a moment but only succeeded in pricking her fingers and pulling dress and thorns into a tighter tangle. Overcome by impatience, she flung the gown aside. She was quite alone here, and it would take no more than a moment or two to get the moccasin out of the tree. That done, she could take her time with the dress.

Glancing around to make sure no one was coming, she slipped out of the thicket and onto the path.

For the space of a few heartbeats, she stood perfectly still, stunned by the feel of being in the open without her clothes. The breeze was so sweet on her bare skin that she shivered with pleasure. She flung out her arms and spun like a giddy child, drunk with the strange freedom of it. She had *wanted* to try out this new sensation, she realized. She had wanted it all along. The moccasin in the tree had only provided an excuse.

Her whole body tingled with awareness as she walked to the brink of the ledge and paused, looking down at the crystal blue water below—water that came close to matching the color of Wolf Heart's eyes. For a long moment she imagined leaping into space, diving head down, arrow straight, as the young Shawnee girls did, then feeling the ring of water explode around her body, the bubbles rippling over the surface of her bare skin. Was it possible? Could she really do it?

She felt goose bumps tighten on her skin as she stared down into the pool, which suddenly looked very small and very faraway. No, she was not ready for such a plunge. And since she planned to escape on the morrow, she likely never would be. She would go back into the thicket, put on her clothes and take the coward's way down to the water.

"Clarissa?" The deep masculine voice, ringing out through the trees, was Wolf Heart's. Her pulse lurched as she heard the faint rustle of the underbrush, its cadence matching the familiar rhythm of his stride, coming closer and closer.

"Clarissa?"

There was no time to grab her clothes, no time to lunge for the shelter of the thicket. As he stepped into sight, Clarissa did the only thing she could think of doing.

She jumped off the ledge.

Chapter Twelve

Clarissa's jump was not a graceful swan dive like the ones she had so admired. It was a panic-stricken plunge, feet first, arms flailing, mouth open in a silent shriek. She hit the water hard and went under, bubbles of air bursting upward around her as she sank.

As the shock wore off, she kicked upward. Seconds later she surfaced, spitting water. Instinctively she stroked for the rocks, intent on climbing out onto the bank. Only as her feet skimmed bottom did she remember, with a sinking heart, that she had left her dress and underclothes in the blackberry bushes at the top of the ledge. She had nothing on except the tiny leather apron.

She hovered uncertainly, hands paddling in the water as her eyes scanned the top of the ledge. Wolf Heart would be up there somewhere, watching her, probably laughing until his sides ached. If she knew him, he would wait until cold and fatigue forced her to come out of the water. Then, as she trudged up the path, naked and shivering, he would taunt her until she seethed with rage. But no matter, Clarissa reminded herself. By this time tomorrow, she would be on her way back to Fort Pitt, where she could put this whole humiliating experience behind her.

"You may as well come out!" she shouted up at him, her voice ringing off the ledges. "I know you're up there!"

No one answered.

"You're not fooling me, Seth Johnson!" she called, thinking the use of his Christian name would surely draw him out. "Come on! Be a gentleman for once in your life, and bring me my clothes!"

The only sounds she heard were the babble of the spring and the mocking echo of her own words.

Now what?

For several long minutes Clarissa paddled in agitated circles, moving to keep warm as she groped for the courage to haul herself out of the water and climb the path to the top of the ledge. The sun hung low above the cliffs. If she could hold out until dark...

But no, her teeth were already chattering. And who could say how much longer she would be alone here? Other women, their bodies hot and perspiring from the practice, would undoubtedly want to swim, too. They would find her dilemma amusing and make a great joke of it at her expense.

"Clarissa."

At the sound of her name, she turned abruptly in the water. Wolf Heart was standing on the bank among the jutting rocks. Suspended from his outstretched hands was—heaven be praised—a red woolen trade blanket.

"It's all right," he said softly, as if soothing a frightened animal. "You can come out."

She glared at him from shoulder-deep water, part of her still angry, part of her desperately wanting the warmth of the blanket and his enfolding arms.

"Why should I?" she retorted defiantly. "You scared me half to death up there! Don't you have any respect for a woman's privacy?"

"Your lips are turning blue," he said, ignoring her question. "Come on out of that water before you freeze."

Clarissa hesitated, but only for a heartbeat. "Close your eyes!" she insisted.

An amused smile twitched at the corner of his mouth, and for an instant she thought he was going to tease her about claiming to be a lady. But then, without another word, he shut his eyes tightly and stood like a tall mahogany carving, the soft crimson blanket hanging from his hands.

Arms crossed over her bare breasts, Clarissa waded, dripping, out of the water. The low sun cast the cleft of the pond into deep shadow, and the breeze, even now in late spring, was chilly. Her teeth were chattering by the time she gained the rocks and stumbled into the blanket's enfolding warmth.

Wolf Heart held her as if she were made of bone china, and she realized their last explosive encounter had stung him as bitterly as it had her. So what was he doing here? she wondered as she ached to burrow against his hard broad chest and lose herself in his arms. Why had he followed her to the ledge, and what was he thinking as he warmed her as gently as one would warm a child?

"You still haven't told me what you're doing here," she challenged him.

"I needed to talk with you alone," he said, and Clarissa's heart leaped.

"Very well, here I am," she said, her calm answer belying her frenetic pulse. Her whole body felt warm now, so warm that the blanket was needed only for modesty. What was the matter with her? Why was she trembling like a silly schoolgirl when she did not even know what he was going to say—especially when, in light of her plans to escape, nothing Wolf Heart had to say could make any difference?

"This may take some time." He eased her back from the water's edge to where they could sit side by side on a flat-topped boulder. Clarissa's hands clasped the blanket from the inside, holding it around her as he let her go. Now that she was no longer cold, the wool was becoming scratchy against her skin, but slipping the blanket off was out of the question.

"We may not have much time," she said. "Some of the women will want to swim now that their practice is over."

"They will wait." Wolf Heart did not explain how he knew, but his words hinted at some conspiracy with White Moon. What could be so important that the women's chief was involved in it?

"They will not wait patiently," Clarissa replied. "If you have something to say to me, you'd best get it said."

He shifted restlessly on the rocky seat, his eyes gazing up at the fading circle of sky above the ledges. "Clarissa, have you been happy here?" he asked.

Happy? She stared at him incredulously. She had worked her hands raw, slept on an earthen floor and worn the same threadbare clothes for two moons! She had taken constant orders from a grumpy old woman and struggled to survive among a people who had started off their acquaintance by beating her half to death. She had never felt stronger, freer, or more sure of herself, Clarissa realized. But happy?

She turned away and looked out across the darkening pool. "I don't know," she said truthfully. "Why should it make any difference? I have no choice except to be here.''

She could sense his gaze on her, sense the strange sadness in it. ''I was not happy here, either, at first,'' he said. ''I missed my father, for all his troubled ways. I had a hard time making friends. The Shawnee boys teased me because of my white skin and because I wasn't good at their games. I had to struggle with the language and with the skills of hunting and fighting. It was painful learning to be Shawnee. Many times, only the fear of shame kept me from weeping.''

''You're suggesting that I could learn as you did? That I could become a Shawnee?'' Clarissa felt an odd prickling sensation at the root of her neck as she pondered the unthinkable. She had found goodness, even kindness, among the Shawnee people. She had found honesty and respect. She had found a man she could love for a hundred lifetimes, if given the chance.

But no, it was out of the question. She was going to escape. She was going home to Baltimore, home to her large brick house, to her fine clothes, her friends and her brother. She was going home to her safe civilized world, and nothing was going to stop her.

Nothing.

Wolf Heart had not answered her question. He sat hunched forward with his elbows on his knees, looking troubled. Clarissa stole a sidelong glance at his rugged profile, fighting the urge to run her hand along the muscular curve of his back, or to reach out and brush a finger along the knuckles of his clasped hands. Was he on the verge of asking her to stay here with him, as his wife? She swallowed the ache in her throat, torn by the unspoken question. As the shadows deepened she grew more and more agitated until, at last, she could stand the silence no longer.

"I've told you as much as I can," she said. "But I can't really answer your questions until I know what you want."

He glanced sharply at her. "I came here in an effort to keep an old woman's heart from breaking," he said, and her heart dropped. "Two days from now, at the feast, Swan Feather plans to announce your adoption as her daughter."

Clarissa stiffened as if she had been stabbed with a long shard of ice. She stared at Wolf Heart, overcome by the openheartedness of Swan Feather's gift but dismayed by her own lack of worth. She could not accept, of course. She would not even be here to accept. But what was she going to say to Wolf Heart now?

"If this is not what you wish, tell me at once," he said. "That way, perhaps, I can find some gentle way to dissuade her."

Clarissa forced her mouth to form words. "As Swan Feather's daughter, would I then be Shawnee?"

"You would be more than Shawnee." His voice held no trace of emotion. "You would be a *mekoche*—a healer."

"And the others, the women, the braves," she whispered. "They would support Swan Feather in this adoption?"

"White Moon speaks for the women, Hunts-at-Night for the men. They have already given their blessing. All that remains is your own consent."

Churning inside, Clarissa slumped forward and buried her face in her hands. The blanket slipped down to expose her shoulders and the upper part of her back. She let it fall, paying no heed to the sudden coolness on her skin.

"Swan Feather plans the adoption to be a surprise for you," Wolf Heart said. "I would gladly honor her wishes, but I would not see her humiliated by your refusal before the people."

Clarissa lifted her face and looked at him. "Do you think I would choose to humiliate Swan Feather?" she asked in a choked voice.

"You told me once that you would rather be a dog than a Shawnee."

"I was angry then. I wanted to hurt you."

"Does that mean your heart has changed, Clarissa? Does it mean you would consent to the adoption?"

His eyes were deep, dark blue in the gathering twilight. Clarissa studied him through the lingering blur of tears, thinking that perhaps, if he had offered her his love, then she would have been truly torn. But she could not give up her own future to keep from hurting an old woman's feelings. There would be no announcement, no public refusal, because she would be gone before the day of the feast. That was the only answer. But it was not an answer she dared give to Wolf Heart.

"What happens if I decide against being adopted?" she asked.

"Nothing. You will go on as before."

"As a slave?"

"That is your word, not mine." He stirred beside her on the rock, and Clarissa sensed the dark cast settling over his mood. "Swan Feather may choose to give you to someone else, since she was hoping to find a daughter, not a servant."

"I see." She nodded her understanding, swallowed,

and forced herself to speak the necessary lie. "I can't give you an answer yet. I need time to think."

"How long?" His voice held no trace of suspicion.

"Until tomorrow." She fought back a shiver of self-recrimination. "Tomorrow after the game you will have my decision."

He sighed irritably, shoulders flexing, long limbs stirring, and Clarissa sensed how many words he was holding back. "I take it your clothes are at the top of the ledge," he said as if she had not spoken.

"I can walk up the trail by myself." She felt his coldness and knew she deserved far worse. "You can have your blanket later. I'll leave it with Swan Feather."

"Tell her to keep it as my gift." He watched as she stood and wrapped the blanket tightly around her body, gripping the fringed ends in her hands. The blanket was a large one. Its long corners dragged on the ground, hiding her feet and making it hard to avoid the sharp rocks that jutted from the trail's surface.

Clarissa lifted her chin and moved ahead, determined to preserve what remained of her dignity. But she was not used to going barefoot, and every step was a new misadventure. When she stubbed her toe for the third agonizing time, Wolf Heart, following a few silent paces behind, stepped forward and scooped her up in his arms, blanket and all.

"That wasn't necessary!" She glared into his unsmiling face, profoundly grateful. "I was doing just fine on my own!"

"Fine? Ha!" he growled, mounting the steep trail as if she weighed no more than a bag of goose feathers. "You were painful to watch. I couldn't stand it any longer."

"Then you could have stopped watching!"

He paused in midstride. "Do you want me to put you down?"

"No."

"Then don't argue!" His arms tightened around her as the trail narrowed. Clarissa settled against him, her senses drinking in the clean hickory-smoke aroma of his skin. The small leather medicine pouch pressed against her cheek, an ever-present reminder of who he was and why it was so useless to love him.

What a splendid figure Seth Johnson would have made in white society—tall, strong and handsome, a man of integrity, industry and intelligence. How proud she would have been to walk at his side, to share his home and bear his children. What a waste of both their lives that he was so stubbornly, maddeningly Shawnee!

Clarissa closed her eyes, clinging to the moment, hearing the low beat of his heart, matching her own breath to the rise and fall of his chest, savoring the warm, strong, infinitely precious feel of him—and knowing it would be for the last time.

Wolf Heart strode up the trail with Clarissa in his arms, his thoughts as turbulent as the churning river. Part of him wanted to set her down, seize her shoulders and shake every word of truth from her deceitful little mouth. Yet another part of him yearned to sweep her into the shadows, spread the blanket beneath them and caress every curve and hollow of her lovely body—to kiss the sweetness of her pink-nippled breasts and press his face against her long white belly; to tease, taunt and love her until she whimpered for mercy.

That brief glimpse of her atop the ledge, her hair like a flying flame as her pale lithe body spun toward the brink, would have ignited any man. He had known desire before and, in time, learned to master it. But this tenderness, this overwhelming need to be near a woman, to know her as intimately as he knew himself, was new to him and he was stunned by its power. Logic and reason fled when Clarissa was close to him, and that was not good, because if ever he needed logic and reason, it was now.

She was planning to escape—her evasive eyes and words had told him that much. And he knew it would be soon. She had promised him an answer to the adoption question after the ball game. Wolf Heart knew that her answer would not be given in words. By the game's end, Clarissa would be gone.

Would he let her go? Could he?

Where the trail ended, the top of the ledge rose dark against the twilight sky. From the crown of a scraggly pine, a great blue heron unfolded its wings, stretched its legs and glided like a silvery phantom toward the river. In the cool shadows, crickets stirred and began to sing.

Clarissa had scarcely spoken on the upward climb—strange for one who was usually so talkative. But in her silence Wolf Heart could sense the working of her mind. She was plotting, planning, weighing one risk against another.

So, when will it be? he imagined asking her. *Will you go tonight while Swan Feather is asleep? Will you go tomorrow while she is helping prepare the bread for the feast? When will you choose to betray her?*

He could confront her here and now. But with no evidence, Clarissa would surely deny everything and call him a suspicious fool. He had no choice except to bide his time, despising his own inaction, until she made a move.

And then what?

She stirred in his arms as they neared the top of the trail. "I can make it from here," she said.

"Where are your things?" He kept his hold on her.

"There. In the thicket." She strained toward the place. "Except for my shoe, which is—uh—in the tree. I threw it at a very insolent bird."

"I see it. I'll toss it to you." In spite of his dark mood, Wolf Heart had to bite back a smile. But they were speaking like strangers, he thought, hiding behind masks of politeness. What would happen if he were to tear his mask away and speak openly? Would Clarissa do the same, or would he only be putting himself at her none-too-tender mercy?

They had reached the thicket. At its edge, he lowered her to the ground. She slid down the front of him, her hands holding the blanket carefully in place. "Until tomorrow, then," she murmured stiffly.

"Yes." He battled the urge to seize her in his arms and make lies of all their proper talk. "Good luck in the game. If you want to play your best, I'd suggest wearing the costume White Moon gave you."

He sensed the rush of heat from her as she drew sharply away from him. "No," she said in a small choked voice. "No, I think not."

He left her then, after glancing around for the presence of wild animals or anything else that might harm her. In spite of everything, she was precious to him, this bright, courageous child-woman. He did not know what she felt for him or what he would do tomorrow when she tried to leave. He only knew that the night ahead would be long and troubled, with no promise of rest.

Clarissa was awake before dawn the next morning—not that she had really slept. It had been all she could do to lie quietly beneath her blankets so as to not disturb Swan Feather. The first paling of pewter sky between the bark slabs had come as a blessed relief.

While the old woman still snored, her withered hands flung upward like a sleeping child's, Clarissa rose and laid kindling on the coals. For a long moment she crouched beside the fire pit, watching the amber-blue flames lick at the splintered wood. This, she vowed again, would be her last day as a Shawnee captive.

Dipping a little water into a pot, she added cornmeal for gruel and placed it on the coals to simmer. More often than not, it was Swan Feather who, out of long habit, rose early and prepared the morning meal. But Swan Feather was growing more frail with each passing day. She needed her rest. From now on—

But what on earth was she thinking? Clarissa brought herself up with a mental slap. By the end of the day she would be on her way back to Fort Pitt. The old woman would have to care for herself or depend on the kindness of others.

That, or find herself another daughter.

Stepping outside, she took up a large empty calabash, slung it on her hip and set out for the river. Even at this hour people were awake and stirring. An air of anticipation hung over the village. The women she passed on the way to the river smiled at her and made signs of victory with their hands. Children, too excited to sleep, sat wide-eyed in their doorways or raced along the riverbank in the dawning light. Clarissa glanced around for Wolf Heart, but did not see him.

As she bent to fill her calabash, she thought of the parfleche, filled with dried meat, corn bread and slices of dried pumpkin that she had buried at the edge of the meadow two days earlier. With careful use, the food would sustain her all the way back to the fort. All that remained was to steal a horse and put a safe distance between herself and the Shawnee before she was missed.

For that, she would need the distraction of the ball game.

Swan Feather was still asleep when Clarissa returned to the lodge with the heavy calabash of water. She stirred the thickened gruel and moved the small pot to the outside edge of the fire pit. Calculating that she had plenty of time, she trotted back to the garden plots, which lay between the village and the river. She would spend some time cultivating Swan Feather's little patch of corn, beans and squash. It was the least she could do before leaving the old woman without help.

Whistling lightly through her teeth—a trick she'd learned from a young corporal at Fort Pitt—she found a digging stick and set to work. The morning was cool, the low slanting rays of sunlight soft upon the land. She thrust the pointed stick into the rich brown loam, savoring the earthy scent that rose to meet her nostrils. Maybe when she was back in Baltimore she would plant a little garden just for the pleasure of working the soil. Instead of corn, squash and beans, she would grow violets and little black-eyed daisies like the ones that grew so profusely in the meadow.

Halfway down the long row of corn, she paused to stretch her limbs and rest her back. She arched toward the sky, her gaze following a long vee of snow geese winging northward against the dawn-streaked sky. Their echoing cries tugged at her heart, stirring a wildness in her, a yearning for something just out of reach—something she could not even name.

Would she see wild geese in Baltimore? Would the

sight and sound of them still stir a longing to take wing and follow?

She finished the garden patch and returned to the lodge to find Swan Feather huddled by the fire, finishing her share of the corn gruel. She looked drawn, shriveled and infinitely weary this morning, Clarissa thought. The work of preparing the sacred feast would be well left to younger hands.

But when she ventured to suggest as much, the old woman puffed up like a small indignant owl. "To be one of the twelve honored women—the importance of that is beyond your understanding!" she snapped as she struggled to her feet. "The honor was given to me for life, and only when I am dead—"

She tottered outside without finishing the sentence, moving stiffly on her little bandy legs. A strange, hard lump rose in Clarissa's throat as she watched her go. Prickly, cantankerous Swan Feather who nagged her, bossed her, scolded her—and loved her enough to want to become her mother.

How she would miss the old woman.

By the time Clarissa had finished her share of the corn gruel, washed her face and tidied up the lodge, the drums were calling people to the clearing. As was customary, the ball game would be played early, allowing the losers the rest of the day to gather the huge pile of firewood that would be needed for the cooking and dancing. Soon it would be time to begin.

Wiping her hands on her dress, Clarissa hurried to join the crowd. She had long since resolved that she would play fully clothed. Modesty aside, she could hardly make her escape wearing nothing but a tiny leather apron. And the clothes, with their trailing skirts, were part of her strategy—an important part.

By the time she reached the clearing, her face was flushed and her pulse was galloping. Thinking about her plan had been one thing. Carrying it out safely would be quite another. The odds of something going wrong were higher than she dared to contemplate, but this could be her only chance.

Laughing people crowded the clearing, shouting out ribald jokes and challenges. Those who'd bet on the outcome of the game had hung their prizes from a painted pole at the far side of the field. Ribbons, feathers and beaded ornaments dangled in the morning breeze, catching glints of sunlight. Children chased and whooped, dodging among their elders; and all the while the drums throbbed, their urgent primal rhythms weaving among the sights and sounds like the threads of a tapestry.

The men's and women's teams were clustering at opposite ends of the field. Clarissa glanced around for Wolf Heart and spotted him at last, standing beside the chief in front of the council house. For the space of a breath, his eyes held hers across the distance, their dark gaze as compelling as a touch. She became aware that she was trembling. Could it be that, by means of some sixth sense, he knew about her plan?

With a shake of her hair, she tore her gaze away and ran to join her teammates. No, it was impossible, she reassured herself. She'd confided in no one. And Wolf Heart, for all his gifts, was no mind reader. Her secret was as safe as ever it could be.

White Moon's smile flashed in greeting as Clarissa joined the huddle of women. Her handsome eyes flickered as they took in the ragged gown, but she said nothing, and soon Clarissa was pulled into plotting the first moves of the game. Guiltily she kept her silence. She had a few moves of her own planned—moves that would do little or nothing to help the women win.

The drums thundered to a climax and abruptly ceased, a signal that the game was about to start. Men and women faced each other across the midline of the field, their naked bodies gleaming like oiled copper in the morning sunlight. Cat Follower had taken Wolf Heart's place as captain of the men's team. He stood with arms akimbo, a confident grin on his face. The women's captain, Dawn Star, was the girl Clarissa had surprised in his bed. Spectators hooted suggestively as the pair crouched almost nose to nose, waiting for the first toss of the ball.

From her place in the rear of the women's ranks, Clarissa waited, muscles tense, nerves screaming, as Hunts-at-Night drew back his arm and hurled the ball high into the air. As the arc of its flight curved and descended, the playing field erupted into a melee of leaping, surging bodies.

Dawn Star emerged with the ball and, clutching it like stolen treasure, streaked down the field with the men in howling pursuit. She was nearing the goal when Cat Follower flung himself against her side, slamming into her with a blow that knocked them both sprawling in a wild, sensuous tangle of legs. The crowd whooped as the loose ball was batted away by another brave. An expert kick sent it flying toward the men's goal, where it was booted between the posts. The men howled in jubilation.

Clarissa had kept to the fringe of the action. Now, as the players readied themselves for another toss-up, she gathered her courage and forced her way into the knot of sweating brown bodies clustered at midfield. She didn't relish the idea of being knocked down and trampled, but if it would provide a way to get her off the field—

She risked a glance at Wolf Heart as the ball went up.

He was watching the game intently. All to the good, Clarissa thought as she flung herself into the scramble that followed the toss-up. Her freedom depended on escaping his vigilance long enough to get to the horses.

Cat Follower and Dawn Star were grappling for the ball. Suddenly it slipped loose and flew straight toward Clarissa. With no time to think, she scooped it out of the air and, clutching it against her chest, wheeled and sprinted full out down the field.

Caught up in the excitement of the moment, she might have outrun her whooping male pursuers, but she remembered her plan in time. With a twinge of guilty regret for the lost goal, she eased off on her long-legged stride until she felt a strong hand close on a fold of her flying skirt. Her own momentum did the rest. She spun to one side, then pitched forward, losing her hold on the ball. By the time she struck the ground, hard enough to hurt, an alert brave had kicked the ball toward the men. Both teams turned and stampeded in the opposite direction, several players charging right over top of her. Clarissa's breath exploded outward with the brief but punishing weight of their moccasined feet. Then they were gone and she lay alone on the grass, stunned and bruised—exactly as she'd planned.

A furtive glance in Wolf Heart's direction showed the worry on his face. But she had counted on the fact that he would not make a public spectacle of himself by rushing onto the field. This time, at least, she had judged him accurately. It was White Moon who paused and extended a grass-stained hand to help her up.

"Are you all right?" she asked, the sincere concern in her black eyes stabbing Clarissa with guilt.

"I...think so." Clarissa staggered to her feet, stood

and took an experimental step. "Oh—" She faked a sharp little moan as she put full weight on her left ankle.

"Bad?" White Moon asked.

Clarissa nodded, teeth clenched against the imaginary pain. "I—must have twisted my leg when I fell. Maybe if I rest for a little while I'll be able to play again."

"No, you'll only risk making it worse," White Moon cautioned as, twenty paces behind her, the men's team erupted into cheers over a second goal. "Forget about playing," she added with a rueful smile. "After all, this is only a game."

"If the men win, I'll help gather firewood," Clarissa lied, despising the necessity for it.

"We'll see. Rest now." The women's chief trotted back to her team as they gathered for the next play. Clarissa limped off the field, Wolf Heart's gaze following her every labored step. He would watch her for a short time, she calculated. Once he'd determined she was not seriously hurt, his attention would be drawn back to the game. He was, after all, an avid player. He would be anxious to see his friends win.

Finding room on the side of the field wasn't easy, but she managed to squeeze in behind a plump middle-aged woman and her very pregnant daughter. The pair nearly hid her from Wolf Heart's sight—again, all to the good. But Clarissa's heart was already hammering in anticipation of what she would have to do next.

For a few minutes she forced herself to sit still and watch the game. She cheered when Red Fawn slipped through the lines with the ball and sprinted down the field for the women's first goal. But her spirits sank when she risked a glance at Wolf Heart. He was still casting sidelong looks in her direction, his face as inscrutable as a granite boulder.

Only when play resumed again did her chance finally come. The rough contest had gotten personal between Cat Follower and Dawn Star. They were bumping and jabbing each other whenever they passed, and their last skirmish for the ball had degenerated into an all-out fight. As the ball came down again, Cat Follower swung his full body against her, slamming her out of the way. For Dawn Star, it was the last straw. Forgetting the game, she flew at him, kicking, clawing and screaming like an angry hawk.

Pandemonium erupted on the field, the spectacle so compelling that even Wolf Heart was distracted by it. Seizing the moment, Clarissa backed quietly out of the crowd and limped behind the far side of the council house. Once out of sight, she glanced swiftly around to make certain she was alone. Yes, it was all right. Only a big brindled dog, dozing in the sun, had opened a sleepy eye to see her go.

A wistful ache filled her as she glanced around the cluster of empty lodges and thought of people she would never see again—Swan Feather, White Moon, Cat Follower and a score of others who had called her friend and sister. And Wolf Heart. Wolf Heart, whose memory triggered a yearning so intense that she almost moaned out loud. The urge to go back, to see him one more time seized her like an attack of sudden madness, and for a moment—

But she was being foolish now. Fate had granted her this one chance to escape. She had to go now or all would be lost.

Glancing around one more time, she plotted the swiftest course through the village and took off at a dead run.

By the time she reached the roped-off enclosure where

the horses were kept, Clarissa's heart was pounding like a blacksmith's hammer gone berserk. Her ribs heaved and her breath came in painful gasps, but she knew she could not stop to rest. To stop would be to think. To think would be to lose her courage and, ultimately, her freedom.

The horses were grazing peacefully, their coats gleaming like wet silk in the morning sunlight. Clarissa's spirits leaped as she glanced around and realized there was no one guarding them. Her plan was moving smoothly—almost too smoothly.

Three of the high-strung animals raised their heads and nickered softly as she approached. For much of the past moon she had visited them daily, bringing them handfuls of dried corn, fresh clover or succulent roots from the meadow. The horses had learned to expect her and to welcome the treats she fed them. But would any of them let her mount and ride? That remained to be seen.

Digging deep into her pocket, she scooped out the kernels of dried corn she'd secreted there. Heart pounding, she stepped into the enclosure, stretched out her hand and made small coaxing sounds in her throat.

A dappled mare was the first to start toward her. Good, Clarissa thought, trembling in spite of herself. This animal she knew to be both swift and docile, and the rawhide thong around its neck would make it easy to catch and lead. Holding her breath, she waited until the velvety gray muzzle pushed into her palm for the corn. Quickly she seized the thong with her free hand and moved, tugging, toward the edge of the enclosure. The mare went willingly, munching the dried corn as Clarissa lowered the rope, guided it through the opening and retied the knot.

Getting the mare into the concealing trees was easy

enough, but there Clarissa hesitated. No, she decided swiftly, she would not try to mount yet. Getting onto the horse could be awkward and noisy, and she would only have to dismount again to retrieve her hidden cache of supplies. She would lead the animal until she had the parfleche. Then she would climb onto the sleek bare back and ride like fury.

The raucous shouts from the ball field faded into stillness as she made her way along the shadowed path. Chickadees piped their calls from the trees. The horse snorted and shook its silvery hide, content to be moving. Pale gold ribbons of sunlight filtered down through the leafy branches, touching clumps of velvet moss and lichen-encrusted stones. How beautiful these woods were, Clarissa thought, how clean and unspoiled their secret trails. One day, if she could find words to describe it, she would tell her children about this place.

She had buried the parfleche at the base of a tall chestnut tree and marked the spot with a large gray stone. Her pulse quickened as she saw it, a dozen paces from the clearing where the trail branched toward the river. Hands shaking, she tied the horse to a sapling. She had all but done it! Minutes from now she would be mounted and galloping for freedom.

She had left the Shawnee world behind forever.

Forcing her feet to move, she ran to the tree, sank to the leaf-strewn ground at its base and rolled the stone aside. Getting the parfleche would be a matter of scraping aside a few scant inches of earth, then—

Clarissa's heart dropped as her fingers jabbed into the soft humus, probing deeper, then deeper still, finding nothing of use. The parfleche was gone.

"Have you lost something, Clarissa?"

The low rough voice behind her stopped her breath. Stunned, she turned to see a tall figure standing in a shaft of sunlight.

She had not escaped after all.

Chapter Thirteen

Clarissa froze at the base of the tree, torn between running, pleading for mercy, and trying to bluff her way out of danger. The morning light cast Wolf Heart's tall form into silhouette. Her sun-dazzled eyes could not see the expression on his face, but her imagination filled in a mask of cold fury. For the first time since that long-ago beginning of her captivity, she was afraid of him.

"What are you doing here?" she whispered, forcing the words through a throat so tight that she seemed to be strangling.

"I might ask the same question of you." The words could have been carved in stone for all the expression they carried. "Were you looking for this?"

Still blocked against the sun, he held something out to her. Clarissa's breath caught as she realized it was the parfleche. "Yes," she said, realizing it would be useless to lie. "That's what I was looking for."

"And this is the answer you would give to Swan Feather?"

"Yes."

"You could have told me last night." Anger still darkened his voice.

"And what would you have done?" she demanded, glaring up at him. "Would you have let me go? Or would you have tied me up like something you owned?"

"I don't own you."

"Swan Feather does!"

"It is her wish to change that."

"Then why didn't she ask me how I felt?" She flung the question at him. "Why was it left to you?"

"Because it never occurred to her that you would be anything but pleased and honored," Wolf Heart answered quietly.

"So what are you going to do with me now?" She scrambled to her feet and stood quivering as she faced him, all defiance.

In answer, he glanced back over his shoulder. Only then did Clarissa notice the horse, a small but sturdy-looking buckskin, grazing in a stand of hickory behind him. "The mare you have taken belongs to Hunts-at-Night," he said. "It is his wife's favorite mount and they would both be unhappy to find it gone. I've brought you a different horse, one of my own."

Clarissa's hand went to her throat. She stared at him, feeling as if the ground had just been jerked out from under her feet, leaving her to fall into a deep pit of her own making. "You're saying I can go?" she whispered, unable to believe her own ears.

"Would it make any difference if I tried to stop you?" He turned slightly, changing the angle of the light, and now at last she saw his face in full detail, saw the tightly reined anguish etched in every line of his features.

"Would you try to stop me?" she challenged him, knowing suddenly that having him stop her was exactly what she wanted. It was what she had wanted all along— a life with this man, whatever kind of life that might be.

But he would have to speak, or at least give some sign that he wanted her. Otherwise she would have no choice except to leave.

"There's the horse," he said. "Take it and go. You're free."

"And Swan Feather?" She hesitated, waiting, hoping.

"Swan Feather would not hold you against your will. I will explain and she will understand—in time."

In time. Clarissa turned slowly away and moved toward the buckskin horse. Every step was weighted by a despair so black that she felt as if she would carry it for the rest of her life. She was free. But she could not thank him. She could not even say goodbye. One more word and she would shatter like unfired clay.

"Clarissa."

At the sound of her name, she spun back toward him. Her heart leaped, then dropped like a stone as she saw that he was holding the parfleche, extending it toward her with both hands.

Fighting tears of anguish, she walked slowly back toward him. His face was in full sunlight now, the jaw set, the eyes narrowed against the glare. What colossal, stubborn pride he had! If only he would speak, or even look at her...

She reached out to take the rawhide case and their fingers happened to brush. The light contact of skin to skin blazed like a flash of gunpowder through her body. The parfleche dropped from between their hands. Struck by the sudden searing heat in his eyes, Clarissa let it fall.

In the next instant he had caught her in his arms.

All barriers between them—pride, distrust, conflict— vanished as he kissed her. Clarissa melted against him, her fingers furrowing his long black hair, her mouth opening, her wanton hips moving, pressing, seeking the wonderful hardness that lay beneath his breechcloth. His breathing deepened, and she knew there would be no stopping this time, no restraint, no guilt. She would give herself to him fully and completely, and he would make her his woman.

With a low moan, he swept her up against his chest, his arms clasping her thighs and shoulders. She clung to him, hearing the wild drumming of his heart as he carried her through the trees to a hidden glade overhung by willows, cushioned with soft spring moss and dotted with tiny white flowers. It was a perfect wedding place, she thought as he lowered her to the ground, more beautiful than any church she had ever seen. She thought of saying so, but as he leaned above her, his eyes hot and fierce and tender, Clarissa knew that the time for talk was long past. They needed no words, she and Wolf Heart. They needed nothing more than here and now, nothing more than what they could give to each other.

Her hand moved upward to caress his face, fingers trembling down the chiseled hollow of his long cheek and over the rugged line of his jaw. His throat moved as she clasped the back of his neck and pulled his head down to her breasts, every part of her wanting him, needing him.

She whimpered out loud as his lips nuzzled aside the flimsy fabric of her bodice and she felt the heaven of his mouth on her sensitive skin, nibbling, tasting, licking. His teeth captured the dark circle of her aureole, nipping lightly while his tongue circled the throbbing, puckered nipple, igniting waves that shimmered out and down, cascading like shooting stars through her body.

His hard belly lay against her hips. Wanting more of him, all of him, she arched upward, seeking the sweet familiar pressure that had all but driven her mad before.

But this time it was his hand that answered, stroking downward, finding her through the ragged tangle of skirts, his fingertips cool against the hot wet core of her need.

"Wolf Heart—" She pushed against him, feverish with yearning. Her urgent fingers groped and tugged, all but ripping away his breechcloth. She gasped as her fingertips found naked flesh. His manhood was as hard and smooth as polished marble, as exquisitely fashioned as a flower. She clasped him with one trembling hand and heard him groan. The rough need in his voice stirred her blood and touched her heart. Yes, she had been born for him, Clarissa thought. Born for this man, for this moment.

She lay open and waiting as he poised himself above her. For the space of a long breath his gaze held hers, fiercely tender and full of promise. Then, as longing burst in them both, she arched to meet his thrust. There was a small burst of pain, then the sensation of sliding into a spiral of ecstasy as he began to move inside her, flesh cloaked in flesh. Marble sheathed in silk. She closed her eyes and lost herself in their motion, in the sweet raw newness of their love as the singing grew deep inside her, swelling, filling every joyous part of her.

As they soared and burst together, Clarissa knew there would be no escape, no return to Baltimore. She belonged with this man, Wolf Heart or Seth Johnson or whatever he might choose to call himself. He was her love, her life.

Spent, they lay together on the carpet of blossoms. Even now she could not get enough of him. She curled against his side, savoring the hard-muscled smoothness of his body and the rich masculine aroma of his skin.

Through the bower of overhanging willows, the sun

cast dappled patterns of light and shadow over their bodies. Next time, she thought, drowsy with contentment, they would make love by the light of the moon. Kokomthena, their grandmother, who had fashioned men and women to enjoy each other's bodies, would be very pleased.

Clarissa's adoption took place the following afternoon. Wolf Heart had refused to tell her about the ceremony, saying only that it was forbidden for her to know the details ahead of time. With no reason to believe otherwise, she had assumed it would be a simple affair—an exchange of words, perhaps, or small gifts. She could not have been more wrong.

The food for the banquet was simmering over the cook fires—built with wood she had helped the women gather—when the drums called the people to assemble in the council house. Everyone—men, women and children—put aside their tasks and came.

Clarissa had never been inside the mysterious log building before. As she stood beside Swan Feather, her gaze explored the cavernous space, the massive roof beams, the battle trophies hung upon the walls—shields, lances, even scalps. This, then, was the heart of the village, the center of Wolf Heart's world, and now her own.

The council house was large enough to hold all the people in the village. Although they entered smiling and chatting through the wide doorway hung with buffalo hides, even the children fell into respectful silence as they arranged themselves in rows on the hard-packed earthen floor. Light streamed in through the windows to glisten on their sleek black hair and coppery bodies.

Wolf Heart strode in and quietly took a seat on her left, his eyes betraying nothing. They had agreed to re-

main apart until her adoption, after which he could ask
Swan Feather for her hand in the proper way by pre-
senting the old woman with gifts. How much did the
village know about what had happened between them?
she wondered, glancing furtively around her. Was it possible to keep any kind of secret in this place?

Hunts-at-Night, with an air of great dignity, stepped
before the gathered listeners and began to speak. His so-
norous voice related the history of the Shawnee as a people, how they had come as wanderers to this, the valley
of the Beautiful River. The recitation droned on for so
long that Clarissa, seated cross-legged on the floor like
the others, began to feel cramped and fidgety.

Her gaze shifted to Wolf Heart's craggy profile. How
majestic he looked today, with silver ornaments gleaming
at his earlobes, his black hair twisted at the scalp lock
and held by a small silver clasp, from which twin eagle
feathers rose. Today he had added a handsome silver
breastplate engraved with his symbol, the wolf. Beside
him, she looked as drab and tattered as an old muskrat
skin thrown out for the dogs to worry. If this was to be
such a grand occasion, why had no one offered her anything to wear?

She was almost caught off guard when Hunts-at-Night
asked her to stand. Reminding herself that the adoption
was supposed to be a surprise, she scrambled to her feet
and prepared herself to look astonished.

"You have lived among us and seen our ways." The
chief's scar-slashed face was stern but his voice was kind.
"Is it your wish to join with the Shawnee as the daughter
of Swan Feather?"

Clarissa glanced down at the old woman's beaming
countenance. Moments ago she'd thought she would have
to feign emotion, but now, as she felt everyone's gaze

on her, the throbbing lump that rose in her throat was all too real. These people who possessed so little were offering her everything they had—their kinship, their support, even their love. Unshed tears blurred her eyes as she nodded and whispered, "Yes."

The chief's grim features broke into a smile. "So let it be done," he said. Without another word, he turned away and down the long center aisle toward the door. There was a stirring in the lodge as all the boys and men, including Wolf Heart, rose and followed him outside, leaving only the women and girls, who edged forward expectantly.

Clarissa stood before them, wondering what to do next. Swan Feather's wrinkled face wore a gap-toothed grin. Some of the younger girls had begun to giggle. The unsettling tightness in Clarissa's stomach was quelled only a little when White Moon stepped forward, beaming.

"Now we will make you Shawnee," she said.

As if triggered by some silent signal, a half-dozen senior women sprinted forward, surrounded Clarissa and began pulling at her clothes. Only White Moon's reassuring smile kept Clarissa from bolting out of the lodge as the worn fabric began to rip and tear. First the skirt went, then the petticoat and the bodice of the gown. Buttons popped off and rolled across the floor to be snatched up by eager hands. The watchers laughed, hooted and shouted encouragement as fabric strained and ripped.

Clarissa gasped as rough fingers split her chemise down the back and jerked it off her arms, leaving her bare from the waist up. "Stop—" she pleaded, clasping her arms over her exposed chest as the hall resounded with laughter. But even she knew where this rough-and-tumble was going. When her underdrawers were ripped away, the stained muslin so threadbare that it offered lit-

tle resistance, she stood naked and trembling before the
gathered women, her hands too small to conceal her body
from their curious eyes. To be sure, few of them had ever
seen red hair down *there*. But did they have to stare at
her so openly?

At a nod from White Moon, four younger women hurried forward, each of them carrying a small earthenware
pot. Only when the first of them dipped her fingers into
the pot and began smearing a thick white liquid clay onto
Clarissa's bare shoulder did she realize what was happening.

They were going to paint her, all of her, from head to
toe!

She forced herself to stand still as the women's hands
rubbed paint onto her skin. The watchers in the hall had
begun to chant—a high-pitched blood-stirring song—accompanied by clapping hands and the throb of an unseen
drum. By the time the song was finished, the white paint
had been spread over Clarissa's entire body. Her face,
her hair, her breasts and her genitals, were covered. Even
the bottoms of her feet had not been missed.

Clarissa stared down at the paint-spattered earthen
floor, her nerves silently screaming. Only the calm presence of White Moon and her whispered reassurances kept
her from bolting out of the council house in a fit of panic.
When she'd expressed her willingness to become a Shawnee, she'd had no idea what that consent would entail.
But if this was the price of Wolf Heart's love, she would
endure it, Clarissa reminded herself. For him, she would
endure anything.

Abruptly the chanting ended. Clarissa waited in the
silence, trembling as she wondered what would happen
next. She did not have to wonder long. Like the sudden
bursting of a rock slide, all the women scrambled to their

feet and rushed toward her. Whooping and shrilling, they swarmed around her and began pushing her in a mass toward the door at the far end of the hall.

They were taking her outside. Painted, naked and blazing with humiliation. *They were taking her outside!*

Clarissa's hard-won composure nearly broke as they passed through the doorway and into the blinding sunlight. It was one thing to stand naked before a group of women. But before the entire village—this was too much to demand of her. "No!" she gasped, resisting for the first time. "I can't do this!"

"It will be all right," White Moon whispered, close to her ear. "See, the women will stay all around you. No man will see what he should not. This is one of the lessons you must learn today—that Shawnee women stand together and protect one another."

And so it was as the women's chief had said. Clarissa passed through the village, concealed in her nakedness by the throng of women who surrounded her. For a moment she glimpsed Wolf Heart's face above the crowd— both of them being taller than most Shawnee. In the brief meeting of their eyes, she read his concern, and she realized how much he had worried about her acceptance of this strange ritual.

Lifting her chin, she forced her paint-smeared features into a brave smile. His gaze softened with love, and in the next instant the swarm of women had swept her away from him, moving swiftly downhill toward the bank of the river.

They skirted the garden plots where corn, beans and squash sprouted in hills of rich river-silt. Clarissa could feel the earth under her feet growing damp, then wet. The women were in high spirits now. When one stately matron began to sing, the others joined in, matching their

steps to the chant as they marched Clarissa hip deep into
the chilly water. There, still laughing and chanting, they
began to scrub away the paint that covered her skin.

There was nothing gentle about the scrubbing. The
women used wadded grass, weeds, even sand to scour
every inch of her painted flesh. "We will scrub away all
the white in you!" the women's chief laughed as she
attacked Clarissa's back with a piece of woven rush mat-
ting. "What is left will be all Shawnee!"

Clarissa clenched her teeth against the sting of her
abraded skin, knowing it would disgrace her to show
pain. The women laughed and sang as they scrubbed,
taking so much time that it was all she could do to keep
from screaming, breaking loose from them, plunging out
of the river and running for the woods. Where were her
clothes? Ruined, to be sure. What on earth was she supposed to wear?

At last, mercifully, the torture ended. Clarissa was
dunked beneath the flowing water to remove the last
traces of the paint. Then, as the women whooped and
sang, she waded out of the river, as pink and raw as a
newborn baby.

The sun was warm but the river breeze still carried a
whisper of spring chill. By the time she reached the bank,
her teeth were chattering and her stinging flesh had puckered into goose bumps. She did not feel Shawnee. She
only felt sore and wet and cold. Even when White Moon
stepped forward with an enfolding blanket she could not
stop shivering.

The two young girls, Red Fawn and Laughing Bird
pressed close and began to comb the tangles from Clarissa's hair. From where she stood, bundled in the blanket, she could see Swan Feather sitting on a flat rock
above the level of the wetness, her gnarled brown hands

clutching a thick bundle. White Moon strode up the bank, took the bundle from her and brought it back to Clarissa.

"This is for you," she said, smiling. "Many hands helped in the making of it, even your own."

Puzzled, Clarissa unrolled the bundle, only to gasp in astonishment as it fell open in her hands to reveal a long fringed tunic of the softest white buckskin, decorated around the neck with an elegantly simple pattern worked in quills and tiny glass trade beads. There were leggings, as well, and a pair of beautiful new moccasins, exactly the size of her own feet.

She clutched the gift, overcome by its beauty and the generosity of the givers. Only then, as her fingers caressed the baby-soft buckskin, was she struck by something the women's chief had told her.

"Such fine work is beyond the skill of my hands," she said cautiously, not wishing to offend. "I took no part in making these things."

"Oh, but you are wrong!" White Moon's black eyes sparkled. "It was you who flensed and scraped the hides! You did the hardest work of all!"

Clarissa's throat hardened as she stared down at the exquisitely worked garments. Those deer hides! Those hateful, awful, smelly deer hides! If only she had known what they would become! Tears blurred her vision and, for a moment, she all but lost the power to speak.

"Put your new clothes on," White Moon said gently. "We need to finish this and get back to preparing the feast."

Laughing, the women helped Clarissa dress. The supple deerskin slipped over her body to hang lightly in place, giving her full freedom of movement—freedom to run, to ride, to work, to dance.

When everything was in place, they led her up the

bank to where Swan Feather sat. A reverent hush had
fallen over the group of women. This, Clarissa sensed,
would be the most important part of the ceremony, the
part that would make her fully Shawnee.

White Moon spoke. "Swan Feather, we have prepared
your daughter. Will you accept her?"

Swan Feather rose to her feet. Her shriveled brown
face betrayed no emotion. *My mother,* Clarissa thought,
and the very notion seemed unreal, like something from
a strange dream. She could scarcely remember her own
mother except that she had been delicate and pretty and
always smelled of rose water. How could it be possible
that this gruff, unkempt old woman had assumed her
place?

This old woman who claimed to love her?

Swan Feather's mouth worked. Then she cleared her
throat noisily and spat into the grass. "Does my daughter
have a name?" she asked.

"We have chosen her name together." White Moon
glanced at the matrons who stood on either side of her.
"Her hair is the color of the red fox's coat, and her movements are swift and graceful. Your daughter shall be
called Dancing Fox."

"*We-sah.* It is good." Swan Feather nodded curtly,
signifying her acceptance. Clarissa waited awkwardly,
wondering what to do next. Should she embrace the old
woman? Should she speak? Take her hand?

Silence hung in the air as the two of them, mother and
daughter, faced each other, Clarissa tense and expectant,
Swan Feather as impassive as a weathered gray stump.
Then, as if nothing of importance had happened, the old
woman turned aside. "The food will burn," she said.
"We should return to the cooking."

Chattering like a flock of blackbirds, the women swept

up the bank, all of them intent on returning to their work. No one chided Clarissa when she tarried on the riverbank, staring out at the roiling greenish water while she turned the new name over in her mind. *Dancing Fox.* She liked the graceful sound of it. Still it seemed a strange fit, like a new pair of slippers that pinched. If the truth be told, everything that had happened today seemed a strange fit.

She was a Shawnee now. Why didn't she feel Shawnee? What was wrong with her?

The morning breeze was cool on her damp skin. She clasped her arms across her breasts, her hand touching the beautiful quillwork on the deerskin tunic the women had made for her. Everything would be all right, she reassured herself. In time, the confusion would disappear. She would feel at home with these blunt-spoken, open-hearted people. She would be one of them. She would belong.

''So it's Dancing Fox now.'' Wolf Heart's voice, coming from behind her, sent a thrill of response through her body. She turned to see him striding down the bank, so tall and splendid that the very sight of him made her throat ache.

Only as he gathered her into his arms did she realize he had spoken to her not in English but in Shawnee.

For the space of a breath she stiffened against him. Then, resolving to let it pass, she lifted her face and surrendered, melting into him, pressing close until she was dizzy with desire. Here was belonging, all she could ever want.

He held her close for a long moment. Then, laughing, he eased her away from him. ''Behave yourself,'' he teased, ''you're liable to start a forest fire.''

''So?''

"Many people come here. Someone could be watching us."

"Would that be so bad?" She answered in Shawnee to please him. "I don't care if the whole world knows how much I want you!"

"Some things are best saved for when people are alone." He took her hand before she could pout, tugging her gently but firmly toward the path that trailed along the riverbank. Clarissa allowed him to lead her, but she felt her spirits darkening with each step. She had thought everything in her life would fall into place when she became Shawnee. But nothing was as she'd expected. Not even Wolf Heart.

They rounded a bend in the river where willows trailed graceful branches in the current, concealing the spot where they stood. Here, at last, he stopped, turned and gathered her into his arms again. She sank against him, feeling dispirited, needing refuge.

"So where is that forest fire now?" he teased, his lips nibbling a light trail along her hairline. "Has it burned out so soon?"

Clarissa shook her head, a storm of emotions churning inside her.

"What is it?" He curled a forefinger under her chin, forcing her to look up at him. His eyes were so blue they almost broke her heart. Biting back a little sob of frustration, she edged away from him until they were a step apart.

"Look at me," she demanded in English. "What do you see?"

His gaze swept over her, then his eyes narrowed beneath the black ridges of his brows. "I see beauty," he answered softly. "I see courage and love. And much as I would wish to deny it, I see unhappiness."

She stood her ground, resisting the urge to crumple into his arms again. "But do you see a Shawnee?" she pressed him. "Apart from the clothes, do you see a different person than the woman you saw yesterday?"

"Clarissa—" He broke off, then stared at her in dismay, realizing that his unwitting use of her Christian name had answered her question. Reaching out with both arms, he caught her shoulders and gathered her close again, cradling her against his chest. "Don't be so impatient with yourself," he murmured, his lips moving against her temple. "Today was only a beginning, like the birth and naming of a child. To grow, to learn, that will take time. Everyone understands that—everyone, it seems, but you. Swan Feather says—"

"You're patronizing me now!" She twisted away from him. "And Swan Feather has said nothing to me! Even after the ceremony, when she'd just become my mother, she simply stood there! Then she turned away and muttered something about getting back to the food! I was afraid I'd done something to offend her—"

"You've done nothing to offend anyone." His hands captured her shoulders yet again, turning her forcefully toward the riverbank this time so that she stood in the circle of his arms, her back not quite touching his chest. She stood in rigid silence, gazing out at the play of sunlight on the water, its brightness hurting her eyes.

"Shawnee are trained from birth not to show emotion," he said, speaking English now so she would understand every word. "It begins as a matter of survival— one crying baby can alert an enemy and bring on the death of a whole camp. As children grow, they learn that to show pain is weakness. A warrior does not flinch. A woman will bite on a stick of wood or a leather knife sheath to keep from crying out in childbirth—"

"But Shawnee laugh," Clarissa interrupted for the sake of argument. "I've certainly heard them."

"Yes, and they grieve, too, but at the proper time, in the proper way. And lovers embrace—that, too, you know—but only when they are alone, if they want to be well thought of. Private behavior in front of others shows disrespect."

Clarissa examined his words, her mind turning them like a curious pebble as she struggled to understand. "And Swan Feather?" she finally asked.

"As you come to know her, you'll learn that Swan Feather feels things deeply. But her way of showing what she feels—" He groped for the right choice of words. "It's the only way she knows."

Clarissa fingered her soft deerskin tunic, remembering the gift, remembering the lessons in the meadow, the infinite patience. Yes, she told herself, things would come right—*she* would come right—in time. She could not expect a simple scrubbing to make her into a Shawnee. But she could learn. For Wolf Heart's sake, she *would* learn.

"Tell me about the dance tonight," she said brightly, changing the subject. "I've never seen Shawnee dance. I take it they don't do jigs and reels?"

He laughed then, clearly relieved that the storm had passed. "We dance with our feet and our hearts," he said, "and the drums are more exciting than any fiddle music you ever heard."

"But what happens in the dance? Do you have partners? Do the men and women dance with each other?"

Again he laughed, softly this time, his breath tickling her hair. "After a fashion. The women dance in a circle, facing the fire. The men dance behind them, in a bigger circle. If a man takes a woman's hands, they dance together."

"Will you be dancing? Will I get to watch?"

"Watch!" His arms swung her around, hard against him. "You're not going to watch! You are Dancing Fox, and you're going to dance tonight like a proper Shawnee maiden!"

"I'm hardly any kind of maiden, let alone proper," she demurred, delighted by the rise of color in his cheeks. "Besides, I don't know how to dance!"

"They don't dance in Baltimore?" he teased.

"Not around a fire, and not to drums." She flung back her damp hair, feeling suddenly bold and reckless. "Teach me!" she demanded.

"It's easy!" He moved to one side of her and began a shuffling toe-heel motion, chanting under his breath to keep the rhythm. Clarissa followed him awkwardly, struggling to imitate the slight bend of the knee, the two-beat striking of the feet, thinking how splendidly savage he would look dancing in the darkness with firelight gleaming on his golden skin. Desire fluttered in the depths of her body as she brushed against him. Merciful heaven, how she wanted this man! If he so much as looked at her, she would melt like hot tallow!

"One more thing," he said, ignoring her sidelong glances. "And this is very important. The women dance holding scarves—White Moon will have one to give you. With the scarf, when a man takes your hands to dance, there are two ways you can dance with him."

"Two ways?" Clarissa gazed up at him, intrigued.

"If you hold his hands through the scarf, he will know that it is just a dance, nothing more."

"And the other way?" she asked, feeling the flutter in her body warm to a slow, licking flame.

A hint of color flared in his cheeks. "If you give him your bare hand, you are offering yourself for love."

"Offering myself for love!" She was teasing him now, enjoying it. "And what if I confused my signals with some bold Shawnee warrior? Will you come to my rescue, Wolf Heart?"

He scowled at her in mock reproach. "If you're foolish enough to think this is a joke, I won't be responsible for what happens."

Clarissa laughed and wriggled into his arms, pressing her face against his chest, savoring the aroma of his warm clean skin. "I like your way of dancing," she murmured, dizzy with wanting him. "Teach me more!"

Veiled by wispy clouds, the moon, home of Ko-komthena, lay above the stark filigree of the treetops. Its light deepened the woodland shadows and brushed the black expanse of the river with soft shimmers of gold. In the clearing where the great bonfire blazed, tiny orange sparks shot into the darkness, swirling upward with the smoke to lose themselves among the glittering stars.

From the ring of light around the fire came the sound of drums, chanting and laughter. The people had feasted on roast venison, stewed beans and fresh corn bread until they were sated. Now was the best time of all, the time for dancing.

Wolf Heart moved distractedly along the fringe of the men's circle, his feet keeping a semblance of rhythm as his eyes followed the blaze of Clarissa's hair. She was dancing with Cat Follower now, and even though the scarf covered her hands, the two of them seemed to be having far too much fun.

She had learned the simple dance steps well. Now she moved as easily as if she had been born to the rhythm. Dancing Fox. The name could not have suited her better. Her bouncing hair glowed like flame in the amber light of the bonfire. She held her small proud head high, laughing as she gripped the crimson scarf and matched her partner's steps, arching her back in a graceful curve that pressed the points of her small perfect breasts against the soft white buckskin. Even like this, watching her from a distance, Wolf Heart felt the surging swell of heat in his loins, and he knew he could not wait to have her again.

Dawn Star, Cat Follower's erstwhile love, danced past him, her bare hands exposed behind her. Her fingers wriggled enticingly, but when he showed no interest, she moved on. Clearly she was looking for a way to make Cat Follower jealous. But she could look elsewhere, Wolf Heart resolved. He had lost all desire for such game playing. Tomorrow he would bring Swan Feather enough beaver skins, blankets, tanned hides and cured deer meat to make her a rich woman by Shawnee standards. Then, before the day was out, he would take Dancing Fox before the shaman and marry her in the old way, the proper way, which many young couples no longer followed. Before the sun, the earth and all the people, he would make her his.

She and Cat Follower had separated now, and Clarissa was dancing alone. Wolf Heart's breath caught as she moved toward him, gazing into the bonfire, seemingly unaware of his presence. Her skin glowed like amber in the flickering light. Her eyes sparkled like the deep green stone he had seen long ago in a wealthy white woman's ring. She was the most beautiful thing he had ever known, and he ached with love, ached to give her the whole world.

The whole world.

Concern darkened his spirits as she danced toward him, immersed in the rhythm of the drums, a dreamy little smile on her face. What she had done today, she had

done for him, he knew. But what could he offer her in
return? How long would she be content with this life,
sleeping on the ground, wearing crude buckskin garments
and working her hands to raw blisters? And what of the
future? What of his terrible vision. Could he, even in the
spirit of love, ask this woman to share what lay ahead
for the Shawnee?

She edged closer, her image blurred by smoke as the
night wind shifted. For all her show of indifference, Wolf
Heart knew she saw only him in the blaze of firelight, as
he saw only her. Her slender hips swayed beneath the
deerskin tunic as she brushed lightly against him, inviting
him to dance.

He felt her bare hands in the darkness, felt them trem-
ble as he took them in his own, and then they were moving together, their bodies burning with need, the sound
of the drumbeats lost in the pulsing of their hearts.

Chapter Fourteen

With a swiftness that dazzled Clarissa's senses, spring ripened into the lushness of summer. The pink-white blossoms that had dotted the blackberry thickets shed their petals and swelled into hard green clumps that bobbed in the morning breeze. Herons reared their spindle-necked offspring on reedy islands in the river, keeping watchful eyes on the naked brown boys who speared fish in the shallows. In the village gardens, the waist-high corn was already sprouting silken green tassels.

On what she might have calculated to be a late June morning, Clarissa awoke to pewter light probing through chinks in the bark roof of the spacious new lodge the women had helped her build. Beside her, Wolf Heart was already awake. He lay propped on one elbow, his eyes gazing down at her, a curious smile playing at the corners of his mouth. Clarissa responded with a drowsy smile of her own, only to moan out loud as she remembered. This morning he would be leaving on a hunt with three other braves. He would be gone for many days—as long as a moon, perhaps, if game proved scarce.

"Do you really have to go?" She spoke her mind to him, as always.

"People need meat. Would you have them go hungry?"

She sighed in resignation and snuggled into the warmth of his body. Providing for the village was a never-ending task, and Wolf Heart could not bear to see any of his people in want. As long as there was need, he would be out on the woodland trails, refusing the comfort of his own warm fireside—and the woman who loved him—until all had been fed. Clarissa knew she would ache with longing every moment he was gone, but she could not help being proud of her man. He was the most skillful hunter in the village and the most generous provider.

His hand slid around her waist, easing her against him. "You have not been to the moon lodge," he murmured, causing her to draw back, startled by his perception. True, her moon was overdue, and for the past few days she had awakened with an odd queasiness in her stomach and a tingling tightness in her breasts. But she had scarcely begun to wonder herself.

"Has it happened so soon?" he asked, pulling her close again, his lips nuzzling her tousled hair.

"I don't know," she whispered, still dazed by his discovery. "How is it supposed to feel?"

"You're asking me? A man?" His chuckle warmed her, stirred her. "You should talk to Swan Feather."

"Would you be pleased if it were so?" She nestled closer pressing into the muscular length of his body.

"Pleased?" He rolled onto his back, laughing as he pulled her on top of him. "I would be the happiest man in the whole Shawnee nation!"

She felt his hardness beneath her and the pulsing heat of her own response. Instinctively her hips began to move against him. Then she hesitated, rising on her arms, suddenly cautious. "No one ever told me anything about having babies," she whispered. "Is it safe, now that I'm—"

His hungry kiss blocked her words as he pulled her down to him again. "Not that I have any experience in this," he muttered against her lips. "But I've heard enough talk among husbands to know that, if all is well, it should be safe now and for moons to come."

"Then…" An ecstatic whimper escaped Clarissa's throat as she arched above him and lowered herself onto the marbled shaft of his manhood. She could not keep him from going on the hunt, she knew. But at least he would be late in leaving.

By the time the sun was up, Wolf Heart had departed and Clarissa had slipped into the rhythm of work that filled her days when he was gone. By now she knew that rhythm well. She would rise at dawn to prepare the early meal of corn mush and cold venison. After leaving a portion outside the entrance to Swan Feather's lodge, she would hurry to the village gardens, in the rich bottomland near the river, to do her share of weeding and hoeing before the sun grew hot.

Other women would be working, as well, some with their babies and toddlers in tow, others with budding daughters. There would be laughter and good-natured gossip to ease the tedium of bending over the growing crops. Who was getting married? Who had missed her time in the moon lodge? How long would Dawn Star continue to sleep with Cat Follower despite their loud and continual squabbling? No subject was too risqué, no matter too personal for discussion while busy hands tended clumps of corn, beans and squash.

By the time the sun had cleared the treetops she would

be on her way back to Swan Feather's for more instruction in the art of healing. This, apart from the time she spent with Wolf Heart, was Clarissa's favorite part of the day. There seemed no end to the variety of herbs the old woman showed her, no end to their practical uses. Every answer opened the door to more questions. What was best for fever in a child? What was best for stopping a woman's blood after childbirth? When was the best time to harvest willow bark? She grasped hungrily at every new bit of learning the old woman offered.

The length of each lesson was coming to depend more and more on Swan Feather's dwindling strength. Clarissa could see her Shawnee mother shrinking before her eyes, a waning Kokomthena who poured out her wisdom with fearful urgency. The old *mekoche* woman's manner was as gruff as ever, her demands on Clarissa, if anything, even more insistent than before. But the shortness of time hung between them, a silent presence of which neither of them spoke.

Each day's lesson lasted until Swan Feather was exhausted. When her words began to falter, Clarissa would help her into her lodge and ease her onto her bed of deer and buffalo robes. While the old woman napped, she would hurry back to her own lodge, to the chores of sweeping the floor, tending the big round stew pot on the coals and dressing the hides that Wolf Heart had brought back from his last hunt. The flensing, scraping and tanning were familiar tasks by now, and she sometimes smiled at the memory of her early revulsion.

It was just as Wolf Heart had said, Clarissa told herself. Little by little, day by day, she was becoming more Shawnee.

Today, as she came over the rise of the bank, she could hear the chatter of the women as they hoed and weeded.

The sudden hush when they looked up and saw her was louder than a shout.

They had clearly been talking about her.

Color blazed in Clarissa's cheeks as she lifted her chin and stalked down the bank toward her section of the garden patch. Some of the women were tight cheeked with suppressed smiles. One young girl tittered out loud, only to be hushed by an elbow jab from her mother. Stung and bewildered, Clarissa hunched over and began jerking at a stubborn pokeweed. Until now she'd believed that she was liked and accepted by the village women. But what was she to think when they gossiped about her behind her back?

As so often happened, it was White Moon who elected to break the leaden silence. Striding between the corn rows, the women's chief stopped beside Clarissa, then swiftly bent and plied her stick to the obdurate root. "Do not judge us so badly, Dancing Fox," she said. "We were only rejoicing in your good fortune."

"My good fortune?" Clarissa staggered backward as the weed loosened its grip on the soil.

A smile dimpled White Moon's face. "Everyone knows you have not been to the moon lodge. We share your happiness."

Once more, color surged into Clarissa's cheeks. Had the choice been hers, she would have kept her secret for a time, holding it like a private treasure between herself and Wolf Heart, but there were no secrets here. For better or for worse, everyone shared.

White Moon turned back to her own work and Clarissa noticed the wistful glint in her ebony eyes. Only then did the realization strike her—White Moon, the chief's younger, second wife and a mother to the entire village, seemed to have no children of her own. Had her children

died or been stolen, or were they nothing more than long-
ings never conceived? Clarissa found herself burning
with a need to understand the sadness that glimmered
within this wise and gentle woman. The questions in her
mind were too painful to ask White Moon directly. But
Swan Feather would know the answers. Swan Feather
knew everything.

Clarissa finished her morning's work in the garden and
hurried up the bank in the direction of Swan Feather's
lodge. She was eager for today's lesson, eager for the
feel of dried herbs between her fingers and her foster
mother's gruff wisdom feeding her mind. She would tell
Swan Feather about the baby, she resolved as she
mounted the narrow trail. The news of a grandchild coming would gladden her weary old heart.

Ahead, through the trees, she could see the low dark
outline of the lodge. By now the old woman would be
up and around, finishing her breakfast, most likely, or
perhaps scraping one of the deerskins Wolf Heart had
brought her from his last hunt. Even when Clarissa protested that she had a daughter to care for her now and
had earned the right to rest, Swan Feather insisted on
doing a full day's measure of work—which was why it
suddenly struck Clarissa as strange that her lodge seemed
so quiet this morning.

A magpie squawked a harsh warning as Clarissa broke
into a run. There had to be a simple explanation, she
reassured herself, an obvious reason why there was no
activity about the place, not even a wisp of smoke curling
through the roof hole. There had to be a reason for it all,
her mind screamed, even as she saw the untouched bowl
of corn mush and venison where she had left it earlier.
The old woman was sleeping, or she had gone off to
relieve herself, or perhaps she wasn't feeling well.

But when Clarissa burst into the dim shadows of the lodge, she knew what she would find.

Swan Feather lay on her back, cradled in the skins Wolf Heart had given her as Clarissa's own bride-price. Her gnarled hands were curled into baby fists, her arms flung upward like a small child's. Her eyes were tightly closed—she might have been sleeping, in fact, were it not for the huge blowflies that buzzed unheeded around her face, settling now and then at the corners of her eyes and mouth, where traces of moisture still lingered. Swan Feather had hated flies.

Clarissa made an instinctive motion to brush them away. Then, as the truth sank home, she felt her knees give way beneath her, and she sank to the earthen floor of the lodge, her nerves screaming. The image of her father, lying in his open coffin in the parlor, flashed through her mind—the summer flies, the cloying fragrance of roses, and the deep, terrible sense of loss.

She clutched her heaving ribs, fighting the paroxysm of grief and shock that was threatening to sweep her out of control. She was the daughter—the healer now—and only by being strong could she honor the memory of the woman who had given her so much.

Her voice rose in the first keening notes of the Shawnee death song, but the effort was so strained, so unnatural in the dim, hollow space of the lodge, that her voice quavered and died in her throat. She knelt in silence, arms clasped around her rocking body. *Wolf Heart!* She needed him here, needed him now! Perhaps if she were to send a rider, a boy, on the fastest pony—

But she knew better than to call him back. The village needed meat, and there was nothing Wolf Heart could do here. Given the choice, he would choose to help the living, not the dead.

With one shaking hand, she reached out and tugged the edge of the soft deerskin robe over Swan Feather's tiny shriveled face. There had been no trace of open affection between the two of them. But Swan Feather had loved her. That much Clarissa knew with a certainty that shook her to the core of her soul.

A small convulsive hiccup escaped her throat, then another and another. Before she knew it, she was sobbing violently, her eyes streaming tears, her body jerking with the shock of emotions she had not even known she possessed.

She was still weeping when White Moon came and found her.

Swan Feather was dressed in her finest robes and buried at the edge of her beloved meadow, her head toward the setting sun. Nothing was left to mark the spot. By summer's end the meadow grass would cover the small mound of earth, and in the spring the wildflowers, nourished by the remains of her body, would bloom there in a glorious profusion of color.

Clarissa sat beside the grave after everyone else had gone back to the village, gazing out across the meadow. In the gathering twilight, she could almost fancy she saw Swan Feather's gnomelike figure striding through the tall grass, her silver-white hair streaming as she drew strength from sun and air.

What would she do now that the old woman was gone? Who would be her teacher? Her mother?

"Dancing Fox?" The voice behind her was hesitant, almost diffident. She turned to see a woman—a widow, still young—who lived at the far end of the village. Clarissa had met her, but did not know her well. Now she was crouched in the grass a few paces away, her eyes wet and imploring.

"It's my little girl, Dancing Fox. I didn't want to disturb your mourning, but she's been down with a fever since yesterday. I've tried to cool her, but the fever is getting worse, and I'm afraid—"

Clarissa's throat contracted as she realized what the woman wanted. "You think *I* can treat your little girl?" she whispered.

"You are the only *mekoche* in the village. Please."

"But I'm only learning! I know so little—"

"You are Swan Feather's daughter! *Please,* there's no one else!"

Clarissa hesitated, but only for a heartbeat. Swan Feather had passed on her gift for a purpose. Whether she felt prepared or not, a child needed her help and she could not refuse.

"Take me to your little girl," she declared, struggling to stand on numb legs that had been folded beneath her for too long. "I'll do whatever I can."

Wolf Heart crouched on his haunches, staring absently into the darkening embers of the campfire. The moon was high, and his companions had already rolled themselves into their blankets for the night. But try as he might, he could not sleep.

"Look at him!" Cat Follower teased from the edge of the dwindling firelight. "When a man can't get to sleep without a roll in the blankets with his bride, that's a bad sign. I tell you, marriage spoils you for anything worthwhile, like war or hunting! Me, I welcome the chance to get away from the women! They're always chasing after me! It wears me out, fighting them off!"

"Don't you ever stop talking?" Swift Eagle grumbled

from his bed at the base of a stump. "Leave Wolf Heart
alone! At least he isn't keeping me awake with his jabbering!"

Wolf Heart ignored the good-natured banter of his two
friends. His thoughts were with Clarissa and his last
glimpse of her, standing outside their lodge, waving as
he rode out of sight. He had left her before, but something about this time had torn at him. Maybe it was the
idea that she might be carrying his child. Or maybe it
was something deeper, a dark premonition that he was at
a loss to explain.

As he watched the slow dying of the coals, the cry of
a wolf, faint with distance, echoed through the forest.
Was it a message from his *unsoma?* Or was it simply
what it seemed—a wolf pack out for a night's hunting?
Wolf Heart's restless fingers picked up a stone and flung
it into the coals, sending up a shower of fiery sparks. He
was being foolish, he lectured himself. Clarissa was
strong and self-reliant, and if anything did go wrong, she
had a village full of friends who would help and protect
her.

But she had looked so solitary standing there beside
the lodge. In all the times he had left her to hunt, her
vulnerability had never struck him so deeply. Even now,
his instincts were pulling at him, urging him to mount
his horse and gallop through the darkness to her side.

But the people needed meat and skins, he reminded
himself sharply. He could not shirk his duty on a whim
of the heart. If all went well, mere days from now the
hunting party would ride into the village, whooping and
singing, the ponies laden with salted game. Clarissa—his
Dancing Fox—would come running out to meet him,
laughing with joy as she flung herself into his arms. The
night to come would be sweeter than a hundred heavens,

and he would laugh at himself for having been so worried.

The wolf calls, one close, another farther away, echoed through the darkness. Yes, they were hunting, Wolf Heart reassured himself. They were speaking to each other, not to him. Here and in the village, all was well.

All the same, he sat by the fire far into the night, watching the coals fade from orange to crimson to gray and listening to the mournful, distant keening of the wolf pack, too restless for sleep.

The widow's little girl was five or six years old, Clarissa judged, but small and thin for her age. She lay uncovered on a bed of ragged skins, whimpering with fever, showing little awareness of the white woman bending over her.

Clarissa's knees went watery as she raised the child's tattered buckskin tunic and saw the fine pinkish rash that covered her small torso.

"Where has this child been?" she asked, forcing the words out of her fear-choked throat.

The pupils of the mother's weary eyes flickered. "Nowhere, Dancing Fox. Only in the village."

"And have any strangers been here?" Clarissa demanded, her pulse racing. "Anyone from outside our village?"

"No!" The woman's hand crept nervously to her throat revealing, at the wrist, a bracelet of cheap gaudy trade beads, so new that the string showing between them was still white.

"Where did you get that?" She seized the woman's arm, jerking the bracelet into full view.

"From—my husband!" The widow was quaking now.

"Yes, from him, a very long time ago! I wear it always—"

"You're lying!" Clarissa flung the woman away from
her, causing the little girl to cry out in fear from her bed.
The plaintive sound stopped her fury like a wall. Anger
would accomplish nothing here, least of all in the undoing of what had already come to pass.

The woman crouched at her daughter's side, cringing
as if she were expecting to be struck. The terror in her
eyes drained Clarissa of all remaining anger. Her breath
hissed outward in a long exhalation. "I'll do everything
I can to help," she said wearily. "But you'll have to tell
me where you've been and who you were with. It could
mean life or death to this village."

The woman's thin body sagged. "There's a place on
the river, two days by canoe, where the French trappers
meet to camp and drink. I took my daughter and went
there before the last dark moon. There were things I
needed, Dancing Fox, and no other way to get them. If
you were alone in this place, with a child to raise and no
man to provide, you would understand."

Clarissa gazed down at the feverish little girl, feeling
light-headed in the warm darkness of the lodge. "But the
village provides for everyone," she protested, thinking
that right now her man was out hunting so that people
like this woman and her child would have enough to eat.
"Surely you do not have to do this thing."

The answering pain in the woman's eyes shattered her
complacency. "We do not starve," she said, reaching out
to clasp her daughter's small hot hand. "But there are
other things, nice things, that must be earned or given.
For me, there is no other way to get them."

The bracelet, a tawdry clump of cheap glass and string,
caught a beam of fading sunlight, the broken reflection

scattering rainbows over the drab interior of the lodge. The little girl's eyes followed the dancing colors, dazzled even in her feverish condition.

"At the camp," Clarissa said, forcing each word, "was anyone sick?"

"A boy—maybe twelve winters." The woman coughed nervously. "But he was only a little bit sick, not like this. One of the men gave him some money to watch my daughter while I—"

"Never mind." With growing dread Clarissa studied the rash on the bony little body. Measles, she surmised grimly. She had easily survived the illness herself at the age of eight. But she'd heard enough talk around Fort Pitt to know that Indians had no resistance to white men's diseases. Exposed, they died by the score, sometimes by the hundreds.

Fighting panic now, she struggled to remember what she knew about measles, which was not a great deal. Quarantine was essential to keep the illness from spreading. For those who did get sick, willow bark tea might help the fever. But would it be enough? Dear heaven, what could she do to save these precious people?

Ordering the woman to raise her tunic, she examined the prominent ribs, the stretch-marked belly. There was no sign of a rash. Apparently the woman had not been exposed at the camp. But she had been with her child and would likely come down with measles later.

"Which children has your daughter played with?" she asked, willing herself to speak calmly.

"Who can say? All the little ones, they run together like a flock of young quail. Two of them came to see her this morning, but she was too sick to play with them."

"And anyone else? Any adults besides you?" She was ice now, afraid to feel any emotion too deeply.

"No. No one else. I—" The woman's eyes widened as she stared past Clarissa, toward the entrance of the lodge.

Clarissa turned to gaze in horror at the commanding presence who had just stepped inside.

"I hear there is sickness in our village," said Hunts-at-Night. "What can I do to help?"

On the seventeenth day of the hunt, Cat Follower was mauled by an angry sow bear.

It happened so fast that Wolf Heart scarcely had time to react. They'd been walking along a forest path, on the trail of a wounded buck, when the she-bear exploded out of the brambles. Wolf Heart glimpsed the two cubs behind her before she struck his friend, her massive weight carrying him to the ground.

Grunting like a giant pig, the bear swung its huge head, maneuvering for a death-bite on Cat Follower's thrashing body. With the two of them at such close quarters, Wolf Heart could not risk a shot with the musket. The sound of his father's death screams echoed in his memory as he seized the gun barrel and, swinging the stock like a club, waded into the melee.

His first blow struck the bear across the face—the only vulnerable part of the huge creature. Stunned, it raised its massive head and bawled with rage.

"Ha!" Wolf Heart swung the musket again, hoping to distract the monster long enough for Cat Follower to roll out of the way, but the bear stood its ground, dropping its head again to worry its victim's shredded, bleeding shoulder. The blow struck the back of its skull and glanced harmlessly away.

In a fury of desperation Wolf Heart flung his full strength into another blow. This one cracked across the she-bear's nose, and this time, with an ugly snarl, the angry animal abandoned Cat Follower and lunged after him. Wolf Heart backed into the trees, jabbing with the musket to keep the beast at bay, but he knew it would do little good. He had seconds, no more, before the bear tired of the game and moved in for the kill.

Swift Eagle had been a few moments behind them with the horses. With luck, he would hear the commotion and come running. Otherwise, Wolf Heart knew his only chance would be to get the musket into firing position—impossible now, with the animal so close.

The bear lunged again. Dodging away, Wolf Heart stumbled over a root behind him, lost his balance and pitched backward. With an angry bellow, the beast came at him. As he braced the musket against the onslaught of slavering teeth, Clarissa's image flickered through his mind. The thought of never seeing her again, never holding their child in his arms, was more terrible than death itself.

With the miasma of the she-bear's breath all but smothering him, he shoved the musket sideways between the huge jaws and hung on. He heard the stock splintering, felt the rigid structure of the weapon giving way as his strength began to ebb. He braced his arms, determined to fight to the end.

The sudden roar of Swift Eagle's musket was so close it almost shattered his eardrums. Incredibly the shot missed, but the bear, startled by the sound, reared onto its hind legs and staggered backward. With its two cubs bawling from the nearby thicket, it hesitated, then swung around on its hindquarters, dropped to all fours and lumbered off into the woods.

Shaken and scratched, Wolf Heart scrambled to his feet and raced back to his fallen friend. Cat Follower was badly chewed around the arms and shoulders. His wounds were streaming blood, but he forced a grin as Wolf Heart eased him onto his back. "Now what am I going to do?" he joked through clenched teeth. "When I was just plain ugly, it was all I could do to fight off the women. With these scars, I'll be downright hideous! They won't be able to leave me alone! I'll never get any sleep!"

"Stop yapping, you fool!" Wolf Heart swallowed the tightness in his throat as he packed the awful wounds with moss. Cat Follower had been lucky. If the bites could be kept free of infection, he would live.

"And you!" Cat Follower taunted the chagrined Swift Eagle. "If you'd been a better shot, we'd be skinning bear right now! Maybe you need a pair of the white man's spectacles, eh?"

"It's a lucky thing we're not skinning you!" Wolf Heart growled as he wrapped Cat Follower's mangled arm. "This hunt is over. We're taking you back to the village."

"Any excuse to get you home to your red-tailed fox!"

"Next I'll bandage your mouth." Wolf Heart's gruff response masked a rush of longing to sleep in his own lodge once more with Clarissa in his arms. The hunting had not been as good as he'd hoped—white settlers were encroaching on the hunting grounds, and game was less plentiful than he remembered. For the Shawnee and their red brothers, hardship loomed beyond the horizon. That much Wolf Heart knew, and suddenly all he wanted was to enjoy the good years that remained—to love his woman, to know the joy of their children. He did not want to waste another day of his life away from her.

Swift Eagle, silent and practical, was already cutting saplings to rig a travois. Cat Follower was too weak to ride. For the next few days, at least, his bed would have to be dragged behind the horse, a painstakingly slow means of travel. The path would be long and difficult. But it was time—long past time for Wolf Heart. They were going home.

Clarissa dipped the bowl of her hands into the pond, scooped up the clear water and splashed it on her face. The shock of the cold startled her, jarring her fully awake. There, she thought. Maybe that would hold her for a few hours.

Slowly she stood up, stretching her weary back. How long had it been since she'd taken the time for a good meal or a full night's sleep? But what did food and sleep matter, when three children and seven adults had died of measles in the past fortnight, and a score of others were still down with sickness?

Only the strict quarantine she'd imposed had kept a full-scale epidemic from sweeping through the village. Perhaps the worst was over. There had been no new cases in seven days. But the encouraging news would not save those who had gone. It would not save the mother and child who had carried the illness from the French camp to the Shawnee. It would not save Hunts-at-Night, nor would it ease the savage grief of White Moon, who had wailed like an animal, ripped her clothes and smeared her face and body with ashes. For the year of mourning to come, White Moon would not comb her hair, wash or even laugh.

Bending over again, Clarissa pooled a little water in her palm, lifted her hand and took a tentative sip. The pregnancy that had been a question on the day of Wolf Heart's departure was now a certainty. Her nausea-racked stomach could not seem to keep anything down. Even the taste of water set off the queasiness. In that faraway other world, she might have rested, might have made excuses for her "delicate condition." But not here. With so many people sick and needing her care, delicacy was not one of her choices.

She stood for a moment gazing down at her own haggard reflection in the pool. Which child would die today? she wondered. Which pretty young girl? Which brave? Which mother? In less than the cycle of a moon, she had seen a lifetime's worth of death. *No more,* she prayed silently. *Please, God, no more.*

She could not recall exactly when she'd begun to think about Baltimore. Maybe it had been in one of the dreams that clouded her rare moments of sleep. Maybe it had been the night the widow's little girl had died, and she had caught herself wondering what it would be like to stand helplessly by and watch her own child slip from life. Maybe it had been the moment of White Moon's bereavement, hearing the wails of unbridled grief, all the while knowing her own man lived in constant danger and she could easily be next.

Whatever the cause, when the world around her became too harsh to bear, Clarissa had found herself retreating into a rose-tinted fantasy that became more familiar each time she entered it. The cozy brick home, built on the land provided by her dowry. The polished hardwood table with its white linen cloth, laden with a breakfast of cured ham, eggs, porridge and flaky biscuits with butter and strawberry preserves. The children flocking around their parents—little girls showing off the samplers they'd embroidered, serious little boys in knee breeches, dressed for school. Herself, presiding over breakfast in a gown of simple blue muslin, hair twisted and pinned sedately on her head. Her tall handsome husband—Seth Johnson—dressed for a day of business in town, gazing at her across the table, reluctant to leave this haven of love even for a few hours. All of them together. All of them safe.

It was a beautiful dream, made all the more tantalizing by the notion that it might come true.

"Dancing Fox!" The breathless voice of a young boy startled her out of her reverie. Was it another person down with fever? Some other poor soul dying? Clarissa turned around and braced herself for more bad news.

The youth, one of a handful of children who had come down with measles and survived, was grinning at her, ribs heaving from the long run. "The hunters are coming back!" he gasped. "Spotted Wings and I saw them from the top of the far bluff!"

"Wolf Heart!" Clarissa felt her soul stir and flutter to life, then freeze as a new fear struck her. "He's with them? He's all right?"

"The hunters were too far away for us to see their faces. But there were three men, two of them riding and one lying on a bed that was dragging behind the horse—"

"No!" Her cry cut off the boy's words as she spun away and raced up the zigzag trail toward the village. *Please,* she prayed as she ran. *Please let him be all right!*

Chapter Fifteen

They lay together in the darkness of the lodge, both of them silent after a raw and hungry lovemaking. Wolf Heart cradled Clarissa's gaunt trembling body as gently as a child might hold a broken doll. Her bones were sharp and hard beneath her skin. She clutched him fiercely, as if she were afraid he might at any moment get up and leave her again.

She had saved the village, his Dancing Fox. That much White Moon had told him. But the terrible days had taken their toll. She looked like a ghost spirit, the flesh melted from her body, her eyes haunted, red-rimmed holes in her chalky face.

What had he led her to expect when he'd asked her to share his life? For all her spirit and passion, Clarissa was a white woman. When she'd caught sight of Cat Follower's wounds and his own scratches, she had turned so pale that he had feared she was going to faint. What must it have been like for her in his absence, with death and illness all around her?

And what if he had died beneath the she-bear? What would Clarissa have done if he hadn't returned at all?

She stirred restlessly against him, and he brushed a

path of kisses across her hairline. "I thought you might be asleep," he lied, knowing better.

"I have something to say." She spoke in English, her body suddenly taut in his arms. "It came to me while you were gone, and now I can't stop thinking about it."

"Then you'd best get it said," he answered softly, a premonition of dread quickening his pulse. He had known something was coming. Known it and feared it.

She tensed, and he felt the strain in her, the frayed nerves, the grief and shock, the bone-deep weariness. "I can't do this," she whispered. "I tried because I loved you so much, but it isn't working. The thought of raising our child here, amid so much death and danger—"

"Clarissa—"

"No, hear me out." She had drawn away from him and lay staring up at him in the darkness. "I want us both to go back to Baltimore," she said in a flat voice. "I have land there, and money enough to get us started. We could have a good life, a safe life for our family."

Wolf Heart pressed his lips tightly together to keep from crying out. If Clarissa wanted to go back to the white world he knew he would not stand in her way. But how could he abandon his own people, even for the woman he loved more than life?

"You could learn a trade," she persisted in the face of his silence. "Or Junius could find a place for you in the cloth business. You're decently educated and a fine figure of a man. Why, there's nothing you couldn't do or be if you put your mind to it!"

Wolf Heart rolled onto his back beside her and stared up at the shadowy ceiling of the lodge. He knew she was waiting for an answer. But how could he crush her spirit with the truth? How could he tell her, now that she had spoken her mind, about his conversation with White Moon that very morning?

He had entered her lodge to pay his respects to the chief's widow, intending to stay for no more than a moment. But she had reached out with one ash-smeared hand, taken his wrist and pulled him down to sit beside her. The whites of her dark eyes were laced with red, her handsome face streaked with dirt and tears. "I won't keep you for long," she had said. "You need to be with Dancing Fox. This terrible time has cost her much strength."

"Yes, I know," he had answered softly. "I have seen her."

"That strength saved our village. If she had not fought to keep the sick ones apart from the rest of us, many more would have died."

"Your husband was a great chief," Wolf Heart had said.

"Yes. Yes, I know." White Moon had stared into the blackened empty fire pit for what seemed to be a long time. "He loved his people, Wolf Heart. You more than any of them."

Wolf Heart had shot her a startled glance. Hunts-at-Night had treated all his braves equally. That the chief had held him in any special regard came as a surprise.

"My husband left no living sons," White Moon had said, her words followed by a pause that left Wolf Heart wondering what would come next. "But I know what his wish would be, because he spoke of it often over the past few moons. He must have sensed that his time would be short. In any case, he made it very clear to me."

Wolf Heart had waited in the unsettling silence. Among the Shawnee the position of war chief was earned by leadership and valor in battle. But the higher position of peace chief, which Hunts-at-Night had held, customarily passed from father to son.

"It was my husband's wish that I adopt you in his name," White Moon had said, letting the words and all they implied hang like smoke in the air between them.

"The honor is too great," he had responded, breaking the silence at last. "There are others who are wiser and more worthy."

"Would you question the wisdom of Hunts-at-Night?" Her gaze had sharpened through the screen of ash-coated hair that hung in her face. "As more and more white people move into our territory, we need a leader whose mind understands their ways and yet whose heart is fully Shawnee. Who else can better see to the survival of our people?"

Wolf Heart had known better than to challenge her words. "As my mother, you could still be women's chief," he had said, thinking of Clarissa and the strain that would be placed on her with a child on the way.

"Perhaps." The shadow of a smile had flickered across White Moon's generous mouth. "But don't underestimate Dancing Fox. She has proven herself to be strong and intelligent and full of compassion for others. She would make a superb women's chief."

With White Moon's words still echoing in his mind, Wolf Heart had walked slowly back through the village to his own lodge. With the measles epidemic abating, people were venturing outdoors again. He heard the sounds of work around him—the rhythmic blows of a hatchet splitting wood, the familiar scrape of sharpened bone on stretched hide. He heard sounds of greeting, even laughter. But on this sunny summer day there was sorrow, and everywhere he looked, there was need.

With each step, the weight of Wolf Heart's responsibility grew heavier. How could he lead these people? How could he care for them in the trying years ahead? Yet, how could he look into their faces and turn away?

He had meant to break the news to Clarissa at once, but as he approached the lodge he was struck by the sight of her, slumped in the doorway, overcome by exhaustion and despair. Clearly she had not seen him. Her eyes were fixed on the ground, their expression so detached, so vacant, that for a moment he wondered if she was ill. As he had hurried toward her, she had glanced up and seen him. Her face had animated at once—too swiftly, too brightly, and suddenly Wolf Heart had realized where his wife's thoughts had been.

Suddenly he had felt his world begin to crumble.

"Are you certain this is what you want?" he asked her as they lay together in the darkness.

"Very certain."

Her answer tore at him. "So certain that you would go back to Baltimore without me?"

"No!" She stared up at him in horror. "Wolf Heart—Seth—I could never leave you! You know that!"

"Then couldn't you learn to be happy here?"

She sighed as she uncurled from his side and stretched out alongside him, gazing up into the darkness. "Once I thought so," she said in a small sad voice. "But when I think of our child—our *children,* heaven willing—growing up in this wilderness, no schooling, no opportunities to make anything of themselves. When I think of them dying young, of disease or animal attacks, or even in a war against their own kind, then I know we have no responsible choice except to go back to Baltimore where it's safe. I can't stay here and watch our children turn into...into little savages!"

Shocked by her vehemence, Wolf Heart had to force

himself to speak. "The white world has its own kind of savages," he said.

"Don't be so stubborn!" she hissed. "You're white—as white as I am! As white as our children will be! I can't go through life pretending to be something I'm not, and neither can you!"

Rigid with anguish, Wolf Heart lay beside her, fighting the urge to seize her in his arms again and love her until all her resistance was gone. It wouldn't work, he reminded himself. If Clarissa was unhappy in his chosen world, not even love would be enough to change her mind.

"You're exhausted," he said, grasping at the last hope. "We can talk about this later, after you've had a chance to rest. By then, things might not look so bad."

"No!" She shook her head adamantly. "I've had plenty of time to think about this, and I'm not going to change my mind! I love you..." She paused and he heard the slight catch in her voice, the jerk of her throat. "I love you more than I can say, but I can't live in constant fear for our children's lives! I can't and I won't—and if you have any sort of conscience, you won't, either!"

Wolf Heart lay silent beside her, not trusting himself to answer. Where did his conscience lie? His loyalty? How could he force Clarissa to live where she was fearful and unhappy? How could he turn his back on his people in their time of need?

The answer, when it came, was as bitter as a blast of icy winter wind. Yet as it struck him, Wolf Heart knew at once that he had no other choice. Clarissa belonged in her own world. He belonged with his people. And if the pain of what he had to do was like cutting out his own heart, so be it.

"What are you thinking?" She had risen up on one

elbow and was gazing at him, her moss-green eyes soft in the darkness. He should have known better than to take her prisoner, then fall in love with her. He should have known that in the end it would come to this.

He drew a deep, anguished breath and slowly released it. ''Get your things ready,'' he said. ''We'll be leaving for Fort Pitt in the morning.''

Clarissa chattered brightly as they rode single file along the wooded trail that paralleled the Ohio River, carrying on a one-sided conversation that filled the void of Wolf Heart's morose silence. ''We won't have to live with Junius, of course,'' she was saying. ''Between what you can earn and the interest on my dowry money, we should be able to rent a small place in town until our house is finished. And that shouldn't take the workmen too long, should it? Surely we won't need more than four or five rooms, including the kitchen. I would so like to be settled before the baby comes!''

Wolf Heart rode ahead of her, barely nodding in reply. Why had he agreed so readily to her plan? She had expected arguments, outrage, even anger. Anything but this disturbingly silent acquiescence.

Bobbing lightly on the improvised saddle, she studied his splendid back—the erect spine, the broad, bare, muscular shoulders, the glossy raven-black mane of hair that streamed down his back. The silver studs in his ears glittered in the sunlight, and he had twisted a single eagle feather into his scalp lock. He looked every inch a defiant Shawnee warrior.

A warrior on his way to becoming a white man.

The irony struck her like a slap as he paused to guide the horses around a fallen tree. She had never asked him whether he thought he could be happy in Baltimore. She had never asked him how he felt about living in a fine brick house, working at a trade and never seeing his Shawnee friends again. She had simply demanded that he take her home and he had agreed with a readiness that startled her.

Ever the considerate husband, he had chosen the gentlest of his ponies for her and padded its back with blankets to give her an easy ride. But his gaze had flickered away as he took her arm to help her mount. Why? she wondered now. What could he be thinking?

Under different circumstances, she would have asked him. It was not like her to hold back anything, including questions. But now, as she studied the proud, rigid line of his back, Clarissa sensed that she would be wise to hold her tongue. Wolf Heart was headed in the right direction. She would be foolish to say anything that might turn him aside.

Sooner or later everything would be all right, she reassured herself. She would *make* it all right. Once they were safely back in Baltimore, she would devote her life to making him exquisitely happy. She would be the perfect wife, the perfect mother! Seth Johnson would never be sorry he had left the Shawnee!

They rode until it became too dark to see the trail. By then Clarissa was so weary she could barely stay on the horse. Wolf Heart had no sooner arranged their blankets on a soft bed of leaves than she collapsed there, too exhausted even to eat. Within seconds she was fast asleep.

The next day passed in a similar manner, and much of the day after. Wolf Heart's silence deepened as they neared the fort. When they passed the careless remains of white men's camps along the trail, Clarissa could sense the tension in him. She could see the suppressed anger in the hardening of his mouth and the rigid set of his shoulders. He seemed almost to bristle, snarling under his breath like a wild animal set down in a place where it had no wish to be. Still he made no suggestion that they turn back. He would come around, she told herself. As Seth Johnson, he had lived the first eleven years of his life in the white world. He remembered the language, the customs, the manners. Given time, he would adapt and thrive.

On the third day, with late afternoon heat blanketing the land, they came over a low rise. Wolf Heart halted his mount on the crest and waited in silence for Clarissa to come alongside. Sensing what lay ahead but scarcely daring to believe it, she nudged her pony up the slope.

Wolf Heart did not look at her as she reached his side. He was staring upriver, his face in profile, his mouth set in a taut line. Shading her eyes with her hand, Clarissa followed the direction of his gaze.

Far ahead, through the blue haze of sunlight, she could make out the place where the gleaming Ohio forked like the tongue of a great serpent to make the Monongahela and the Allegheny. At the confluence of the two rivers, dark against the summer green of the landscape, rose the stockaded walls and ramshackle environs of Fort Pitt.

Stifling an exclamation of relief, she glanced at Wolf Heart. He was too quiet, she thought, too grim. This was not an easy thing he was doing for her sake. She would need to remember that in the difficult days ahead.

"Are you ready?" she asked softly.

He nodded, scarcely looking at her as he urged his mount to a walk. Was he angry? Worried? She did not dare press him until they had reached the safety of the fort.

They were, perhaps, within a mile of the settlement when he halted once more in the shelter of a hickory grove. "You go on ahead," he said, motioning her forward. "With your red hair, no one on the parapet will mistake you for a Shawnee. But with me along, one of the guards or some nervous citizen might decide to shoot first and ask questions later. I don't want to take a chance on either of us being hit by a musket ball."

Clarissa stared at him. "But we were going in together!" she protested. "No one is going to shoot at you! Just take that feather out of your hair and stay close to me!"

"No, it's safer this way. Trust me." He twisted the feather out of his scalp lock and dropped it carelessly to the ground. Then he swung off his horse, caught the reins and looped them over a stump, a clear indication that he meant to go nowhere. "You ride in alone and ask for your aunt and uncle. Once you've found them, you can tell them the whole story. Then your uncle can send an armed escort to bring me in. That way there'll be no trouble." His mouth smiled, but not his eyes. "Go on, now. I'll be fine."

Clarissa edged her pony forward, then hesitated, still uncertain. He was right, she told herself. There could be people in the fort or the town who hated Indians so much that they wouldn't hesitate to fire at one on sight. And even with the feather gone, with his sun-bronzed skin, flowing black hair and buckskin breeches, Wolf Heart looked more Shawnee than white.

She hadn't come this far to see him shot, reason argued. Caution was the wiser course here. But the very thought of parting from him now, even for such a short span of time, seemed more than her soul could bear.

"Go on," he urged her gently. "You'll see. It's best this way."

Clarissa gulped back her fear as she urged the pony

forward to the edge of the trees. There was no reason to believe anything would go wrong, she reassured herself. An hour from now, sooner, perhaps, she and her husband would be sitting at Aunt Margaret's table, enjoying cold cider from the spring house and contemplating the start of their new life together.

"Clarissa."

She glanced back over her shoulder at the sound of his voice. He was standing where she had left him, one hand toying restlessly with a lock of his horse's mane.

"I love you." The words were little more than a whisper.

"And I love you." Suddenly it was all she could do to keep from flinging herself off the pony, running to his arms and ending this foolishness once and for all. She didn't have to go back to Baltimore! As long as Wolf Heart was by her side, she could be happy anywhere on earth!

But she was being foolish now. She and Wolf Heart were white. Their unborn child was white. What they were about to do was only right and fitting.

Summoning her courage, she nudged the pony to a trot and forced herself to look ahead to the fork of the rivers where the walls of the stockade rose dark above the shimmering landscape. She fixed her eyes on the faint white speck of the Union Jack and told herself once more that everything would be all right.

Wolf Heart stood in the trees and watched his love grow small with distance. Only when her bright hair was no more than a speck of fire against the green did he turn and mount his horse. This was the only way, he told himself for perhaps the hundredth time. Clarissa belonged with her own people. He belonged with his. Perhaps in time she would understand and forgive him.

His throat tightened as he paused for one last moment, gazing toward the fort where she had already disappeared.

"Tanakia," he whispered, touching his heart. Goodbye.

Then, before he could weaken and change his mind, he wheeled the horse and galloped west.

Chapter Sixteen

"Slow down, child! You're not making any sense!" Clarissa's uncle, Colonel Benjamin Hancock, scowled at her over the rims of his spectacles. "You say you've been with the Shawnee, you have a husband, and he's out there on the woods? Good Lord, girl, are you saying he's an Indian?"

"Leave her alone, Benjamin!" Aunt Margaret's arm tightened protectively around Clarissa's shoulders. "Can't you imagine what she's been through with those savages? The things they do to women?"

"Please!" Clarissa tore herself away from her aunt's embrace and flung herself toward her uncle. "My husband is a white man! His name is Seth Johnson! But he was with the Shawnee for so long he's afraid of being mistaken for one of them! Send someone out to protect him! That's all I ask!"

The colonel sighed. "All in good time, my dear. But first we have to get some food down you and get you to bed. You don't look well."

"Please!" Clarissa was beside herself, and the smell of roasting pig from the kitchen was making her nauseous. "He's not far, but someone has to go now!"

"Oh, very well." The colonel removed his spectacles and rubbed his prominent hooked nose. "I'll order a detail out. But you may as well know the men won't like it. There've been some nasty rumors of Indian trouble lately—soldiers being led into ambush and such. If they suspect a trap—"

"For heaven's sake, Benjamin, just do as the poor girl asks!" Aunt Margaret snapped. "I'll take care of her. She looks as if she's about to—"

The rest of her words were lost in the sickening black swirl that flooded Clarissa's senses. The floor opened up into a yawning hole and Clarissa pitched into it, spiraling down, down until there was nothing left for her to see, hear or feel.

Clarissa awakened in her aunt's bed, surrounded by the scent and crackle of fresh linen sheets. A frantically exploring hand revealed that she was wearing a flannel nightdress, buttoned up to the top of her throat. The dimly lit room was stifling.

"You're awake! Thank goodness!" Aunt Margaret bustled in carrying a tray with a small china teapot and matching cup and saucer. "How do you feel, dear?"

"I—I don't know!" Clarissa muttered, still dazed. "My dress—"

"That dirty buckskin rag? I told Molly to bury it in the yard. The clothes you brought with you for your visit are still here in your trunk. But something tells me you won't be wearing them for long." She sat down on the side of the bed. "Clarissa, why didn't you tell us you were with child?"

"There wasn't exactly time." Her eyes closed wearily, then shot open. She sat bolt upright, her gaze darting frantically around the small bedroom. "My husband! Where is he?"

"Shh!" Her aunt pressed a firm hand to Clarissa's chest. "Lie back. Too much excitement isn't good for a woman in your condition."

"Where is he? I want to see him!"

A long shadow, cast by the light from the doorway, fell across the bed. For an instant Clarissa's heart leaped, but when she looked up it was her uncle she saw.

"My men combed the woods where you said your husband was waiting," he said. "They never found a soul. He's gone—if he was ever there to begin with." His eyes narrowed skeptically as Clarissa stared at him open-mouthed, too dumbfounded to speak.

"They did find one thing," he continued, ignoring her obvious distress. "Does this look at all familiar?" He drew an object from behind his back and held it out for her to examine. Clarissa felt her heart drop.

It was a slim gray eagle feather—the same feather she had asked Wolf Heart to take from his hair that very afternoon.

"Give it to me!" She snatched the feather from her uncle's hand and clutched it to her body, quivering with anguish. It all made sense now—Wolf Heart's willingness to come back to the fort with her; his withdrawn silence on the way; his insistence, finally, that she go in ahead of him. How could she not have seen it? How could she have talked herself into believing that he would ever forsake his people, even for her?

He had been planning this all along, Clarissa reasoned, her fury mounting. He had betrayed her, abandoned her without so much as a civil goodbye!

As she stared at the feather in her hands, her chest began to jerk uncontrollably. Sobs erupted from her throat, mingled with the senseless laughter of the bereft. Her shoulders heaved as scalding tears streamed down her face. She had forced Wolf Heart to choose, and she had lost him. She had lost everything.

The colonel backed away in mute horror, shaking his head. "Send for the doctor!" he muttered to his wife. "It's quite obvious the girl is hysterical!"

Clarissa sat quietly in her rocker, watching the bright golden sycamore leaves flutter past her upstairs window. How she would like to be a leaf, she mused, to blow free wherever the wind might take her. To fly over the land, then settle, perhaps, on the sparkling surface of a stream, to be carried along in its current all the way downstream to the mighty Ohio. To float from there all the way back to the land of the Shawnee.

But such freedom was an idle wish, she reminded herself. She might as well be a prisoner in her brother's house, shut away in this small upstairs room. Poor Clarissa, who, according to neighborhood gossip, had been captured by the Shawnee and forced to endure the most unspeakable violations of her body. Poor Clarissa who, it was whispered, would never again be fully right in her head.

As she shifted in her chair, she felt the familiar kicking and stirring inside her. Tenderly she cupped her hands over her bulging belly, protecting and caressing the tiny life that grew there. Time was growing short. Three months at most, she calculated, and her baby would be born. She would hold Wolf Heart's child in her arms and cherish all that remained of the love between them.

Junius was a decent man—that much, at least, she had discovered on her return to Baltimore. He had agreed to support her and the child until such time as she might choose to remarry. But he had exacted his own terms in exchange. To avoid embarrassment to the family, Clarissa was not to leave the house for the duration of her pregnancy. To pay for the extra expense of her care, she was to give up the fifty pounds of gold that had been part of her dowry and, after her confinement, take over most of the housekeeping duties from the aging Mrs. Pimm. The safe, secure life she had longed for in the Shawnee village was hers.

Oh, Wolf Heart! Wolf Heart!

Straining forward, she stared into the autumn sky as if she could will herself away from this place and fly to his side. In the early weeks of their separation she had been furious with him. But she had long since forgiven his deception. She had pushed him too far, and Wolf Heart had made what he judged to be the only right decision.

She had no one to blame but herself.

From the street below, the sound of children playing tag filtered through the closed window. Clarissa pressed her face to the cool glass pane, trying to imagine Wolf Heart's child growing up in this so-called civilized world. It would not be such a bad life, she reasoned. There would be ample provisions for food, shelter and clothing. There would be books to read, plays and concerts to attend. If her child was a boy, Junius might even be kind enough to pay for his education and, later, take him into the business. If a girl, she would learn the arts of managing a home and, heaven willing, grow up to marry a good man.

But Wolf Heart's son would never creep through a thicket on moccasined feet to bring down a deer with a single arrow. He would never dive into an icy river to earn his *pa-waw-ka* or seek out a spiritual vision to guide his life. Wolf Heart's daughter would never walk through Swan Feather's beloved meadow gathering herbs to heal the people who revered and trusted her. She would never dive naked and free into the deep, cold water of the rocky pool or prance joyously to the rhythm of dancing drums.

And as for herself—Clarissa touched her cheek where a solitary tear had left its cold wet track—she would never again awaken to the scent of hickory smoke and the sight of sunbeams trickling through chinks in the roof of a bark lodge. She would never again know White Moon's gracious smile or Cat Follower's teasing laughter. She would never again lie on a bed of soft skins, cradled by Wolf Heart's arms, both of them warm and damp from the sweet fire of their lovemaking.

What a stubborn, pathetic fool she had been! During her early weeks here, when she might have been able to return to the Shawnee, pride had held her back. Now that same pride had crumbled away to longing. But her change of heart had come too late. With winter almost here and her pregnancy advancing into its last trimester, it would be difficult to make the strenuous journey to Fort Pitt and, from there, down the Ohio.

Difficult, yes. And dangerous.

She closed her eyes, and it was as if she could see Wolf Heart standing on the bluff, watching the river. She could feel the loneliness in him, feel him reaching out to her and to their child, and suddenly she knew that, whatever the odds, she had to go to him. It was that or live with bitter regret for the rest of her life.

Impatient now, she bolted out of the chair, flew to the door of her room and flung it open. As she descended the steep staircase, one hand gripping the banister for balance, she realized she was already breaking one of Junius's rules—that she remain on the second floor except when she had his express permission to come downstairs. To keep peace in the house she had complied with his demands. Today she no longer cared.

Mrs. Pimm flashed her a startled glance as she strode past the kitchen, but Clarissa did not stop to apologize or explain as she crossed the dining room and headed straight down the hall for Junius's private office. She had done enough apologizing to last her for the rest of her life.

She found her brother at his desk, going over the accounts in his huge ledger book. He scowled at her as she burst into the room, thin eyebrows meeting above the pewter rims of his spectacles. "What is it now?" he asked irritably, as if this were the tenth time she had bothered him that day.

Clarissa resolved not to mince words. "I'm going home, Junius," she said.

"But you are home." His spidery fingers, ink stained where they gripped the quill, paused above a long column of figures. Junius Rogers might have been a handsome man except for the pinched, perpetually sour expression on his face. "You were born in this house, and whether you like it or not—"

"That's not what I meant." She faced him across the desk, as defiant as the figurehead on a man-of-war. "I said I was going *home*. Back down the Ohio, to my husband. I want my child to be born Shawnee."

Junius sucked in his breath, staring at her in disbelief. "You're insane!" he hissed. "I've defended you over these past months, but now I'm beginning to believe everything people say about you is true!"

Clarissa allowed herself a bitter smile. "If that's the case, I don't belong here in Baltimore, living off your money and causing you no end of embarrassment, do I?"

Junius rocketed to his feet. "But that's preposterous! What will people say?"

"I don't care a fig what they'll say."

"I won't allow it, Clarissa."

"And why not?" She stepped closer to the desk, stretching on tiptoe to bring her eyes even with his own. "You've already taken my dowry money, but I still have my land—land that's growing in value every day. You can buy that land from me, Junius, for the price of my passage, and be rid of me in the bargain!"

She heard the small catch of his breath. It was an incredible offer—the land was easily worth ten times what she was asking. Still he hesitated, the left corner of his mouth twitching in a small nervous spasm.

"So?" she prodded him, anxious for an answer.

"You may not believe this, but I do have a conscience," he said. "You are my sister, and I want to do right by you."

"Then let your conscience rule for my happiness!" She seized his thin hands and gripped them tightly, something she had not done since childhood. "Take my offer, Junius. Take it and let me go!"

"Clarissa—"

She saw the welling of emotion in his eyes, the strain of his self-imposed isolation. "You deserve some happiness of your own," she said softly. "Find a good woman who'll care for you. Have a family. Fill this gloomy house with laughter and music and love."

She saw his throat move as he swallowed. "I'll have the papers drawn up for the transfer of the land," he said. "And I'll arrange safe escort for you to Fort Pitt and down the Ohio. You'll want for nothing on the way."

Impulsively she leaned across the desk and kissed her brother's taut, dry cheek. "Let me know when everything's ready,'' she whispered. ''I'll be upstairs packing my things.''

By the time the flatboat had reached the confluence of the Kanawha and Ohio Rivers, snow had begun to fall. Clarissa huddled in the lee of the deck house, watching the white flakes melt into the icy green-brown water. The damp cold air crept through her woolen cloak, chilling her to the bone. She had not been warm, it seemed, for weeks. But the cold was nothing compared to the fears that haunted her days and the images that stalked her dreams. What if she did not find Wolf Heart at the end of her journey? What if he had succumbed to fever, perished in battle or been killed by a bear or puma?

What if he had taken another woman—a woman born Shawnee—and no longer wanted her?

''Ma'am?'' The boatman's gruff voice broke into her thoughts. ''We'll be putting you ashore sometime this afternoon. You're sure you know the place?''

''I know the place.''

''And you're right certain you want to do this?'' The man's grizzled face was furrowed with concern. Junius, true to his word, had hired an experienced and reputable crew to take his sister down the river. They were good men and had treated her with the kindness and respect due a woman in her condition.

But even they could not be persuaded to venture beyond the open bank of the Ohio. Clarissa would have to walk the last three miles, up the tributary that fronted the Shawnee village, by herself.

''Ma'am?'' The boatman waited for an answer to his question.

''I'm certain,'' Clarissa said. ''I haven't come this far to lose heart.''

"Once we put you on the bank you'll be on your own. We can't stay and wait in case you change your mind. The men won't stand for it. They're already as jumpy as spooked rabbits."

In truth, Clarissa would not have asked the flatboat crew to wait for her. Their presence so close to the village would only create dangerous tension. To keep the trust of the Shawnee she would have to return alone.

"I understand," she said.

"Then God help you, ma'am," the boatman muttered as he turned and walked away.

The snow grew heavier as the day wore on. Clarissa watched the bank through a swirl of white flakes, grateful for the dense cloak and sturdy boots she had worn. She would need them to reach the village safely.

But what would she do if her worst fears came true and there was no Wolf Heart to welcome her? After days of agonizing the answer had finally come. She was not just returning to the man she loved; she was returning to the way of the Shawnee. She would remain as a healer to her adopted people, and she would raise Wolf Heart's child among them.

But to live without seeing him…without holding him…

Clarissa watched the moving bank and silently prayed.

The sun was low in the gray November sky when she saw the mouth of the small river. Her chilled lips parted as the memory flashed through her mind—the racing canoes, the chanting braves and Cat Follower's jubilant laughter. She was home at last.

Minutes later, without ceremony, she was helped onto the bank. The nervous crewmen poled at once for the middle of the river, anxious to put distance between themselves and the Shawnee. They would toil their way upstream to one of the remote settlements that had sprung

up below Fort Pitt. There, with luck, they might trade
their boat timbers for horses to ride the rest of the way
home.

But Clarissa could not waste precious daylight watching them go. The sun was already burning red above the
trees. If she did not strike out at once it would be dark
before she reached the Shawnee village.

Shouldering her pack, which contained little more than
biscuits, a few necessities and some small gifts for her
friends, she strode up the bank. By the time she reached
the familiar trail at the top she was gasping for breath.
The long idle months in Baltimore, coupled with her
pregnancy, had cost her dearly. But no matter, she reassured herself. Even at her labored pace, the village was
scarcely an hour away. Soon the delicious smells of roast
corn and venison would float down to her on the river
breeze. She would hear the welcoming birdcalls from the
lookouts and the laughing shouts of children, and she
would know that Dancing Fox had come home at last.

Please let Wolf Heart be there, she prayed silently.
*Please let him be well and safe. Please let him still want
me.*

Silence blanketed the twilight—a silence filled with
softly falling flakes of snow. The darkening river caught
amber glints from the setting sun.

By now Clarissa had come more than halfway to the
village, and she had seen no canoes on the water, no fresh
tracks on the ground. The only sound that reached her
ears was the sigh of rushing water, broken now and then
by the melancholy cry of a circling crow.

But everything was all right—it had to be. Any moment now, she would hear the bark of a dog or see the
curl of smoke from a cook fire. Any moment now, someone would see her from the top of the bluff. The shout

would go up, and people would come running down the trail to meet her.

She crossed the garden patches where nothing remained except a few standing cornstalks and tangled squash vines, brown from frost. Above her rose the high bank that separated the village from her sight. Clarissa's heart pounded as she climbed up the last few yards of the trail. Soon she would be safe and warm. Soon, heaven willing, she would be with Wolf Heart.

She reached the top of the bank and stopped cold.

The village was gone.

Clarissa's eyes swept over the desolation—the bare sapling frames of the lodges, their coverings stripped away; the blackened fire pits filling up with snow, the empty council house, its floor littered with leaves that had blown in through the wide uncovered windows and doorways. Her breath came in stuttering gasps of disbelief.

Something tugged at her memory, something she had heard and forgotten until now. What was it? She groped for the recollection, then sank to the ground in dismay as it came.

Winter camp. Someone, perhaps Wolf Heart, had mentioned that the Shawnee left their villages in wintertime and broke up into small groups. This scattering made it easier to find enough game during the long moons of cold and hunger.

How could she have glossed over such a simple vital fact? It was more than a foolish mistake—it was a fatal error, and the price of her folly could be her own life and that of her child.

Darkness was gathering swiftly, and the wind had turned the snow to stinging pellets. Scrambling to her feet, Clarissa made for the council house which, despite

its gaping doors and windows, was the only solid structure remaining in the village. She had a flint for making
fire and enough biscuits to last for a day or two. But how
long could she really survive here? How long before she
starved or froze or—

A distant sound, echoing on the twilight wind, stopped
her in her tracks. She paused, her heart in her throat, as
it rose again, a haunting, mournful wail that continued
for the space of a dozen pulse beats, then dropped in pitch
and fell once more into wintry silence.

Clarissa's arms crept protectively around the tender
bulge of her unborn child. There was no mistaking what
she had heard.

It was the cry of a hunting wolf calling to its pack.

Once again Wolf Heart's quest had not gone as he had
hoped. He had returned to the cave above the rockslide,
seeking a clearer vision to guide his people. But after
four days of fasting and waiting, nothing had come to
him—nothing except memories of Clarissa bounding
across the sunlit meadow; Clarissa dancing in the fire
circle with golden light blazing on her hair; Clarissa lying
in his arms, her face aglow with love.

He was incomplete without her—that much he had
known since the day of their parting. But there was no
undoing the past. She was with her own people now,
where she belonged by choice, and he was still searching
for the wisdom to carry on alone. He was still waiting
for the guidance of the wolf spirit.

With a weary sigh he shouldered the pack and musket
he had left in a small cave at the base of the slide. His
time would have been better spent hunting, he groused.
He had left the people in his camp with plenty of meat,
but by now the supply would be getting low again.

Maybe on the way back he could bring down a deer to justify his absence.

He would be wise to check on the other camps, as well, he mused as he trudged downhill through the snow. As peace chief, he felt responsible for all of his people.

Through a blur of falling snowflakes, he could see the full moon rising above the bare trees. Even Kokomthena looked cold on this chilly night. It would feel good to return to camp and bed down beside the fire in his solitary lodge.

He was crossing the path to the river when he heard it—the long keening cry of a wolf, rising and falling to mingle with the howl of the night wind. He raised his head, listening intently.

The call had come from the direction of the deserted village.

Driven by an urgency he could neither deny nor understand, he plunged through the swirling snow. As he neared the village, his keen nostrils caught the scent of smoke on the wind. Someone was there—someone in trouble, perhaps, who needed his help. Or some enemy bent on harm, he reminded himself as he slowed his approach, moving cautiously on silent feet.

He could see firelight now, flickering through the open windows of the council house. And he could see the gray phantom shape circling outside in the darkness—a huge pale wolf shape that vanished like a ghost as he came closer.

Then, suddenly, he could see the slender figure—achingly familiar—silhouetted by firelight in the wide doorway, a blazing tree branch clutched in her hands.

He raised the loaded musket to defend her, if necessary, but the wolf was gone. There was only Clarissa, crying out at the sight of him, dropping her torch and flying to meet him through the swirling snow.

He caught her and held her fiercely, feeling her hot tears against his cold face, feeling the sweet solid bulge of their child between them. Later there would be time for food and warmth. There would be time for talk, for understanding and for planning their future together. The years ahead would be difficult, even heartbreaking, Wolf Heart knew. They would both need to be very strong. But right now only one thing mattered.

She had come home to him.

Epilogue

"So what happened after that, Grandmother?" Six-year-old Red Arrow's eyes widened with wonder. "Did Grandfather go out and shoot the wolf?"

Dancing Fox smiled, the creases deepening at the corners of her sharp green eyes. "No," she said. "The wolf was gone. Later, when we looked around the village, we found no trace of it, not even its tracks in the snow. What do you think of that?"

The little boy considered the question gravely, his scowl a miniature version of Wolf Heart's. "I think it was a spirit wolf," he said. "It was Grandfather's *unsoma,* and it told him where to find you."

"Perhaps." Dancing Fox laughed as she hugged her grandson, knowing he had heard the story countless times before and that his answer was always the same.

"And then what did you and Grandfather do?" Ten-year-old Spotted Fawn, darkly beautiful like her Shawnee mother, spoke from her place beside the fire. "Where did you go?"

"Your grandfather took me back to the camp where the other Shawnee were waiting." Dancing Fox concluded the story that had become a family legend. "I became women's chief, and later that very winter your father, Silver Wolf, was born.''

She closed her eyes, remembering the perilous joy of that day. The passing years had been filled with danger and hardship, but Wolf Heart had led his people wisely. He had kept them together, kept them beyond the reach of white civilization. They lived, now, in an isolated northern valley, hoping each day that they would remain safe here.

"I want Father and Grandfather to come home!" Red Arrow declared. "It's getting dark outside."

"Be patient." Dancing Fox rumpled her grandson's wavy black hair. "You know they'll come home when they've found meat for us."

"I hear horses—they're back!" Spotted Fawn leaped up and raced out into the snowy darkness.

"I'm going, too!" Red Arrow bounded off his grandmother's lap. "Maybe they've shot a deer, or even a buffalo!"

Dancing Fox rose from her place beside the fire, her heart singing in quiet joy. One hand smoothed her silver-streaked hair as she waited, all but dancing with anticipation. He would come to her at once, as he always did.

The deerskin flap stirred and lifted. Then he was there, stepping into the lodge, tall and strong, his iron-gray hair glistening with fallen snow. Wolf Heart. Her love. Her life.

She lost herself in his arms.

* * * * *

Come escape with Harlequin's new

Series Sampler

Four great full-length Harlequin novels bound together in one fabulous volume and at an unbelievable price.

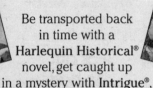

Be transported back in time with a Harlequin Historical® novel, get caught up in a mystery with Intrigue®, be tempted by a hot, sizzling romance with Harlequin Temptation®, or just enjoy a down-home all-American read with American Romance®.

You won't be able to put this collection down!

On sale February 2000 at your favorite retail outlet.

HARLEQUIN®
Makes any time special ™

Visit us at www.romance.net

PHESC

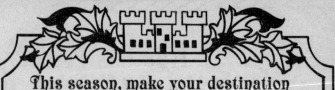

This season, make your destination
England with four exciting stories from
Harlequin Historicals

On sale in December 1999,
THE CHAMPION,
The first book of *KNIGHTS OF THE BLACK ROSE*
by **Suzanne Barclay**
(England, 1222)

BY QUEEN'S GRACE
by **Shari Anton**
(England, 1109)

On sale in January 2000,
THE GENTLEMAN THIEF
by **Deborah Simmons**
(England, 1818)

MY LADY RELUCTANT
by **Laurie Grant**
(England, 1141)

Harlequin Historicals
Have a blast in the past!

Available at your favorite retail outlet.

HARLEQUIN®
Makes any time special ™

Visit us at www.romance.net   HHMED10

3 Stories of Holiday Romance from three bestselling Harlequin® authors

Valentine Babies

by

ANNE STUART

TARA TAYLOR QUINN

JULE McBRIDE

Goddess in Waiting by Anne Stuart
Edward walks into Marika's funky maternity shop to pick up some things for his sister. He doesn't expect to assist in the delivery of a baby and fall for outrageous Marika.

Gabe's Special Delivery by Tara Taylor Quinn
On February 14, Gabe Stone finds a living, breathing valentine on his doorstep—his daughter. Her mother has given Gabe four hours to adjust to fatherhood, resolve custody and win back his ex-wife?

My Man Valentine by Jule McBride
Everyone knows Eloise Hunter and C. D. Valentine are in love. Except Eloise and C. D. Then, one of Eloise's baby-sitting clients leaves her with a baby to mind, and C. D. swings into protector mode.

VALENTINE BABIES

On sale January 2000 at your favorite retail outlet.

HARLEQUIN®
Makes any time special ™

Visit us at www.romance.net

PHVALB

Harlequin® Historical

is proud to offer four very different
Western romances that will
warm your hearts....

On sale in December 1999,
SHAWNEE BRIDE
by **Elizabeth Lane**
and
THE LADY AND THE OUTLAW
by **DeLoras Scott**

On sale in January 2000,
THE BACHELOR TAX
by **Carolyn Davidson**
and
THE OUTLAW'S BRIDE
by **Liz Ireland**

Harlequin Historicals
The way the past *should* have been.

Available at your favorite retail outlet.

HARLEQUIN®
Makes any time special ™

Visit us at www.romance.net

HHWEST5